MW00938981

# HOT BOSS

## HOT BILLIONAIRE DADDIES BOOK 1

### SUZANNE HART

© Copyright 2020 by Suzanne Hart - All rights reserved.

In no way is it legal to reproduce, duplicate, or transmit any part of this document in either electronic means or in printed format. Recording of this publication is strictly prohibited and any storage of this document is not allowed unless with written permission from the publisher. All rights reserved.

Respective authors own all copyrights not held by the publisher.

WARNING: This Book contains sexually explicit scenes and adult language. It may be considered offensive to some readers. This Book is for sale to adults ONLY.

Please ensure this Book is stored somewhere that cannot be accessed by underage readers.

# CONTENTS

# 1

## NINA

*I* clutched my bag's shoulder strap tightly as I walked down the hall. I was returning to my dorm room alone. Just like most other days in the past three years of my college life, I'd spent today in the library too. If I didn't have classes to attend, I preferred to spend my time reading and re-reading books. The library was a safe and quiet space. In there, nobody bugged me with questions or made suggestions of going out. I enjoyed the silence, where the only sound around me was that which the pages made when they were being turned.

As far back as I could remember, this was who I was. One half of a pair of twins, the younger sister of Raina Jones, daughter of Mac, belonging to Chicago's south side but not quite belonging anywhere. I was a quiet kid growing up, even though my twin brother Corey was the exact opposite. He always had something to say, whether you asked him a question or not.

My older sister Raina was strong and capable. Technically, she was my half-sister, but she'd looked after Corey and me like we were her children. Our mother was never a part of our lives. What happened there? Nobody really explained it. From the bits of information I could gather growing up, through snatched conversations or arguments between our dad and Raina, it was obvious our mother never wanted to be a part of our lives.

So, when Dad died, and we were quite young then, it was up to Raina to take care of us.

She did everything in her capacity to give us a good life, but we lived in the *south side*. Our dad was involved in the drug trade, and we had a family history of drug abuse. All these factors hung on our backs like a dark shadow the whole time we were growing up.

I knew I would always carry them as my burden.

Raina wanted to make sure that Corey and I never got involved in anything like that. She wanted to give us a good life. She worked hard, even though she was just a teenager, to provide for us and to force a good education on us. No matter how much we resisted it. She had her mind set on getting us out of the south side, and she did.

Nobody would have ever predicted that I, Mac Jones's daughter, would be in college. That I would prefer the library over getting drunk or doing drugs at some nightclub on a daily basis. Being in college made Raina proud. Corey wasn't the college kind, and that was all right. At least she'd succeeded with one of us.

I told myself I was doing this to make Raina happy. After everything she had done for me.

But just because I was in college didn't mean I had to live the life of a college student. Nobody could make me do that.

As I walked down the hall toward my dorm this evening, my fellow students passed me by in streams of chatter and good spirits. It was Friday evening, and everyone was going out. There was going to be a party in every corner of this building and everywhere else on campus. I was glad I hadn't made any friends here.

Except Karen.

She was sitting up on her bed when I entered our dorm room. A dark lipstick in one hand and a small oval mirror in the other. She was putting on makeup.

"Hey, you," she said, without looking up at me.

It had taken us a while to get along when we first found ourselves living together three years ago. Karen was outgoing and popular. I was quiet and had no friends. We were polar opposites and we clashed.

In time, Karen came to realize I was the only person she could actually trust in this place. I was never going to tell on her, no matter how strange her secrets were. I would never judge her. I always had her back. We relied on each other now. The only other person besides Corey and Raina whom I could trust was her. Even though I had no other friends in this place, I was glad I had Karen.

"Going out?" I asked, throwing my bag on my single bed and flinging myself on it too.

"I didn't want to, but Jake is going to be there and tonight might be our night!" She sounded excited. She snapped her mirror shut and slid it into a shiny purse she was going to carry.

"Well, you look great."

Karen had had a crush on Jake for several weeks. Just like all the other guys she'd had a crush on since coming to college, she wholeheartedly believed that Jake was 'the one' for her.

She jumped off the bed and gave a little twirl, showing off her new dress. "You like?"

We didn't have the same tastes. While Karen loved flashy colors and always wore makeup, the only thing I adorned myself with was foundation to cover my freckles. Even eyeliner was a farfetched idea in my mind.

"It's a lovely color, suits you."

She was happy with that. She knew I never paid empty compliments. I wouldn't have said anything if I didn't genuinely think her dress was nice.

"Well, wish me luck too. If that boy doesn't make a move tonight, I'm seriously going to give up."

Unlike most other guys who were always asking Karen out, Jake was a stone wall she was repeatedly banging herself against. Even I couldn't figure out what was wrong. He was single, straight, interested in spending time with her, but he had yet to admit he 'liked' her. It was driving the poor girl crazy.

"You know what my thoughts are on this. You shouldn't be wasting your time on a guy who doesn't want to be with you," I said.

I pushed my back up against the wall and pulled out a book

from my bag. Karen rolled her eyes and started getting ready to leave.

"Sometimes, Nina, you just have to put in an effort. It's part of the chase. I know he wants me, you're wrong about that, and not everyone is like you. It doesn't always come easy to everyone to just speak their mind. There could be something else going on with him."

I shrugged. These were Karen's choices. If I was in her place, I would have gone out with a guy who showed obvious interest. If my life had taught me anything, it was that most human beings were unreliable anyway. There was no point planning your life around any of them. But Karen wasn't like me, she wasn't a lone wolf.

I hadn't looked at the time for ages. Karen had been gone for some time now. I'd shimmied from a seated-up position against the wall, down to lying on my single bed. I was bundled up amidst my pillows and sheets, deeply engrossed in the book I was reading on Political Theory. All I knew was that it was dark outside.

A knock on the door made me jump up.

I looked at my wristwatch. It was close to midnight. It couldn't be Karen. She had a key. Unless she'd lost it. Was she drunk? Was she okay?

Panicked thoughts rushed through my head as I went to open the door. Instead of Karen, I found *him* again. He was standing on the other side, with a wide sleazy grin on his face. His hands were stuck deep down in the pockets of his polyester jacket. He was middle-aged and balding.

"What the fuck?" I cursed as a defense mechanism. This was creepy. If I hadn't been afraid of him before, I was now. What was he doing here? How did he get into the building? Where was security?

"Hello, Nina. I hope I didn't wake you up. I thought maybe we could talk."

"Talk about what? I told you I don't want anything to do with you or your business. Just leave me alone!" I tried slamming the door on him but he blocked it with his foot. Alarm bells went off in my head. He pushed his way into the room with his elbows. His hands were still in his pocket.

"I don't think you're really hearing me. Your family owes me money."

The smile faded from his face now. He glared at me with his beady little dark eyes. I wished our dorm room was better lit. I moved away from him, backing up against my bed. I hoped he couldn't see how utterly horrified I truly was.

"My family doesn't owe you any money. Our dad did. He's dead now. What do you want us to do about it?"

Raina had worked so hard to get us out of the South. To give us a different life than the one we were born in. Our father dying, though devastating for us and tough, was like a chance at a new start.

But here I was, being threatened by a man who used to work with our father.

"I'm sure you know how these things work, Nina. Your dad

owed me money. Now he's dead, but the debt carries forward. You're in college. You can figure this shit out, right?" He was smiling again. He thought this was funny, threatening a twenty-one-year-old?

"How did you get in here?"

"It doesn't matter. I'm here now."

He moved closer to me and I gulped. Could I scream? Would anyone hear me?

I knew there was nobody close by. Everyone was busy partying and getting drunk. If I screamed, it was likely I'd get no help.

"Look, babe, I don't want to do anything stupid, so don't tempt me."

*Babe*? Was he seriously going to call me that? But it was the least of my problems right now, and I made no comment. Maybe he could see the lingering fear in my eyes, and that was making him act cockier.

"How about I make this easier for you?" His gaze roamed over me, from head to toe. It seemed like he was checking for something.

"You'll do well at my club."

"Your club?"

He'd mentioned this before. I didn't know much about his business, but I had the feeling this was the kind of club I would never find myself in on a night out.

"All you have to do is serve drinks, collect tips...and trust me, you'll make a lot of tips." He studied me again, his stare settled on my breasts and he wasn't about to look away. "You trust me, right?"

How could I answer that question? While he was standing in my dorm, capable of doing actual physical damage.

"I need to think about this."

He looked up at my face again.

"Good. Yeah, think about it. If you can't come work for me, you need to figure out some other way to repay the debt. Do you understand?" This last part he said with threatening intensity. "You'll make a lot of money if you work for me. My clients are very generous." That grin appeared again. He was pleased with himself and he was making me sick.

"Please leave."

He shrugged. "Sure, I'll go, but I need an answer from you soon. Or the money. Figure this shit out, Nina Jones. I'll go now but I won't be gone for good."

He went to the door, turned, and looked at me one last time before he left. I locked the door behind him and sat down on my bed with a thump. A chill ran down my spine. For a moment, I seriously considered taking up his job offer. I needed the money. I needed him off my back. I didn't want Raina or Corey to find out that our dad's ghost had come back to haunt us.

What else could I do?

For starters, I needed to leave this dorm and make sure I kept this danger away from Karen.

## 2

### ERIC

*M*iles met me at a café he'd suggested. I felt like I was new to Chicago, even though we'd been living here for close to three months now. It wasn't like I'd really had a chance to go around exploring the city yet. I had a fussy five-year-old to look after rather than go sightseeing.

I hadn't even had a chance to really catch up with my old buddy, Miles. His company posed great potential for a business investment. This was the main reason why I moved here. This and the fact that I wanted to get my son away from Seattle.

Miles was waiting for me. He'd already ordered us coffees and I took the chair across from him.

"Sorry about the time. James was having a bad morning. He didn't want to go to playschool today." I shrugged as I spoke. This was my life. Every morning was a struggle to get my son out of the house and off to his new playschool in time.

He didn't like it. He didn't like Chicago. He had no interest in making new friends.

I knew my son was struggling and I wanted to help him, but this was the only way I knew how. Continuing to live in Seattle was not an option for us. We had to get away from Cynthia.

"Let me know if I can help in any way. I bet it's hard for you to make such a big move with a kid." Miles was like a changed man since he met Raina. It was like he suddenly understood what family was about. I was happy for him, that he'd found a woman who could give him that.

We'd known each other in the military. We were in the same squad of the Marines and had been on many missions together. That was a different life. Now, even when I tried to think about it, I couldn't really remember. It was a long time ago.

I had no plans on quitting the military, and I probably would have had a similar career as Miles, but then Cynthia wrote me a letter saying she was pregnant. She hadn't wanted the baby. I had no choice but to quit and go home. I'd done every-thing I could to convince her to keep it. I'd promised to raise the baby myself, alone if I had to. I took full responsibility. That was six years ago, and here I was, keeping my promise.

"Yeah, thanks. We'll be okay. Just teething problems. It's a new place and James is a sensitive kid. I'm sure we'll settle down soon enough."

Miles nodded. "What can I do?"

I shrugged. "You could find me the perfect babysitter?" I said with a laugh. I wasn't actually expecting Miles to come up with a solution to that. How would Miles know anyone who could babysit James?

But he clearly wanted to help. He was serious about it and was nodding. "I'm on it!"

I laughed. "I was kidding, don't worry about it. If there is the perfect babysitter for James out there, she's definitely not in Chicago. I'm pretty sure I've interviewed everyone available. My son has the special ability to drive any sane woman nuts if she's charged with taking care of him."

Miles looked at me sympathetically.

"I'm okay, I'm fine. Tell me about the business," I said. As much as I loved my son, the truth was that I needed to switch my mind off him for a bit. Just to take a break.

Miles started pulling out a file from the bag he was carrying. "I have all the financial paperwork here. It's been six months since we've been in business, and everything is here for you to see."

I flipped through the file quickly. I was going to take this home with me and study it better.

If everything looked good financially, my plan was to invest in the business and help Miles grow it. The idea was simple. It was basically an app which connected vets to job opportunities around the country. More often than not, it wasn't easy for a vet to find a job once they were out of the military. Some were injured, some just didn't have the skillset needed to work at a regular office, and some didn't know how to even start looking for a suitable job. These vets waited too long for the government to find them jobs and most of them weren't even the right fit.

This app that Miles was developing was all set to change the game.

They'd conducted the necessary market research. They'd recruited the right organizations from around the country. They were now in the process of spreading awareness and marketing it to vets who would be able to use the technology to their benefit.

The potential that this business had was practically limitless in our country, and I would have been a fool to miss out on an opportunity like this.

"Just give me a week and you'll have my answer," I told Miles.

He was more than happy to hear it. I knew they needed investment, and who better to get it from than a friend who understood the industry? I would be the perfect investor for them. I had industry experience, as far as the military was concerned, and I also had experience running a business.

But like every business decision, as I had been taught by my father while he was alive, I would have to go through their books first. It was my money, after all. I needed to invest with my mind and not my heart.

Miles sat back in his chair now and watched me tuck the file into my briefcase.

"I'm glad we might be working together. I'm glad you're in Chicago, man," he said.

I drank some of the coffee he'd ordered for me. "I'm glad to be here too."

"How are you *really* doing, though? What's happening with Cynthia?" he asked.

Miles knew the bare basics of my situation. As much as I'd revealed to him.

He knew Cynthia was James's mother. He knew it was her pregnancy which forced me to quit the Marines and move back home. He also knew that I'd left Seattle with my son because I didn't want her to be a part of our lives.

I ran a hand frustratedly through my crew-cut hair. "She's suddenly decided she wants to be a part of her son's life."

"And that would be a bad thing?" Miles asked.

He only knew *about* Cynthia. He didn't actually know her at all.

"She wasn't around when our son needed her the most. I was the one staying up with him all night, rocking him to sleep when he was a baby." There must have been bitterness in my voice because Miles sat back now and sighed.

"But maybe it might be a good idea for James to get to know his mom?"

My hand fisted on the table, I tried my best to hold back the anger that was building up inside me. Miles caught that. "I'm sure you know what you're doing," he said quickly, and I looked away from him.

I had a flashing image cross my mind, an image of Cynthia from back when I used to know her. When I was so sure she was the girl I was going to spend the rest of my life with.

When we were teenagers, Cynthia had told me one night, as she nibbled my earlobe, that she'd always been in love with me. That I was the only guy for her. I believed her. I recalled that moment, the way she sat beside me, our legs dangling off the ledge of the roof. We used to do that a lot. Sit up on the roof of her father's house at night when everyone else was asleep.

That was what my adolescence had been about—Cynthia, Cynthia, and more Cynthia.

She was my first kiss...my first everything.

I'd always imagined my life to unfold with her. And then everything changed.

"You okay, man?" Miles' voice interrupted my thoughts, and that was probably for the best. I had better things to do than think about her. For the sake of my son. He'd thank me later.

"I'm fine, I just need to get James settled in here and everything else will work out fine."

"I'm going to look around and find you a good babysitter."

I didn't want my friend feeling sorry for me. I could see it in his eyes now. He pitied me.

"Don't worry about it," I told him. "What's happening with you guys? Besides the business?" I wanted to change the subject.

"Things are going really well. I found a good woman. Well, I was lucky enough that we found our way back to each other," he said. Miles was smiling now. Maybe a few years ago, I would have laughed at how silly in love he looked, but the years had taught me how important that was. And how rare.

"Raina seems amazing. We should have dinner together again." In my head, I knew that wasn't going to be possible unless a suitable babysitter for James magically appeared, but I didn't mention it to Miles.

But he snapped his fingers like he'd just woken out of a daze. "That's it! I can ask Nina!"

I just stared at him blankly. "Who?"

"Nina, Raina's younger sister. She's not exactly a professional babysitter, but I know she's looking for a job."

I sat back in my chair. I didn't know how to break it to my friend. If none of the experienced and professional babysitters were able to handle James, I was sure this Nina wasn't going to be able to do it.

Miles was smiling. "This could actually work."

I shrugged. "I wouldn't bet my money on it, but sure, I'll introduce her to James and we can see how things go from there."

Miles already had his phone out in his hand and it seemed like he was texting someone. "I'm going to tell Raina to speak to her the next chance she gets. This could be the perfect job for her."

Things were moving too quickly. I wanted to tell Miles to take it easy. I hadn't even met this Nina person. She hadn't even met James. My son wasn't easy.

"Hey, man, I just want to clarify that I won't necessarily give her the job because she's your sister-in-law."

Miles looked up from his phone and stopped typing for a few seconds. He nodded then. "Yeah, sure, of course. You do whatever suits you, of course. I just think you should give her a chance. She's twenty, studying political theory in college. She's well-read and calm. She could be a good influence on James. That's just my opinion."

"Sounds good. Get her in touch with me and we'll work it out," I told him. Miles was smiling again, pleased by my response.

"I will. I'll make it happen. I mean..." He lowered his phone to the table. "She's a twenty-one-year-old college student. She's a bit of a recluse and all that, but she's a good person."

I nodded. I had no faith in this person working out for James. The only reason I was agreeing to meet her was because Miles seemed so eager.

"Cool. I'm looking forward to meeting her," I said. I was already trying to think of ways of breaking it gently to Miles later about why I couldn't hire her.

Things never worked out this easily for me and I'd stopped expecting it to.

## 3

# NINA

*A* few days later, Raina met me in college. She liked to drop in like that from time to time. She claimed it was because she had some free time with nothing else to do, but I knew she was specifically checking in on me. She rarely ever got to see Corey because he had such an active social life. With me, she felt like she still had some insight into my life.

She came to my dorm room and spoke to Karen for a bit, after which we decided to get a coffee and go for a walk around campus. Raina was delighted to see me, as always, and stopped to give me a tight hug every chance she got.

There was only one weakness I allowed myself, and that was being hugged by Raina.

Even though she was just a few years older than me, she had always been like a mother to me. I felt comfortable and safe with her. Which was why I wasn't going to tell her about our father's ex-associate who had been stalking me these last few weeks.

Raina didn't need to know that. She'd be worried and scared for me. Besides, it wasn't like she'd actually be able to do anything about it. The last thing I wanted was for her to be desperate enough to be driven to ask Miles for the money. He'd already done enough for us.

I could handle this on my own.

"Still want to move out of the dorm?" she asked. We were walking side by side, with thick scarves wound around our necks. It was a chilly fall day. I nodded.

"Why though? You never explained. I thought Karen and you were getting along just fine."

"It's not about Karen. Yeah, we get along great. I just need my own space."

I wanted to keep that man and my family's problems away from Karen, away from the college. I didn't want this affecting my education in any way, or Karen's life. But I couldn't explain any of this to Raina.

"Okay, I see. That's fair enough."

"I'm trying to find a job that'll help me afford a place of my own."

She was smiling at me now, like she knew something I didn't.

"What?"

"I may have something for you," she said.

My brow crinkled. "What does that mean?"

She ignored my inquisitive tone. Raina was used to it by now, after all these years of dealing with me.

"I told Miles about how you're looking for a job and a place of your own, and he said he has this friend of his who is searching for a babysitter for his kid. I think he's five years old. Like a permanent babysitter who'd watch the kid."

"So, like a nanny?" I asked, coming to a halt.

Raina stopped in her tracks too and shrugged. "Sure, whatever you want to call it."

"You want me to become a *nanny*?" I glared at her in disbelief.

Raina was still smiling. "What's so bad about that? I think it's a very honorable job, helping to raise a child, you don't think?" She sounded awfully casual about the whole thing.

"It's not about the nature of the job, I'm just in shock that you think this would be suitable for me."

"Why not?"

"Because I have never been around kids. I can't remember the last time I even spoke to one. I'm just not a kid person. Wouldn't you have figured that out about me by now?" I stood in front of her with my hands hooked on my hips. I was seriously surprised by all this. What was she thinking?

Raina reached a hand out to me and placed it on my shoulder.

"Oh, c'mon, you're thinking too harshly of yourself. You'll be great. You're a calm person. In fact, you're too mature for your age. You'll be a good influence on the child. A good role-model."

"I don't know how to deal with kids!" I shouted the words a

little, which made Raina take in a deep breath and nod.

"Okay, yeah, sure. I guess this will be a new experience for you. I'm sure there's a learning curve involved, but something tells me you're a natural."

I looked away from her. I would've hated to disappoint her, but I couldn't babysit a kid. It was just not going to happen.

"Raina..." I began to protest and she smiled widely at me again.

"You're going to say no. That's okay. We're not trying to force you into doing something you don't want to do. No promises have been made. It would just be nice if you could go meet this man, Miles's friend, maybe spend a little time with the kid. After that, if it's not working for you, we can all move on. It's just that Miles gave this guy his word."

I ran a hand through my hair and sighed. "Sure, yeah, whatever," I mumbled. I knew they were trying to help, but it seemed like they were only complicating things even more for me. I probably shouldn't have told them I was looking for a job or planning to move out of the dorm.

Raina leaped at me, taking this opportunity to hug me again. "Excellent! You're a lifesaver!" She rubbed my back affectionately and I smiled at her.

"Just so you know, I'm going to say no. Maybe you should prepare Miles for that to happen."

She nodded. "Okay, yeah, do what you have to do. Just meet them so we can say we tried."

After that, Raina and I walked a little longer around campus. She talked about Miles, and I did very little talking.

We both discussed Corey and how little we saw of him these days. Then we hugged again and she left, promising to drop by again soon.

As much as I acted like a recluse who was happy to be left alone, the truth was that I loved Raina and I was going to do my best to make this problem with the man go away before she found out. She'd had enough problems for one lifetime.

It wasn't until four days later that things took a more serious turn.

I'd very close to forgetting about the babysitting gig. I hadn't heard anything from the man either, so I was hoping he was now going to leave me alone. But then I returned from class and found the door of our room wide open.

It was very unlike Karen to do something like this. She valued her privacy too much. Even before I'd walked into the room I knew something was wrong. When I did, I found Karen kneeling on the floor. She was picking up makeup and putting it into her vanity bag.

"What happened?" I asked. Now that I looked around the room, things were strewn everywhere. Her makeup and clothes, my books and shoes. Our beds were stripped down and the linen dragged to the corners. Karen's posters of Brad Pitt were scratched off the wall. The fairy lights we hung around the room were deliberately cut, like with scissors.

A cold chill ran down my spine before Karen replied.

She looked up at me and there was this anxious expression on her face. "I don't know what's going on with you, Nina. I wish you'd told me you were in trouble." She zipped up the bag and flung it on the bed. Then she straightened up to face me. It was more than just anxiety that I saw on her face now. She was worried, scared.

"Trouble? What are you talking about? What happened?" I knew that man was somehow involved in whatever happened in our room, but I needed to hear it directly from Karen. She sighed and shook her head.

"There was a man here, in our room. I have no idea how he got in. He was just walking out of the room when I was coming down the hallway. I got pissed off when I saw him. There were people around in the hall, so I wasn't scared to confront him. When I asked him what he was doing in there, he told me to tell you he was taking care of maintenance."

I gulped, barely able to hold Karen's gaze now. Her nostrils were flared. She was visibly upset.

"What's going on, Nina? Who was this man? I walked in here and finally saw the state this room was in." She looked around the place. I did the same. It was obvious that he'd just flung things around, ripped the posters off the wall...all as a warning because I hadn't arranged the money for him yet.

"Nothing is going on. Nothing serious. You don't have to worry," I tried.

I turned away from her but she kept talking. "Who was he? How did he get into the building? All the way up here without being noticed? Why did he trash our room?" She'd walked up right behind me. I kept my face turned to the wall.

This was exactly the kind of situation I was trying to avoid. I didn't want Karen involved. I didn't know what this man was capable of. People from the south side were capable of anything, especially if they thought you owed them something.

"I don't know. I'm going to look into that."

"This is serious, Nina. What kind of trouble are you in? I don't even know..."

I turned to her and forced a smile on my face. Just to make her see I wasn't worried.

"It's nothing. It's more like a joke."

"A joke? He's completely trashed this place. My lipsticks are broken. Some of my clothes are ripped. What kind of a joke is this?" Karen squealed in half-anger.

I sat down on my bed, feeling like a rush of energy had just left my body. I couldn't even feel my feet anymore.

"I'm sorry," I said, shaking my head.

Karen sighed again and then she sat down beside me. She found my hand and squeezed it lightly. "Nina, what's going on with you? You know you can tell me anything. I can see you're hiding something."

I looked into her eyes then looked away. I shook my head. There was no way I'd get Karen involved in this. I'd caused enough trouble already.

"I know, thanks. I'll get this sorted. I'll clean up. Tell me how much the damage cost. I'll find the money for it."

"It's not about the money, Nina. This is serious stuff. We

should get campus security to investigate. If you're in trouble, we should get help..."

I stood up from the bed with a jerk and ran a hand through my hair. "No. None of that is necessary. You won't have to deal with this for much longer. I'm looking for a place of my own."

I hadn't spoken to Karen about this before and she looked like she was in shock.

"Nina..."

I pulled out my cell phone and started typing a text to Raina.

*Set me up for that meeting for that babysitting job.*

I sent it and then I looked up at Karen again. She looked even more worried now. Like she'd just break in half.

"I thought we were best friends, Nina. I thought you told me everything. And now you're planning to leave?" Her voice cracked a little as she spoke. I hated doing this to her, but it was for her own good, for her protection. Maybe I'd be able to explain it to her after this was all over.

I shrugged my shoulders. "Nothing is permanent, Karen. We all move on."

She jumped off the bed and ran past me, out of the room. I'd felt her push against my shoulder as she ran out. She was hurt, upset, angry, and confused. I wanted to make things right with her. She was my best friend, but now we needed to rip this off like a Band-Aid. I couldn't involve her in my family's problems.

## 4

## ERIC

*M*iles got back to me a week after our coffee. He wanted me to meet his sister-in-law, Nina, whom he thought would make a great babysitter for James. I knew I couldn't get out of this situation. I couldn't outrightly be rude to a friend I was about to go into business with. But the truth was I had no faith in an inexperienced college student to be able to manage my son.

I told Miles I would meet her at the park near our apartment. It was one of the only places I was able to take James to without him having a complete meltdown.

It was Saturday afternoon and not too cold outside. We'd walked together to the park, and James had been especially grumpy all morning, despite us making pancakes together for breakfast, which he usually always enjoyed. Today, that hadn't cheered him up at all.

"All okay with you, buddy?" I asked as we walked to the play area. There were other kids there, playing together and enjoying themselves. James seemed to be eyeing them like he didn't trust a single one of them. He hadn't answered my question.

"Hey, buddy, look at me." I knelt down beside him, to get on his eye-level, and gently I tugged him so he would face me. He was staring at the other kids, already upsetting himself at the prospect of having to play with them.

"James." I said his name to get his attention and he finally looked at me. We had the same blue eyes. I saw so much of me in him every day. "You don't have to play with them if you don't want to. We can go somewhere else." I wasn't the kind of parent who forced their kid into anything. I wasn't an expert at parenting either. Most of the time, I was just winging it because I had no idea what I was doing.

The only rule I lived by was to keep James healthy, happy, and safe.

He stared at me and I could see his lower lip quivering a little.

"I miss home, Daddy," he said in a soft voice. I sensed he was having an especially bad day because he never spoke this softly. James usually had no problem voicing his opinion aloud.

"But this is our home now, buddy, we talked about this." I didn't expect a five-year-old to fully grasp the importance of moving. I knew this was going to be a difficult move, but it had to be done. Our lives had reached a standstill in Seattle, and then there was the problem with Cynthia.

"But why?" James pleaded.

"Because of my work here, because we'll be happier here eventually, buddy. You'll see." I tried to explain the situation to him the best I could. We hadn't exactly made progress on that front. James still hated Chicago and he wasn't trying to like it either.

He scrunched up his face in anger and glared at me. "Why can't you work in Seattle? Why? Why? Why?" His voice was rising now. I could sense a tantrum coming. We weren't going to be able to stay at the park for very long. I didn't even care about this Nina person anymore. My focus was entirely on James.

"Okay, I get you're angry. Maybe we can go home and talk. Do you want to leave now? Don't you want to play?"

His brows were crossed and his little pink lips were trembling as he glared at me. In these moments, I could see James's true personality emerge, even though he was just a five-year-old. He was headstrong and stubborn, and he never just took no for an answer. He was a fighter. Although I was proud of these personality traits of his, they were getting in the way of his happiness at the moment. If only he opened himself up to new experiences...

"I hate you," he hissed out of nowhere as we stared at each other.

"You don't mean that, James," I said, still kneeling in front of him. I looked into my son's eyes and for a moment I actually worried that he legitimately hated me. Then I remembered that most kids hated their parents. Or at least they thought they did. It was a part of gaining independence.

But my son was eyeing me like I'd physically hurt him.

"I hate you!" he shrieked.

"Okay, we're going home," I said and started to straighten

up. I wasn't about to let him have this tantrum out here. We'd had enough of them already.

"This isn't my home. I hate Chicago. I hate you!" he squealed. His voice pierced my ears and before I knew it, James had zipped away from me. I was barely even standing up and I definitely wasn't expecting him to do a runner. He'd never done one before.

"James!" I growled, shooting after him.

Somehow though, when I wasn't expecting it, my son proved to be a master escape artist. I had no idea how and when he'd picked up this new skill. He was running around people, zipping past joggers, not stopping once until he was out past the park gates. I was close behind him, but he was frisky.

"James! Get back here!" I shouted at him after he ran out of the gates. He turned to look at me once and then kept running.

"Stop!" I screamed. He wasn't watching where he was going. Now he was about to walk right into traffic. My son was going to have an accident and my whole world came to a standstill.

All those years of military training, but I wasn't prepared for this.

She seemed to appear out of nowhere. I hadn't noticed her standing there on the side of the road. I was focused entirely on James and now he was about to step into traffic. I knew I wasn't going to be quick enough to grab him. But she did.

She seemed to make the split-second decision to just reach out with one arm and grab him. Her arm blocked his run and she pushed him back, and then twirled that arm around his chest. A bus whizzed past them at just that moment. I saw the way it made her dark, straight hair flutter.

James seemed to be hanging from her arms now, hooked to her. She'd managed to lift him off the ground and was carrying him away from the street. He thrashed his legs like a little fighter and started screaming. I ran up to them. My brain still wasn't working correctly. My son could have died.

"James! Are you all right, buddy?"

I should have been mad at him for pulling a stunt like that. He should have known better. But I couldn't, not at this moment. I just needed to know he was okay.

The girl put him down, releasing him from her grip. James twisted his face up to stare at me. He was still angry.

"You can't do that again. You know how dangerous that was. You know the rules, buddy. You could have been seriously hurt." I spoke to him in a quiet respectful manner, but my son whipped away from me and turned to the girl.

"You okay there?" she asked him, tucking loose strands of dark hair behind her ears. James nodded at her, even though he hadn't yet responded to me. It seemed like he was more interested in her.

"Close call, huh? Running into traffic is a dangerous thing to do. I'm sure it was just a mistake though, right?" She was smiling at him. This was the most casual reaction to a near-death experience I could have expected. I glared at them both as I watched them bond.

James nodded.

"There are way more interesting games to play than this," she continued. James looked at her intently and she smiled back at him.

"Nina," she said and stuck her hand out at my son, a five-year-old. As far as I could remember, James had never been greeted this way. He stared at her hand for a few moments and then shook it lightly. "It's nice to meet you."

When she looked at me, seemingly for the first time noticing my presence, she had an amused look on her face.

"You're Miles's sister-in-law," I said, matter-of-fact. She seemed alarmed by this for a moment, and then she nodded. I'd already made the connection.

"And you must be Eric, and this is James."

I didn't want to comment on how funny it was that we met this way. She had just rescued my son from a possibly fatal accident. I felt relief in my soul.

"Thank you for stepping in. We're having a bad day," I told her. Nina nodded again and didn't seem to take notice of her heroic act. "You saved him."

"I did what anyone would have done."

"I would like to repay you for this. Let me buy you lunch," I suggested.

"That won't be necessary." She gazed at my son and smiled at him again. James seemed fascinated by her for some reason, like he'd never seen a human being before.

"Well, we need to talk anyway, right? That is why you're here. There's a small pizza place just around the corner that James likes. We could walk over there. What do you say, buddy?"

My son didn't have any time for me. He wasn't even looking in my direction. However, he did have a response to my suggestion. He inched closer to Nina and gently reached for her hand. He hadn't said a word.

Nina clasped her fingers around his hand and held it steadily. "Well, if James recommends it, we have to go check it out."

That made him smile.

When our eyes met again, I saw the softness of her face. She had thick, dark hair that was cut sharply at shoulder-length. She was slender and small, with no makeup. Her eyes were green and large and seemed to take up all of her face. She was wearing a pair of lightly ripped jeans and a stretchy green blouse that matched her eyes.

We started walking in the direction of the pizza parlor.

Nina walked slowly, with her hand still clasped around James's. He had never taken to another person like this before, especially a stranger. I wasn't expecting this to happen. He'd already rejected six of the babysitters I'd interviewed since arriving in Chicago. James had simply refused to talk to them. He threw a fuss with each of them and ran to his room and remained there until they left. I was close to giving up hope of ever finding someone who'd be able to spend some time with him.

But Nina...she was a natural. They simply clicked.

She was chatting to him now, even though he didn't make a single verbal reply.

"Do you like coming to the park? I used to love the swings. Have you tried out all of them?"

James smiled at her from time to time and that seemed to be enough encouragement for her to keep up the conversation.

"What kind of pizza will you get? I love anything with cheese. And pepperoni. Oh, my God, pepperoni! Do you like pepperoni?"

James nodded.

Nina was patient with him. She seemed to have even more patience than I did with my son. For a girl so young, she seemed to have the composure of a hundred-year-old monk.

We arrived at the parlor and paused at the door for a moment. I turned to her and shrugged. "This is it, nothing fancy."

Nina smiled and walked past me, with James in tow. "It's perfect," she said.

## 5

# NINA

*I* wasn't really thinking when I pulled James off the street.

I was headed in the direction of the park and saw a kid running my way. His little face was scrunched up and red, and he seemed upset. Then, before he could step out into oncoming traffic, I pulled him back and held him in place. He fought it initially, upset by the intrusion, but then he calmed down quickly. I smiled at him, trying to reassure him it was all okay. He was just a kid. He didn't know what he was doing. The last thing he needed was someone bearing down on him.

It was only when his father showed up, worried and relieved, that I realized these were the people Miles and Raina had set me up to meet.

These were not the circumstances I was expecting to meet them in, but I was glad I was there to pull James back.

Now we'd walked to a pizza place. James was sitting beside

me at the booth, his father was across from me and for some reason, I found it extremely difficult to meet Eric Hall's eyes.

And not just because they were this deep, azure blue, or the fact that he had the most perfectly shaped jawline. There was something else about this man. He just seemed... honest. I got the feeling that he used his words sparingly, but when he did say something, he meant it.

He didn't want to meet my eyes either, apparently. He just kept staring at the pizza menu in front of him, even though it only had six items on it.

"Do you know what you want, buddy?" he asked his son, without looking up at him.

"Cheese and pepperoni." It was the first time I heard James's voice. I'd tried but failed to get him to talk earlier, but he, too, like his father, seemed like a boy of just a few words.

I didn't know how it happened, but just in a matter of fifteen minutes, I felt like I'd known them a lifetime. There was no formal awkwardness between us.

James sat close to me at the booth, leaning toward me like he trusted me with his life. I continued to talk to him. It didn't offend me that he barely ever replied. He was a kid. He needed time to open up to me. I used to be the same way when I was his age...in fact, even when I was older. The only people I really spoke to were Raina and Corey.

"Maybe we'll share a pizza," I suggested and James nodded excitedly.

Eric ordered for us, and asked for nothing but a water for himself. He was built like a man who never indulged in fast food.

I got the feeling he was a military man like Miles. Maybe that was how they knew each other.

He had the same closely cropped hair. It was bright yellow, which made his blue eyes pop even more. He wore dark jeans and a black tight t-shirt. When I chanced a gaze at him, I could see the structure of his muscular torso, his biceps, the veins on his arms. He wore a thick sporty black watch on his wrist and that was his only accessory.

This man screamed no-nonsense.

"Have you ever worked with kids before?" He asked me that question, finally breaking the silence between us. We hadn't spoken much, even though this was technically supposed to be a job interview.

Before I met them, I wasn't sure if this job was going to be for me. I needed the money, sure, in fact, I was desperate for it, but babysitting a five-year-old wasn't something I thought I could do. I'd already decided I would have to go looking for something else.

I shook my head. "Never worked with kids, no."

That made him smile and he looked in the direction of his son. "That's not the impression I'm getting."

"The only way I know how to treat a kid is like I would treat everyone else. Like any other friend. I'm not sure if that works for everyone."

"It seems to be working with him."

James looked up at me and we exchanged smiles. Eric was right. This was working. I liked this kid.

"Nobody wants to be treated like a baby, right?" He had the cutest toothy smile.

I found Eric looking at me closely when I met his eyes. He was trying to assess me. Was he considering me for the job?

I had no idea how much he was willing to pay me, but if I got this job, then I'd soon be able to save some money and move out of the dorm. Maybe I'd even be able to save enough to repay the man who was stalking me. Maybe things would be all right after all.

"I'm not sure how much Miles has told you about us. We used to live in Seattle, moved here just a few months ago. I'm going to be working with Miles. We've been friends for some time now."

"You were a Marine like him?" I asked and Eric nodded. Not surprised.

"Basically, we don't know many people here, and James hasn't exactly been pleased with the move."

I nudged the kid with my elbow gently like we had an inside joke. "This place isn't that bad. I know just the places we can go and have some fun." Even though he didn't say anything, I could see the excitement in his eyes. As far as job interviews went, this seemed to be going pretty well.

"And why did you move to Chicago? Just to work with Miles?" I turned to Eric again.

He looked away from me. "I have my reasons," he replied sternly, and that was the first time I saw there was more to this. His face darkened and his jaw clenched. I got the sense that he was running away from something in Seattle. I'd asked him a casual question, but he hadn't taken it casually.

Our food arrived at just the right time. Eric wouldn't have to talk about Seattle anymore. This was the perfect distraction.

I helped James with the slices and we started eating. Eric sipped his water and I turned my attention to the kid. I was feeling nervous all of a sudden, since that question about the move. I knew I'd stepped on his toes. I shouldn't have felt this comfortable this soon. It was just that...I never felt this easy with people so quickly. Karen would have been proud of me if she could see me now.

Eric was quiet for some time while James and I ate and talked. He was beginning to say a few words to me now. I could sense Eric watching us closely. He was still studying me, possibly studying the way I interacted with his son.

"If I give you this job," he spoke finally. "You'll have to come live with us."

I stared at him. He'd caught me by surprise. A slice of pizza dangled from my hand. I couldn't seem to be able to take my eyes off his rugged, handsome face. There was more to this dynamic. I could feel it in my fingers now, in the pit of my stomach. It wasn't just about James and me getting along. I was attracted to Eric. If I accepted this job, he would be my boss.

"Okay," I said.

"Good," he replied and emptied the glass of water down his throat in one long chug.

It was late by the time I returned to the dorm. I'd left James and Eric soon after we finished our pizzas and gone over the finer monetary details of our babysitting arrangement.

Since then, I'd wandered around the park and taken the long way back to campus. I wasn't sure if this was the right decision. There were too many factors to be taken into consideration here.

For starters, I'd never done this before. Even though James and I got along well, evidently, I didn't actually know the first thing about childcare. Did Eric really want to trust me with his child?

And then there was the matter of Eric himself. I was attracted to him, from the first moment I laid eyes on him. I'd tried to maintain a distance. This was supposed to be a professional sphere...but I knew he was going to be on my mind often. How was I going to deal with that on a daily basis if I was to be living with them?

But the deal was done. I'd already accepted the job offer. I told Eric before I left that I would make the move in the next few days once I got everything sorted out in college. Now, I wasn't so sure if this was the right decision. I barely trusted myself.

Karen was awake when I walked in through the door.

Even though she wouldn't admit it, I knew she was trying to stay awake these days until I was back. She was afraid of the man returning. The one who'd ransacked our room, and it was all because of me.

She'd been watching something on her laptop and now she snapped it shut.

"You're never out this late," she commented.

"I was at a job interview."

Karen furrowed her brow. "At this time? What kind of a job is that?"

"I kinda lost track of time after the interview. I got the job. I'm starting soon."

Karen looked suspicious. She still hadn't forgiven me when I told her I was looking to move out. How was I going to tell her now that it was actually happening?

"Okay, where will you be working?"

"With a family. As a babysitter, well, more as a full-time nanny. They've offered me a place in their house."

Karen gulped and her face was still pinched. She wasn't happy at all. She wasn't saying anything, probably because she didn't know how to react.

"So, you're leaving?"

"Just the dorm. I'm still going to see you on campus. We can hang out all the time."

"Yeah, right. How are we going to do that if you have a full-time job as a nanny to some kid?" she snapped.

I sat down beside her on her bed and sighed. "I'm sorry, Karen. I know this seems like a ridiculous idea, but I need to do this. I need the money and I need to move out."

"You never told me you're having trouble with money..."

I shrugged. "There are a lot of things I don't tell anybody."

## 6

## ERIC

*O*f course, I offered the job to Nina because she would be great at it. She was exactly the person I was looking for in Chicago. Magically, James and she were getting along just fine. Given that she was related to my friend Miles, I also knew that I could trust her with my son.

It was only two days since our meeting at the park and James was getting restless already. He wanted Nina to move in quickly so he could have some company. I told him it would take her some time to move out of her dorm in college and start the job, but he'd been waiting so long to find some joy in Chicago that now he couldn't wait any longer.

I found myself looking forward to her arrival too.

Since I met Nina, I thought about her often. I couldn't get that scene out of my mind. Her quick step to the side, the way she stuck her arm out and pulled James in. The bus whizzing past them just a nanosecond later. Anything could have happened. The thought of James getting hurt made my stomach churn.

Before she left the pizza parlor that day, she'd said she would get in touch with me regarding her starting date, but I hadn't heard from her since. It was possible that she'd changed her mind. Just because I considered her to be a good fit for us didn't mean she thought the same of us.

Then on the third day, when James and I returned to the house from his school, we found Nina standing on the steps of our front door.

"Nina!" James squealed with delight and went running to her like he'd known her a lifetime. She dropped her backpack to the side and welcomed him into her arms.

"How are you, my cutie?" She hugged him tightly as I stood back, a little surprised.

My gaze roamed over the short dress she was wearing. It clung to her body loosely, but I could see the shape of her breasts underneath it, the curve of her slender hips and thighs. She wore canvas shoes and a denim jacket. All casual. But there was nothing casual about the way she made me feel when my stare landed on her.

She looked up at me all of a sudden and caught me staring.

"Hi, sorry for dropping in like this. I got your address from Miles. Did he tell you I was coming?"

I slid the house keys out of my pocket and stepped past them to open the door. "It must have slipped his mind."

"Oh, I'm sorry if I'm intruding. I can start tomorrow or some other day if that suits you."

That was when I noticed the two small packed bags that were on the steps too. She'd clearly come prepared for the move.

"No! You will stay with us tonight. I can show you all my toys." James was a real chatterbox today. His mood was instantly lifted when he saw Nina standing there at our door.

"It's no problem. You can start today. There's a room ready for you," I said and lifted her bags and took them inside.

"How was kindergarten?" I heard her ask James.

He started describing his day to her, even though he'd barely spoken to me the entire journey back home. What was it about her that made my son open up to her so easily? She was definitely different. I felt it when we first met. She wasn't like most girls. There was something distinctly unique about Nina.

James led her inside and I could hear them in the living room now. I took her bags up to the spare room. It was a pre-decorated room which I hadn't been inside since we first moved into this house. I'd just hired an interior designer to decorate all the rooms and take care of that part of my responsibilities.

Now I looked around the room more closely and hoped it would be sufficient for Nina. I wanted to do right by Miles, to treat his sister-in-law well.

I left her bags by the side of the bed and went back to the living room. James was down on the rug, pulling out all his action figures from his toy box. Nina was down beside him, admiring each of his toys with awe. She was doing a good job of keeping him interested, and James continued to babble. He was never this excited, not even with kids his age usually.

"James, I'm going to borrow Nina for a few minutes and show her to her room and around the house."

"I'll be back soon, cutie," Nina said and stood up.

James wasn't too happy, but it seemed like he wasn't going to go against what Nina said. She asked him to wait and play with his toys in the meantime and that was what he was going to do.

I was pleasantly surprised by this behavior. Around Nina, my son was like a different boy. Well-behaved and obedient.

She was quiet now as I led her to the spare room.

"I've left your bags in there," I told her and she stepped in behind me.

"Oh, wow! This is gorgeous. I'm guessing you didn't personally pick out the bedding yourself." She twirled around, taking in the décor of the bedroom and then finally looked at me. She was smiling as she said this, with one neat eyebrow raised.

I grinned too. "No, I'm not exactly an expert at complementary colors," I replied.

It made her smile wider. "How does a guy in the military get this rich? I mean, your house is beautiful, Miles said you're investing in his company...I'm sorry, I don't mean to pry." Nina was clearly the kind of person who spoke her mind. She wasn't going to be polite about her questions. She was just going to ask me whatever she wanted to know.

I leaned against the doorframe and nodded. "That's a fair enough question. I, of course, didn't make any of my money from my time in the Marines. My dad ran a successful business in Seattle, and I took over once he passed away, which was after I'd left the military already."

Nina searched my eyes. Her expression told me she was trying to think of something funny to say. "You're telling me you're some kind of a business tycoon?"

"Those are not my exact words."

My gaze drifted down her body before I even tried to stop myself.

I knew she was much younger than me. She was twenty-one, I was thirty-five. I was her boss. She was my friend's sister-in-law. There were a million reasons why I shouldn't have been looking at her that way, but I just couldn't stop myself from picturing her naked. Sprawled on that bed. Underneath me.

I watched the way her neck moved as she looked around the room. How delicate and soft it was. How her sleek dark hair was like a curtain that fell around her face. Did Nina know just how beautiful she was? She seemed like she wouldn't believe any compliment anybody gave her.

"Were you any good?" she asked, interrupting my thoughts. This was the first time I was paying any attention to her voice. It was silky smooth, pleasant to my ear. I wanted to be close to her. My animalistic desire for her had been awakened. I wanted to wrap her legs around my waist. My stomach tightened at the thought of her thighs rubbing against mine.

"At what?" I said. I wasn't sure if my voice was hoarse now. Could she see the desire in my eyes?

"At your business." Nina's eyelids looked heavy as she spoke. Somehow, she'd managed to inch closer to me now. We were standing directly in front of each other. I could see the rise and fall of her perfect breasts.

"I kept the business running, yeah, I managed. I was never going to be as good at it as my dad."

She tipped her head to the side, then her glance glided over me. Just like mine had done over her body a few moments ago. It was like she purposely wanted me to see that she was watching me closely.

"And now you want a different life."

I gritted my teeth and a small smile crept up on her face. "Don't worry, I'm not going to ask you again why. All of us are entitled to our personal reasons," she said.

I took a step forward. The more she spoke, the more I wanted to push her back against the wall and rip her clothes off. Nina parted her lips, just a little, and licked them. I knew she could sense it. She had to! The sexual tension between us was palpable.

"Is that a cue to me that I shouldn't be asking you too many questions?" I said and her smile grew wider.

"You catch on quick, Eric Hall," she replied and for a moment, I thought she was going to get on her toes and reach up and kiss my cheek. I cleared my throat. She was obviously not going to do that.

"I should text my sister and let her know I've moved in and everything is going great," she said.

That was all I needed to hear to step back. A jolt of a reminder of who she was. Nina Jones wasn't just a regular babysitter. She was my friend's sister-in-law. I had some degree of responsibility here, to ensure that I didn't take advantage of her position.

I ran a hand through my hair and nodded "Yeah, you do that, and I'm going to go check if our housekeeper's made enough dinner for all of us."

Nina didn't try to stop me as I left her room. She probably wanted me gone and some privacy while she settled in. I felt like a jerk, like I'd taken things a little far with her. I hadn't tried to hide the fact that I found her sexy. A college student. Fifteen years younger than me. What the hell was I thinking?

## 7

## NINA

Their home was beautiful, James was great, and this bedroom I was going to live in was the biggest, most gorgeous place I'd ever lived in. The bathroom had a luxurious tub made of marble. They had a house-keeper who cooked them their meals!

This was the perfect job.

I couldn't have asked for anything better. I couldn't have imagined anything better.

And yet, I felt a certain uneasiness now as I unpacked my stuff in the wardrobe.

It was because of Eric himself. Because of the way I felt every time I saw him. What was wrong with me? He was my boss. I needed to be professional and formal with him. I *needed* this job!

I'd flirted with him.

Well...I'd done what I considered as flirting, anyway. Maybe he hadn't noticed it at all. I couldn't stop staring at his body, those blue eyes, and his handsome smile melted me. I wanted to know if he could lift me up with just one hand, if his stubble would leave a burn on my cheeks if he kissed me. What would his lips taste like? Would his tongue be forceful in my mouth?

I shuddered at the thought and shut the wardrobe. As much as I tried, I couldn't get those thoughts out of my head, and I'd been trying for the past three days. Since I first met him.

I knew there was the danger of a sexual attraction if I took up this job.

I didn't want to do anything stupid. James liked me and trusted me. If I made a fool of myself here in their home, it would affect James too.

Once my bags were all unpacked, I kept them away and then went to the bathroom to wash my face, hoping it would help me calm down a little. It did. I took a few deep breaths and tried to focus on what was important.

I needed to keep this job. I was here now, somewhere safe and out of Karen's way. I was buying some time. Hopefully, it would take that man a while to figure out where I was. Maybe he wouldn't stalk me here, in Eric's house. Eric definitely looked like the kind of man you don't mess with.

And more importantly, I was earning money now. A lot of money. In a few months, if I budgeted myself correctly, I would have enough to pay off my father's debt without getting anyone into any trouble.

So I needed to keep this job. I needed to live here without any hiccups, for which, I needed to stay away from Eric.

Besides, it wasn't like he would ever want to be with a girl like me.

Eric Hall could have any woman he wanted. Why would he choose a nobody college student like me? I had nothing to offer him but sarcasm and social anxiety.

I focused on my reflection in the bathroom mirror and decided to step outside. James needed me.

We spent the next few hours playing. James showed me the toys in his toy box in the living room and then proceeded to show me the toys in his bedroom too. The boy had a lot of toys, and it was evident that his father spoiled him. He was given everything that he asked for. Was Eric trying to compensate for the mother figure that was missing from James's life?

This was something else I didn't know about this little family. What happened to James's mom? Was she around at all? I was curious, but I didn't want to pry either.

Eric had informed me that he would arrange for dinner to be ready by seven. James was usually in bed by eight. We were going to have dinner together, and I couldn't help but look forward to that. I couldn't help but think about seeing Eric again. He'd taken over my thoughts completely.

In James's room, while he started arranging his action figures in a row, I knelt down beside him on the rug and helped him.

"How is playschool?" I asked him. I wanted to know every-thing there was to know about this kid. I figured that would be the best way for me to help him and to be supportive of him. James was quiet for some time, and he remained focused on his toys.

I reached for his shoulders and gave it a little squeeze.

"You know you can tell me if there's something wrong. Now or whenever, okay? I want you to know that."

The kid looked up at me. He had the same blue eyes as his father and that startled me for a moment, but I managed to smile at him. "I know it can be tough going to a new kindergarten and trying to make new friends all over again. I'm here for you from now on, okay? You're not alone. Even if you feel like you can't tell something to your dad..." I had more to say, and I was trying to gain James's trust, but before I could finish saying it, he threw himself at me.

I wrapped my arms around him and held him close. My suspicion about this boy was correct. He was feeling lost and lonely in this new town, far away from the only home he'd ever known. Far away from his friends whom he'd grown up with. Maybe he blamed his father for this move and this change. That was why he didn't want to discuss his true feelings with him, because he didn't think his father would understand.

I stroked James's soft golden hair and planted a kiss on top of his head. I didn't know I could feel this way about a kid, a child I barely even knew, but I felt protective of him. While he remained tightly enclosed in my arms, I rocked him back and forth. I wanted him to feel safe with me.

After several moments passed, he wriggled and looked up at me.

"You are my best friend, Nina," he said, which made me smile. Things were so simple around a kid. They spoke their minds. They didn't play games with your feelings. He was trying his best to express how he felt about me and I stroked his cheek.

"And you are mine," I replied.

"Daddy is sad, too," James continued.

He'd taken me by surprise. I tried not to stare but I wasn't sure he knew what he was talking about. "What do you mean, honey?"

James shifted out of my arms then and went back to playing with his toys. He was distracted again.

"James, honey, what do you mean by what you just said?" I knew I probably shouldn't have been prying or asking him personal questions about his father, but I couldn't help my curiosity either.

"He didn't want to live in Seattle because he was sad there. But he is sad here too. Daddy is always sad." James wasn't looking up at me as he spoke. He continued playing with his toys while I sat there in silence. I had no idea that kids could be this perceptive, if this was even true.

What did he know about sadness? How could he tell what his father was actually feeling? I found myself hoping he was wrong. I hoped Eric wasn't sad.

"I'm sure it will be all fine, honey. It isn't something you need to worry about, okay? Your daddy is strong and good. He'll be able to handle it himself. Do you understand? He just wants *you* to be happy."

I didn't know if I was doing a good job of talking to this kid. I'd never done something like this before. I wasn't sure of the right words to use in a situation like this. Was I making things worse?

James looked at me and presented me with a crooked smile.

"Do you understand what I'm saying, James? You don't have to worry about your daddy."

He nodded.

I felt Eric's presence at the door at that moment. It was open. I hoped he hadn't overheard our conversation.

"Dinner's ready. It's time to eat, buddy, and then off to bed."

James immediately forgot about our conversation. It was time for him to whine and protest against his father's orders. Eric was barely even looking at me.

I jumped up to help, coaxing James to eat his dinner with us, and then I promised to read him some bedtime stories and help brush his teeth before bed.

"I'm not joining you guys for dinner," Eric said while I led James to the dining room. I stopped and turned to him, a little surprised. I thought we were all eating together, and this declaration disappointed me. But this was my job, and I had no reason to complain. This was exactly why I'd been hired in the first place. So that now Eric would have free time to do his own things, instead of looking after James all the time.

Eric said nothing to me. He just gave his son a stern look. "In bed by eight, James, and listen to whatever Nina says," he said and then he was gone.

This was the part that I was most worried about when I took up this job—bedtime. My inexperience with kids meant that I wasn't confident about being able to put James down to sleep smoothly. Surprisingly, though, it wasn't as difficult as I thought it would be. He *did* go down without a fight.

We ate together, then we went back to his room where I helped him change and brush his teeth. By the time he was in bed, it was just a little before eight. I had to read him a few stories before he actually drifted off, but I didn't mind that at all. I waited some more time, sitting beside him on his bed, watching him sleep and breathe softly. I didn't leave his room until I was absolutely certain he was fast asleep and wouldn't wake up. It seemed like all that excitement of the evening had finally worn him out.

I was tired too, but not so tired that I wasn't wondering where Eric was.

Not that it was any of my business.

The house was quiet now and I felt like I was all alone here, in this big home. There was no sign of Eric and James was asleep. So I went to my bedroom. I sat on my bed reading for some time and then decided to draw myself a bath.

That helped relax me.

By the time I was out of the bath and changed into a pair of pajamas, it was already past ten. I could have just gone to sleep at this point, but I was craving a snack. I figured I could just help myself to a spoon of peanut butter in the kitchen and that would suffice.

I knew Eric was in the house the moment I stepped out of my bedroom. It was like I could actually feel his warm presence around me.

Earlier, after James had fallen asleep, I'd turned off most of the lights around the house. Now there was a dim light pouring out from the living room. That was where Eric was —I could feel it. I moved closer and closer to the room and I could hear my heart beating in my chest.

Why was I reacting this way? What was so special about him? Why did I wish he'd stayed for dinner with us?

I reached the door of the living room and looked inside.

Eric was standing at his drinks cabinet, pouring himself a glass of something. I gulped because of how good he looked right now. I could almost imagine those big strong arms wrapped around me. Since when did I care about big strong arms? I scolded myself.

"How was he?"

Eric spoke, but he hadn't even looked up. He startled me and, for a moment, I couldn't find my voice. How did he know I was standing there? Did he know I'd been staring at him?

The back of my neck burned with embarrassment now.

"James? Yeah, fine. He's asleep now. He's great." I fumbled with the words, nervous.

When he finally looked up at me, those blue eyes were sparkling and I could barely meet his gaze.

"Want one?" he asked. But he was pouring me a glass of it without waiting for my response.

I wasn't much of a drinker, in fact, I rarely ever drank because I rarely ever went out to socialize and yet tonight, I was sure I needed that drink.

Eric came up to me with the two glasses in both his hands. It could have been whiskey, but I wasn't sure. I didn't want to ask him either and embarrass myself. I took the glass from him and took a sip. The brown liquid burned the back of my throat. It was exactly the sensation I needed.

I struggled to not cough, but surely he could see I wasn't great at this.

He smiled. "You don't have to drink it if you don't want to," he told me. I rubbed my mouth with the back of my hand and put the glass down on the coffee table. I could feel his eyes on me.

Suddenly, I was self-conscious about what I was wearing. Just a pair of old pajamas and a skimpy silk camisole which noodle straps kept falling over my shoulders.

Eric was in his usual blue jeans and a black t-shirt.

I didn't know what to say. Did he expect me to stay or leave? Maybe he needed some time to himself and I was intruding?

"I was just on my way to the kitchen to grab something to eat," I said quickly, looking up at him.

"Are you hungry?" he asked but didn't sound concerned.

I shrugged my shoulders. "Not really. I just didn't have anything else to do I guess."

He took a large sip of that bitter, stinging drink, but it didn't seem to affect on him at all.

"What else did my son say about me, other than that he thinks I'm always sad?"

I wasn't expecting that. I didn't have a reaction or an answer prepared. He looked at me closely, like he was watching me for a reaction. Like he could detect exactly what I was thinking.

I didn't know what to say. I'd hoped he hadn't heard James talking about him earlier. "I'm sorry, I didn't want to meddle," I said in a soft voice.

Eric twirled the drink in his glass and shrugged. "I'm not accusing you of anything, Nina. Honestly, I'm glad he's opening up to you because he's been quite shut off from me and everything else lately." He ran a hand through his hair, like he was trying very hard to keep it together.

"He didn't say anything else. He just sounded concerned for you."

Eric put his glass down beside mine and came closer to me. I could feel my throat going dry with anticipation. I wasn't expecting this night to go like this. I felt unprepared. What did *he* want?

A part of me just wanted to turn and run away from here, because I was so afraid of my physical reaction to him. Then there was that part of me that wanted to stay and experience everything.

"And you told him not to worry. I heard that," Eric continued.

"He's a kid. He doesn't need to concern himself with what's going on with you."

"So you do think I'm sad?" Eric came even closer to me now.

"It's not my place to form opinions on your private life. It's not like we're friends," I said.

Eric was standing over me now. Tall and strong. I looked up at him, at his strong jaw. Those big rugged shoulders. There was a tightening in my belly I couldn't explain.

"No, we're not friends. You're right," he said.

"You're my employer," I added, gulping now.

"Right again."

Eric's voice was deep and heavy. I could feel something going on. Something out of the ordinary. I just couldn't tell what would happen next. What did he want? I knew what I wanted.

"And here you are, standing in my living room in that top."

He was direct. His gaze cruised down my front. I knew my nipples had hardened under the silky material of my top. He could see them, and that was what he was referring to. For some reason, I wasn't the least bit embarrassed anymore. I didn't care that he could see just how much he turned me on.

I tilted my head so I could face him even more directly.

"I have no choice. I live here now. You're going to have to see me in these clothes occasionally." I was taunting him.

There was no denying the fact that we'd crossed all boundaries of an employer-employee relationship by now. It was like neither of us was really thinking about what we were saying anymore. It didn't matter.

"And you do know what seeing you like this is going to do to me," he added.

This time, my stare went down his body before I even tried looking away. I gazed at the bulge between his legs. I gulped. There was nothing more I wanted at that moment than to reach out and touch him. To hold him in my hands. To feel the strength of him and to see the effect I had on him.

Maybe me watching him like that spurred him on. Eric reached for me. His arm wound around my waist before I knew what was going to happen. He pulled me to himself and slammed my body to his. I gasped, out of breath.

This was getting way out of control, and I liked it.

His hot breath fell on my face as I clung to him. I could feel those muscles now. Tight and strong all over his torso. Picking up some courage, I wrapped my left leg around one of his. He leaned closer. I knew he could now feel the warmth and maybe the wetness between my thighs.

"This is insane," he mumbled in my ear as our breaths grew heavy.

I didn't know what I was doing. I'd never seduced a man this way before, and certainly not an older, more experienced man like him. I was sure I'd fail miserably. In a few moments, he was going to push me away or break down laughing.

But Eric nibbled my earlobe and a shot of electricity ran down my spine. I parted my lips and moaned softly. His hands were on my waist now.

"I've been thinking about this since we first met," he said.

"Me too."

His mouth moved away from my earlobe and he tasted my neck. I threw my head back, pushing up against his body even more now. I circled my hips so that I slowly rubbed up on his leg. Eric groaned.

"Fuck, Nina, your body is beautiful," I heard him say softly, like I was in a dream and imagining this whole thing.

This had to be a dream, right? How did we even land up here?

His hands traveled all over me now. He felt my hips, my butt, then up my back until he was cradling me by my neck. His hands were gently placed around my throat. I moved against him, shuddering. Rubbing up against his thigh as we stood entwined together. I could feel his breath falling on my neck. He tasted me again, my salty skin.

I moved my hand around his waist. Just waiting for the moment when I'd have enough courage to simply slip my hand down his jeans. I wanted to feel his cock in my hand, and not just through his jeans.

"Eric, I want you," I murmured. I'd forgotten myself. Maybe I didn't even hear myself speak. His left hand was splayed on my butt, he had me pinned to himself. His other hand reached for my breasts. No bra. He flicked one erect nipple and I gasped.

"I want you too," he said, but suddenly, I noticed there was a change in his tone. I was dripping wet. My legs were wrapped around his. I'd been stroking my throbbing pussy against his body...and now...now it sounded like he was about to change his mind.

I looked up at him. He was already watching me.

"But this has to stop right here," he declared and I felt like someone was shattering glass somewhere. It physically pained me to hear those words come out of his mouth.

The sensation I was experiencing now was akin to having a big pail of icy cold water washing over me. For a moment, even after Eric had said what he said, I remained frozen to the spot. Still pressed up against him, breathing his air. Surprisingly, he didn't make a move to push me away.

I couldn't believe I heard him correctly the first time. He must have seen the confusion on my face too because he repeated himself.

"We can't go ahead with this. We need to stop now."

I jerked away from him. I wasn't great at or confident about a thing like this in the first place...and then rejection? I wasn't sure I would ever recover from this incident. I shuddered, suddenly very cold, my lips quivering. I was embarrassed and aroused, angry and relieved all at the same time.

We were separated now. I should have just walked away. Walked out of that door and left the house. Quit my job and never return, but I couldn't move. I just stood there with my feet stuck to the ground.

Eric sighed aloud and placed his hands on his hips like he was just about to give orders to a military regiment. I glanced at him, at his body, at the spot between his legs. I was so close to feeling everything, but that would have been a point of no return.

"I apologize that I allowed things to get too far," he said.

He wasn't the only one who was involved in the scene. I wanted to say something, but all I did was stare at my feet.

"Nina, I want you to know that if you decide to stay on, I promise to keep my hands to myself."

I looked up at him. Was he sincerely apologizing to me? Did he seriously think that I would quit this job because I wanted to get away from him? I gaped at him and he continued to speak.

"The way you have connected with my son is just amazing. He wasn't even this compatible with our nanny in Seattle. I can see he is going to be very happy with you living here, and my son's happiness means more than anything else to me."

"I love spending time with James too," I managed to chirp, to which Eric nodded.

"Good, I'm glad to hear that. I shouldn't have allowed myself to lose control like that. We need to keep it professional," he added.

"Right, keep it professional," I said, feeling like my chest was going to collapse.

"You understand."

I nodded. Of course, I understood. The logic wasn't complicated. I just wished Eric wouldn't keep repeating it to remind me that he'd pushed me away.

"Goodnight, Nina. I have an early day," he said and walked past me. Our half-drunk glasses were on the coffee table and I picked them up and took them to the kitchen. The housekeeper would have cleaned up after us the next morning, but I needed something to do. I wasn't prepared to go to my bedroom and be alone with my thoughts just yet.

This had actually happened. Eric Hall had really touched me. We were so close to more. There were goosebumps on my arms as I thought of that, washing my hands under the kitchen faucet.

I wanted him...no matter what *he* thought was the right thing to do. For the first time in my life, I was a hundred percent sure of what I wanted, but I couldn't have it.

## 8

## ERIC

*N*ow that I didn't have to worry about James being left alone in the house, I had the time and freedom to hit the gym early in the morning. I left a note on the refrigerator door, saying where I was gone. Nina had put up her class schedule for the week there, so I was aware of the few hours in the week when she wouldn't be able to watch James, which weren't that many. This arrangement was working out perfectly. Other than the minor hiccup from the previous night.

No, it wasn't *minor*. I shouldn't have offered her that drink.

I most definitely shouldn't have stepped that close to her where I could smell the sweet delicious scent of her warm skin.

I shouldn't have pulled her close to me.

This morning, working out helped me clear my head. I was hoping that when I returned to the house next and even if I saw Nina there, I'd be able to keep it together. What was so difficult? She was just a girl. She had arms and legs and a mouth like every other woman out there.

In the gym, my gaze landed on a woman who was running on the treadmill in front of me. Long legs in shapely running tights. I looked away. The only thing on my mind was Nina and what she'd looked like pressed up against me last night. We were so close. A few more minutes and I would have been inside her, feeling her warmth.

I would have given anything for that.

Anything but sacrificed James's happiness and comfort. He was the most important thing in my life and any complication with Nina would lead to this arrangement being ruined. How was I going to make him happy again if she left? I was already running out of ideas.

So I ran on the treadmill and lifted some weights to push that energy out of my body. I needed to get Nina Jones out of my mind. For the first time, working out didn't seem to be clearing my head. Frustrated, I left the gym and went in for a shower. This was ridiculous! What was so special about her?

I changed into fresh clothes for the day and stuffed everything into my gym bag. That was when my phone rang and I saw it was Cynthia calling again.

She'd been calling my number and leaving voice messages for over a week now. I'd ignored each one of them, but all of a sudden, talking to her seemed like the perfect solution to get Nina out of my mind. It sounded crazy, but I was willing to give it a shot.

"Eric! Thank God! Finally." I heard her voice on the other

end and my jaw clenched together. There was a time when I liked listening to her speak, when I didn't really know the things she was capable of. Now, her voice put me on edge.

"Why are you still calling me, Cynthia?" I tried to sound as distant and business-like as possible. She didn't deserve my time or my compassion.

"I'm calling to find out about the wellbeing of my son. Is that really so hard for you to imagine?" She sounded mock-offended.

"He's fine. You were never worried about him before," I replied. I was on my way out of the gym but this phone call was slowing me down.

I could picture Cynthia's lip curling now. "Oh, Eric, sweetheart, you sound upset."

"I am upset, Cynthia. I told you categorically to leave us alone."

"But how can you expect me to just forget about my baby? About you?"

I sighed. I should have known she'd play this angle if I took her call. "Well, you did forget about him, for several years."

I was out of the building now, but I lingered near the doors with the phone pressed to my ear.

"I was expecting you to be more supportive of me, Eric. Things have been difficult for me. You, of all people, should know what I've been through."

There was so much I could have said to her then, but I didn't want to. I was not up for a confrontation. Not another one, with the mother of my child.

"What do you want from me, Cynthia?" I stopped in my tracks. I wanted to clearly hear her answer my question.

"You know what I want, Eric. I want to be a part of my son's life. I want to be where you are." Her voice had dropped low, soft. She was trying to gain sympathy and I had none to give her.

"You can't be a part of our lives. It's over."

"Why do *you* get to make that decision? We're both in this together, you know? I'm his mother!" Her voice wasn't soft anymore. She was beginning to lose her temper, just as I'd predicted she would.

"Where were you when he needed you? When all he wanted was to be with his mommy." It stung me to say those words. It was difficult for me to admit that I had needed help.

I'd thought I could raise James alone. I was determined to do it, but nobody warned me how difficult it would be. Cynthia was gone.

"I was trying to find myself, Eric. You know that. You make it out like I abandoned my son and my husband. I was just trying to be the best mother I could be."

I pressed my eyes closed and took in a deep breath. There was a time, not too long ago, when I would have fallen for this shit. I would have given Cynthia the benefit of the doubt because she'd been such a big part of my life. But now I knew better. At this moment, nothing mattered to me more than the happiness of my son.

"Goodbye, Cynthia."

"Eric, wait!" She was trying to keep me on the line.

"I've let you have your say, but now I have to let you go."

"You can't do this to me, Eric! Where are you?"

"Take care of yourself. I hope you find what you're looking for."

"No! Eric! Please! I want to see my son. I want to see you. How can you be this cold?" She was screaming into the phone now.

"I can't give you another chance. I am not going to play with my son's future."

"Our son, you mean."

"Cynthia...goodbye."

I ended the call. We would have continued to argue forever if I didn't stop this now. I wasn't afraid of her. She had no legal standing in this situation. She could drag it out in court if she wanted to. I had the money to fight her on this, and she knew it. She wasn't going to try that. Emotionally blackmailing me and trying to win James over were her only ways out, and I wasn't going to allow it.

Slipping the phone in my pocket, I looked up at the sky. My life felt like a mess. I had no control over it. Having a kid did that to you, I knew it, but I still felt helpless.

I wanted Nina and I couldn't have her either because I was watching out for my son. I'd moved cities, trying to start a new life because I wanted what was best for James. I'd forgotten what it was like to do something just for myself, and that was okay. I didn't resent James for it. Keeping him and raising him alone were my decisions. I was going to stick by them.

I couldn't think of Nina now without feeling disappointed in myself. That phone call with Cynthia was just the reminder I needed that I had a bigger shitstorm to deal with. I didn't have time to pursue anything with Nina. Especially something casual and temporary. What James needed was stability. Nobody could give that to him but me.

I walked back to the house and a part of me wished that I wouldn't find Nina there. I hoped she'd taken James out somewhere. I didn't want to face her just yet.

I'd spent the entire night fantasizing about her. What it would be like to remove all her clothes and thrust myself inside her. What if she saw that in my eyes today? How were we going to make it work if she knew I couldn't forget about her?

## 9

# NINA

*I*t was very early when Eric left for the gym. I found his note in the kitchen when I went in there to make breakfast for myself and James. It almost seemed like he was trying to get away from the house. Was he trying to get away from me? Did he really regret last night that much? Was everything ruined now?

I tried not to think about it. I had a job to do. I needed the money. I was here with a purpose and now that I had the chance, I was going to fulfill it.

In the kitchen, I made some scrambled eggs with spinach and cheese, along with toast. I prepared the table with glasses of orange juice and milk. I wasn't sure if kids ate that, but it seemed like a healthy enough breakfast for a five-year-old.

After that, I went to wake up James who was initially too sleepy to want food, and then too excited to eat. He wanted to play with his toys instead.

We sat at the kitchen table eventually and started eating

together. The only reason he was eating was because I was there and having the same food along with him. The housekeeper, Sarah, arrived a few minutes later and we introduced ourselves to each other for the first time.

In that hour since I'd woken up, I'd managed to keep my mind busy and off Eric. Slowly, I was beginning to feel more confident about the possibility of making through this without crumbling into pieces over him.

I chatted with Sarah for a bit and then got James ready for the day. He seemed excited to spend the day out, but first, there was playschool to be tackled.

We were just about to step out of the house when Eric returned. He walked through the door in gym clothes, looking more muscular and sexy than he had before. I felt my knees go weak and I grabbed on to James's hand a little tighter.

"Hi."

"Hi."

Sarah was around, dusting the house. I wondered if she could sense the awkwardness between Eric and me. Was it obvious or was I just panicking?

"Good morning, buddy. Where are you headed?" Eric chose to direct the conversation to his son now. James hugged his dad and told him I was taking him to playschool and then we'd hit the park.

"Sounds like a great day. Be good and enjoy yourself. I want to hear all about it later."

"Will you have dinner with us, Daddy?" James asked.

Eric ruffled his hair. "I'm going to try," he said and glanced at me. Was it a hint that he would avoid having dinner at home because of me? I was upset by the idea of that.

"I hope you have a nice day too," he then said directly to me.

I was taken aback by it a little. I was expecting him to ignore me completely.

"Thanks," was all I could manage. Then I was tugging James out of the house while he continued to chat with me.

We shut the door behind us and I fixed his jacket and his hat. Just as I was about to turn and leave, I got the feeling that we were being watched. I looked up and saw Eric at a window. It might have been his bedroom. I wasn't sure of the house layout yet. He was looking down at us, and even though he caught me staring up, he didn't budge or look away.

"C'mon, you, we're going to be late for kindergarten," I said to James and hurried him away.

Even as we were walking away, I could sense his eyes on me. Just knowing that he was watching me was enough to make me shudder with desire. How was I going to get through the rest of this job feeling like this?

I dropped James off at his playschool and went over to my college campus. I'd set up a coffee date with Karen and I went to meet her directly.

"What's the kid like?" she asked me, bursting with curiosity. I was curious about her new life too. I knew she had a new roommate in the dorm, but all she told me was that they didn't really get along yet.

"He's sweet, a little lonely. They moved to Chicago recently from Seattle, so he still needs some time to settle in."

Karen watched me closely, nodding her head absent-mindedly.

"I wouldn't have taken you for a *babysitter*," she said. "And why are you so into this job anyway?"

I shrugged. "Yeah, I never considered myself good with kids either, but it seems to be working for us. The kid actually likes me. And the only reason I'm in this job is for the money and a place to stay."

Karen looked away from me. "Yeah, and you're not going to explain the situation to me, right?"

We'd had this conversation before I left. Karen was suspicious, and rightly so, of why I was in such a hurry to leave the dorm room and find a job. Moreover, the man who'd ransacked our room made her even more suspicious.

"There's nothing to know. I need the money and I wanted to move out of the dorm."

Karen shook her head like she didn't believe me. "And what about that guy? Are you going to explain the situation there? Who is he and why did he make a mess of our room?"

"Karen, I..."

She sat back in her chair and rolled her eyes. "That's right, you can't explain that either."

"You have nothing to worry about, that's all you really need to know, right?"

"If I really am your best friend, you're going to tell me what's going on. Why did you really leave the dorm? Was it because of him?" She was persistent.

"Can we talk about something else, please?"

Now would have been a good time to mention what nearly happened with Eric. That would have been the perfect distraction, to steer her away from asking about the other man. But I just couldn't say it. I couldn't get the words out.

Eric's rejection made me suffer. I was embarrassed by my own actions and my feelings. Not that I actually knew what I was feeling.

"Fine, let's talk about something else. How about the idea of going on a blind date?" She was sitting back in her chair with her arms crossed over her chest. Now there was a smile on her lips. Karen knew she'd backed me into a corner.

"You want to set me up on a blind date? Is that what you're saying to me?"

"Yes, that's exactly what I'm saying."

"Why? Why would you even dream of such a thing?" I couldn't help but laugh at the idea.

"Because he's my brother's friend and I think you would be good for each other."

"Are you serious?"

"Dead serious. Unless you're willing to give me some answers, I'm not going to drop it."

I sighed and took a large sip of my coffee. "Why are you

doing this, Karen?"

She took a piece of the oatmeal cookie she'd bought but forgotten. "I'm trying to do what I think is best for you. You should go out, meet someone, get into the dating game so you can socialize more."

"Why should I do any of that?" This conversation was starting to exhaust me.

"Because you're going to be stuck in a rut—of college, your job, that kid...just boring stuff. And now that you're living away from me and I'm not there to keep you company, you're also going to get very lonely very soon."

I gulped. As much as I wanted to disagree with what she was saying, I knew there was some truth to it.

It had been just a day and I already felt lonely. Especially after I'd made a fool of myself with Eric.

"Fine," I declared.

Karen's eyes grew wide like she couldn't believe her plan had actually worked. "Excuse me?"

"I said fine, set me up on this date if you want to."

She jumped out of her chair and lunged at me. Karen was hugging me now over the table and squealing excitedly.

"You two are going to get along, Nina. You totally are. I can feel it. His name is Matthew and I've met him a couple of times with my brother. He's a really nice guy, you'll see."

I nodded and wriggled out of Karen's arms. "You don't have to oversell it, I've agreed to this date already."

Maybe going on a date with a stranger wasn't such a bad

idea after all. This would give me a chance to see that there were other fish in the sea. That Eric was just a passing infatuation.

"Okay, okay. But I'm going to text my brother right now so we can get the ball rolling." Karen was more excited about this than me.

I didn't want to be late picking James up from his playschool, so I arrived there early. I'd been waiting for close to twenty minutes before the doors opened and the kids started pouring out. James walked slowly out of the doors and I saw he was the only kid who was making his way out without anyone else for company. It was clear to me that he hadn't made any friends in kindergarten yet.

"James! Sweetie! Hi!" I waved enthusiastically at him, and his face instantly brightened. My heart melted when I saw him running toward me. I was warmed by the affection I felt toward this child, knowing that he trusted me completely. That he considered me his best friend.

"How was it today?" I lifted him up briefly in my arms because I felt like he might have needed a hug.

"We did colors today," he replied.

"Will you show me at home?"

"Can we go to the park first?" He hadn't forgotten my promise.

"Of course we can." I slid him down and held on tightly to his hand as we started walking to my car.

I tried to get him to talk more about his class and the other kids, but James didn't seem to want to do that. I was curious because I wanted to make sure his teachers were looking out for him and that he wasn't being bullied. I was well aware of how the new kids got treated.

"Is there anybody in class you talk to?"

He shook his head. "No, I don't like talking to them. They are stupid."

I buckled him into his car seat. "Maybe we shouldn't be talking about our friends that way. That is a rude thing to say, sweetie. You know better than that, don't you?"

"They are not my friends. I hate them!" He crossed his arms over his chest in a show of protest. I gulped, at a loss now. I had no idea how to handle a situation like this. What was I supposed to say to him?

"Okay, we can talk about this later when you're not this angry. This discussion isn't over though, kiddo. Think about why you think you hate them."

James wasn't even looking at me as I spoke, like he wanted to shut my voice out. Clearly, discussing his classmates was his least favorite thing to do.

I could have simply ignored it and moved on. Technically, this wasn't a part of my job description, but I knew I couldn't let this go. I needed to get to the bottom of why James hated his classmates and disliked going to kindergarten. I wanted to help him.

But I couldn't do this alone. I would have to tell Eric about this. James was his son, after all, and making parenting decisions wasn't up to me.

## 10

## ERIC

*I* came home for dinner because I'd told James I would try. My instinct was to avoid it because I wanted to avoid Nina. I knew it would be hard for me to not feel the same things I did last night. To not want to rip her clothes off.

She'd helped Sarah set up the dinner table for us when I got home. James was already sitting in his chair, waiting for me to sit down across from him. Mealtimes were usually hard in our household, but it seemed like James didn't mind them so much anymore with Nina around. I didn't know what her trick was, but she was doing *something* right.

While we ate, I asked James about his day, and as usual, he said nothing about playschool but was very excited about all the stuff he got to do at the park. Nina and I avoided eye contact. She clearly had the same idea as me—to get the job done and not bring up the previous night. I was relieved.

I was worried about her ability to her job. The last thing I wanted was to have ruined the good thing we had going for

James here. I was glad she was able to keep this professional.

After dinner, Nina declared she was going to give James a bath and then it was bedtime. I promised to read him a book.

I was about to stand up from my chair when she finally said something directly to me for the first time all evening.

"Can we talk later? Once James is asleep?"

She looked serious. I held her gaze for a few moments. Her large green eyes were dark now, like she had a lot on her mind.

"Sure, whatever you want," I replied.

She nodded once and then she was gone from the room. James had followed her so I was left alone in the dining room. This worried me. Just when I thought things could go back to normal, Nina wanted to 'talk', which I assumed could only mean one thing—she wanted to quit.

I clenched my fists on my lap as I sat there. I should have known!

I was mad at myself for ruining it.

All I could do now was wait for this to come apart.

James had his bath, he'd brushed his teeth, and he was ready for bed way before his usual bedtime. Nina had clearly worked her magic. He behaved so well around her and now this would be over. My search of trying to find the perfect babysitter for him would have to begin all over again.

Nina came to find me in the living room to say James was waiting for me to read to him. I tried to catch her eye again, to predict what she was about to say, but she left the room before I even had a chance to respond.

I found James in his bed when I went to his room. He was in a much better mood than usual.

We read his favorite book together, then I gave him a long tight hug and wished him goodnight. I met Nina on my way out. She was waiting there to take over.

"I'll be in the living room if you want to come find me later," I told her. All she did was nod before she went back into James's room.

It seemed like my son took some time to fall asleep because I'd been waiting in the living room for close to an hour before Nina finally showed up.

I was on my second whiskey and tonight, unlike last night, she wasn't in her pajamas. But Nina seemed to have this unique ability of making just a simple pair of jeans and a blouse look sexy. My gaze fell on her breasts rising and falling under that blouse. The deep neckline. Her slender milky neck and her bow-shaped pink lips. I wanted to kiss her.

It was strange because I hadn't wanted to kiss a woman in a long time.

In my mind, there was a huge difference between wanting to fuck someone and kiss them. I looked away from her, mad at myself for having these thoughts—minutes before she was going to quit her job.

"How may I help you this evening, Nina?" I said when she

entered the room. I could sense her wanting to keep her distance from me tonight. She stood at the edge of the room with her hands clasped together in front of her. I'd decided already that I wasn't going to offer her a drink tonight. I didn't want her to think I was making a move on her.

"I wanted to discuss the situation of James with you."

Our eyes met and I gritted my jaw. "You can spare yourself the awkwardness. I know what you're meaning to say."

"You do?" Her neat brows crossed.

I was sitting on the couch and I wondered if it would be appropriate to offer her a seat too. Or would she assume I was hitting on her again?

"Yeah, you want to leave," I replied and ran my forefinger over the rim of my glass. The condensation felt cool against my skin. Nina's brows remained crossed.

"What?"

"You want to quit. I get it. I don't need an explanation from you," I said.

She breathed in deeply and slowly shook her head. "No, Eric, I'm not here to quit."

I stared at her in surprise. She still wanted to work here? After what happened between us last night? "All right. That's good news."

She gave me a half-smile.

"Because last night—" I began but she interrupted me.

"That's forgotten. We were being stupid. We weren't thinking."

Was that really what she thought of last night? That we were being stupid?

I could see she was blushing. Her cheeks were hot red and I could feel my muscles stiffen. Did she have to look at me like that? With her eyes narrowed under her heavy lids.

"Yes, we were," I said.

A few beats of silence passed between us.

"So, what is this about?" I was trying my best to not let her see how relieved I was by the news. I was glad I hadn't fucked this up for my son.

Nina sighed and took a few steps closer to the couch, like she was finally comfortable doing it.

"It's about James's playschool. Today when I went to pick him up, he came out alone, while all the other kids had friends."

"Okay, yeah. He just needs some more time to make friends. What is the big deal? He's a shy kid."

Nina nodded and licked her lips. "Fair enough, but then when I asked him about making friends in kindergarten, he said all the other kids are stupid." She stared at me with her green eyes bright and widened, like she was expecting me to have all the answers.

"Yeah. James doesn't take to new people very well. Which was why I was so surprised to see the two of you getting along so easily."

Nina's eyes softened and I could see she was actually worried, instead of being impressed by my compliment. "I think you should maybe talk to the playschool, discuss this issue with his teachers."

"Why?" I snapped.

"Because a five-year-old should not be this judgmental about people, especially other kids in his class. He should be making friends. If he's not, there could be an underlying problem there."

"What are you trying to say?" I stood up from the couch to face her.

"He could be getting bullied. Someone needs to watch out for him in class. Maybe his teachers. I don't know... it's just my suspicion. I could be wrong." That worrisome look remained on Nina's face. I came closer to her and she shyly followed my movements with her eyes. I was standing over her again. Just like last night. For the sake of my sanity, I held on to that whiskey glass tightly.

"I don't want to make a big deal of him not having friends in playschool. It would embarrass him," I said.

Nina tucked some loose strands of her dark hair behind her ears. She continued to stare at me, almost without blinking. "I'm just trying to help. I just think it could be worth looking into. He's probably too proud to admit it, and he's still so small."

"Thank you for your concern," I said and she remained very still. "I'll think about it."

I could see the perfect shape of her chin now, the way her pink lips curled. What would her tongue taste like in my mouth? I could feel my cock hardening in my pants. Could she feel it too? I wanted to push her up against the wall and slip my hand underneath her blouse.

But I was grateful she wasn't quitting. James's happiness and peace were worth much more than my sexual desire for this woman.

Nina parted her mouth a little, and her tongue ran over her lips in a smooth sweep. Why was she doing this? Was she trying to tempt me on purpose?

"Okay, sure. Whatever you think is best for him. I just thought I'd bring it to your notice," Nina said. I'd almost forgotten what we were discussing.

"James would have told me if something like that was going on in his playschool."

Nina nodded.

"I know he might seem difficult to you, and sure, he can be a handful sometimes, but he knows he can speak his mind with me. He doesn't need to keep secrets from me," I said.

She nodded again.

Without another word, she turned and was about to walk away. I reached for her hand and grabbed it tightly. Without knowing what I was doing, I yanked her back to myself. I heard her gasp when she fell toward me.

"And last night wasn't stupid. It was just a bad idea," I growled. My voice was low and animalistic. I almost didn't recognize it myself. Her eyes narrowed. She stuck her chin up and stared up at me proudly.

"It doesn't matter. Like you said, we can't jeopardize my job here."

I let go of her wrist. Why did she have to talk like this? Why did her mouth have to look this sexy?

"No, we can't."

"So I'm going to walk away now," she added, like it was a warning. She had nothing to worry about. I wasn't going to pull her back.

"Goodnight." That growl again. I had this sudden urge of wanting to slam my fist into the wall. Just so I could feel something. To relieve this pressure I felt all over my body.

She took a few steps back, watching me still, and then she turned and walked to the door. When she turned to look at me, I knew she was going to be thinking about me tonight. The sexual tension between us was undeniable. Even if it was just for fun. We were two adults, thirsty for each other, living under the same roof and separated because of a kid we both wanted the best for.

Nina was gone in seconds and I sat down on the couch with a thump. This was the second night in a row since her arrival that I was left here drinking my whiskey alone.

I ran a hand through my hair, feeling frustrated. How many more nights of this was I going to have to put myself through while she was around?

This was insane.

There had to be a solution.

Maybe I needed to find something else to distract me, *someone else*, just a temporary solution.

*M*y skin felt like it burned where Eric had touched my wrist the previous night. When he pulled me back to himself again and held me there, I was so sure I'd melt into a puddle. That I wouldn't be able to resist kissing him. Just being around him was a bad idea. Simply looking into his eyes was as dangerous as staring at the sun. I had no self-control as far as he was concerned, and now I was grateful to Karen for the distraction she had provided me with.

I was supposed to meet Matthew for a drink at a bar near the college.

Eric had stayed suspiciously out of my way the whole day. When I finally had a chance to talk to him in the evening, I asked if he would be home at night so I could go out for a few hours after James was asleep. Eric spent just a couple of moments in my presence, long enough to acknowledge the fact that he had heard me and that he'd make himself available while I was gone.

And now I was standing here at the bar, in the only going-out dress I owned, waiting for a stranger to show up—and all I could do was still keep thinking about Eric.

Matthew arrived ten minutes late, just before I would have walked out of this place. Like Karen had described, he was a very good-looking guy. He wasn't too tall, but well-built and stocky. He had longish dark hair and was dressed stylishly, like he was at a cocktail bar.

Karen had said we would be compatible and she knew me well. So I was willing to give this guy a chance.

"You must be Nina," he said, walking up to me with one single red rose in his hand. It was the cheesiest thing he could have done and I tried my best to hold back every comment that passed through my head. I wanted to laugh, but I felt sorry for him. He was making an effort, and besides, like Karen said, he was probably a really nice guy.

We sat at the bar and ordered drinks. Apparently, he only drank beer, and because I rarely drank anything, I ordered a whiskey. Eric had given me a taste of it. I didn't like it, but I wanted to try it again. Just to see what Eric liked about it.

"Wouldn't have pegged you for a whiskey drinker," Matthew commented as we took our first sips. We were sitting close together on barstools. He must have been around my age, early twenties at the latest, but he had an air of being much younger. He seemed nervous about the date too.

"I'm not, I'm just giving it a shot. Trying out something new for a change." The whiskey tasted bitter in my mouth. I wished I'd ordered some juice instead. How did Eric drink this every night? I wanted to spit it out, but I didn't, preserving my dignity.

"Karen's told me a little about you. You're studying English and Philosophy?" he continued.

"And she's told me nothing about you. Other than that you're her brother's friend."

I knew very little about Karen's brother too.

Matthew smirked.

"Yeah, we play on the same basketball team. We hang out sometimes too. Karen heard about my breakup and said she wanted to set me up with her best friend."

"Breakup?" I was surprised to hear that. Karen hadn't mentioned it to me.

Matthew sighed and took a large gulp of his beer. "Yeah, I was with this girl for over four years. It was a serious thing, you know?"

So Karen thought I would be good as a rebound for this guy? This was what she'd set me up for? I could feel the anger creeping under my skin. I wanted tonight to be a distraction from Eric. I didn't come here to listen to some other guy's sob story!

"Okay. I'm sorry about that. We don't have to do this. I had no idea," I said. I started to get off the barstool but Matthew reached out and grabbed my hand. The gesture reminded me of the way Eric had grabbed my hand the previous night. My reactions to both of them were so different.

I tugged my hand away from Matthew.

"S...sorry about that. I didn't mean to startle you. I just...I think you should stay. This is nice. I need this. Could you stay?"

I sat back down on the barstool. This was a disaster. Karen had set me up to serve as this guy's therapy dog for the night. This was hardly a date. There was no attraction here. He just wanted to talk. I toyed with the rose stem on the bar counter and then took another sip of the horrid whiskey.

"Sure, I'll stay. I just want to make something clear—nothing is going to happen between us tonight."

Matthew peered at me for a few moments and then nodded. "Of course. I get it. I understand."

I gulped and forced a small smile on my face. It was unlike me to indulge someone, especially a stranger—to let them talk about themselves, but there was nowhere else I could go right now where I wouldn't have to think about Eric.

"You want to tell me what happened with her? I can see you're not over it yet."

He sighed and looked down at the bottle in his hand. "She just woke up one day and told me it was over. That she just wasn't feeling it anymore. I didn't know what to say or how to react to that. I still can't make sense of it."

He stared at me like I might have had the answers.

I shrugged. "She just didn't want to be with you, man. It happens. There's nothing you can do about it."

Matthew had been talking about his ex for what seemed like hours. When I checked my watch, looking for any excuse to leave this place, I saw it was ten. I'd only been here an hour.

"I should get going," I said, sliding off the barstool. The two whiskeys I drank made me feel weak in my knees, or maybe it was something else. Either way, after sitting there listening to Matthew, my head felt heavy. I had no advice to give him but to just take each day one at a time.

"It'll get better in time. There really is no solution to the way you're feeling, other than waiting for time to do its thing." I was trying to be supportive and give him good advice. Although I didn't actually know this guy and I would probably never see him again.

Maybe a part of me was giving this advice to myself too.

The only way I could successfully get over what I was feeling for Eric was by putting some distance between us and giving it time. Neither was practically possible. I had to be in this job. I needed the money and also...I wanted to be there for James.

"You've been a big help to me tonight, Nina. You don't even know it!" Matthew stood up and gave me a hug. Normally, I would have yanked away from a gesture like that, but tonight, I realized I needed that hug too.

"It was no problem at all," I said, smiling at him.

"This was probably the worst date of your life, right?"

I shrugged. The truth was that I hadn't really been on many dates in my life. I'd never been in a long-term, serious relationship either. If Matthew knew those things about me, he would have known not to ask *me* for advice.

"Don't beat yourself up over this. You're having a rough night, and tomorrow will be better."

"Well, I can tell you, this has probably been one of the best

dates for *me*. You're beautiful and kind, wise and under-
standing. Karen clearly knew what she was doing when she
set us up!" Matthew was smiling as he spoke but I could see
he wasn't kidding. He was totally serious about this.

"Would you like to do this again? I promise, I've gotten it all
out of my system now. We won't have to talk about my ex."
He was reaching for my hand now, but this time I stepped
away from him.

"It's not going to happen, sorry. I can't date you," I said it
quickly, agitatedly.

"I thought we were getting along," he continued, but I was
prepared to leave now.

"As friends, for a quick talk, not....in any other way. I'm sorry,
Matthew, I have to go. Bye. Take care of yourself."

I rushed out of the bar, not waiting to see if he had anything
more to say to me. Outside in the cool air of the night, I felt
like I could finally breathe again. Matthew was nice. He was
handsome and honest. Would it be so bad if I gave him
another chance? I could be attracted to him...in time.

But I couldn't think about him now. I couldn't think of
anyone else because the only man on my mind was Eric. My
boss. The man I couldn't have.

I hoped I wouldn't have to see Eric when I returned to the
house. I knew my heart wouldn't be able to take that kind of
strain tonight. Definitely not after the whiskeys, which were
making me feel so unearthly and light.

I tried to sneak into the house, shutting the door as quietly as possible behind me. James was asleep, and the house was quiet.

I was still standing by the door, trying to slip off my shoes so they wouldn't make a sound. Eric stepped out of the living room into the dark corridor, several feet away from me.

"How was your date?" he asked in a low, grim voice.

It almost sounded like he'd been up this whole time, waiting for me to come home, and he wasn't pleased by my delay. I wasn't expecting him to stay up for me.

I hadn't even told him I was going on a date. How did he know?

"It was okay," I replied. There was no point denying it now that he'd guessed the truth already.

"Just okay?" he came closer toward me while I remained stuck to the spot.

"Yeah, it was just okay. Nothing special. Just a blind date my friend set me up on."

Eric nodded. His hands were deep in the pockets of his pants. Even in the barely-there light of the corridor, I could sense him watching me. I wished I had more control over myself because I was beginning to feel like I would fail at this.

"Well, I hope you find what you're looking for," he said grimly.

I could sense something like anger in his voice now. "It doesn't sound like you're actually wishing me well." I crossed my arms over my chest. He took a few steps in my direction, but he was nowhere close to me. I *wanted* him to come closer. I wanted to see his face clearly as he spoke to me. There was so much more I wanted to feel too, but I couldn't admit.

"Okay, then how do you want me to say it so you'll believe me?" he asked. His movement was stealthy and I knew this was dangerous.

"You don't have to actually say anything."

"Okay, I won't."

Eric came closer and I felt like my breath was stuck in my throat.

"There is only one thing I want tonight."

He came to a stop now, directly in front of me. What happened to us at night? In the day, we could barely look at each other, and now our gazes were locked. Our bodies were just inches apart. I could touch him if I wanted to.

"You can tell me what you want, Nina," he said and reached for my hair. He hadn't even touched my skin, just took a bunch of my smooth dark hair between his fingers and felt it like it was the texture of fabric. But I reeled. Like someone had just punched me in the stomach.

I realized then that I'd wanted him all day. I was hungry for him. This cycle between us was never going to end unless we did something about it.

"I want you," I said aloud. I wasn't going to be afraid of this feeling. He wanted to know, so I was going to be honest about it. If he wanted to fire me over this, then so be it.

Eric searched my eyes like he was trying to figure out if I was serious.

His fingers moved from my hair to my cheek. I stood firmly in front of him, both arms on my sides now, staring up at him. Challenging him with my eyes to do more.

His fingers were on my cheeks, down my neck, and then on the straps of my dress on my shoulders.

"I vowed to stay away from you tonight, Nina. But I just couldn't handle the thought of you on a date with another guy." Eric drew closer. His breath was in my hair now, our bodies were touching. My breasts squeezed up to his chest. His hands rose up to my waist then slid down my butt.

"All I did on that date was think about you," I said in a whisper, and we looked into each other's eyes. It was the truth, I wanted him to see that. Eric leaned toward me.

"You are so fucking gorgeous," he mumbled just before he took my mouth in his. I leaned toward him, hands on his shoulders and his tongue dug into my mouth. I lost all my senses, the wind was knocked out of me. This was the most intense experience of my life. He was finally kissing me. I thought this would never happen.

Our tongues clashed thirstily and our bodies tumbled together.

Eric's hands were on my waist and then he whipped me around. My back was against the wall now. He pushed me up against it. His hands were on my dress, forcefully pulling the straps down over my shoulders. I thrust my hips out toward him. I wanted to feel his cock against me and now I did.

He was aroused, his cock was hard in his pants. I cupped him just as he found the sleek zip on the side of my dress. I moaned when I felt the rock-hardness of his bulge in my hand. Eric started to tug the zip down.

"This has to come off or I'll go crazy. I need to see you naked."

I pressed myself to the wall while he undressed me. My arms were spread on either side. I stood with my legs wide apart too. I felt no shame, and I wasn't self-conscious. The only thing that mattered right now was how soon Eric could be inside me.

He slid my dress down to my ankles and took a step back to look at my body. He said nothing, just a grunting sound of approval. I was just in my lingerie. Black lace, like the dress.

Eric pulled off his t-shirt and I saw his lean, muscular torso, flat abdomen, and six-pack washboard abs. A cry escaped my lips. I couldn't hold it back. That made Eric smirk. He lunged toward me again, grabbing my face in his hand and pulling me to himself so he could kiss me.

"I want to fuck you, Nina Jones. Is that all right with you?" he whispered the words hoarsely in my ear. I was wet between my legs. A pressure was building up in the pit of my stomach. I wanted him to touch me there. I wanted to feel every inch of his muscular body.

"That's what I want too. I want to be fucked by you," I said. We stared heavy-lidded into each other's eyes. I couldn't believe I'd even said those words to him. How did I know what to say? Sex had always been so casual, so eventless before. With Eric, every moment felt like a bomb of emotions exploding inside my body.

My hand slid down the front of his pants and now his cock was in my hand. I couldn't help but be fearful he was going to stop this again. Just like last time.

I wouldn't be able to handle it twice in a row.

But Eric kept going. He had me pinned to the wall, with his hands holding my arms up. His body pushed up against mine while I stroked his big throbbing cock. With one hand now, he started to work on my lingerie. He snapped my bra off first, then he started to roll down my panty. All I could do was shudder and quake and stroke his cock.

I was naked now. Not an inch of clothing on me. Eric kissed my bare shoulder first and then leaned further down to take my right breast in his mouth. I tilted my head up and my eyes rolled back. I couldn't reach his cock anymore so I wound my arms around his neck.

He sucked on my taut pink nipple for a few seconds before moving further down. One hand massaged my breast, flicking my wet nipple, while he made his way to that wet hot core between my legs.

"Eric..." I moaned his name and my fingers streaked his hair. He was crouched down on the ground now, between my legs. His thumb found my swollen clit first and I nearly screamed with pleasure. How was it possible that I felt like I had never been touched before? This was crazy!

He stroked me there and I kept crying out from the sensation of complete surrender. Eric had all the control over me. The way he stroked my clit made me feel like I'd be stuck here forever. I wanted to feel like this forever. He was on his knees in front of me, looking up at my face, watching my changing, intensifying expressions while he took control of my body. His fingers moved over and around my clit until I was out of breath, until he knew I was going to come.

But he didn't want me to come like that. He had other ideas.

He slid his finger into me, just his thick forefinger while he straightened up. I felt my body crash back against the wall.

"Oh, my God." I said the words but I couldn't hear myself speak. I couldn't even feel myself move. All that existed was the crazy feeling of surrender with his finger inside me. I knew I would come any moment now.

Eric grabbed me by the back of my head. With a fistful of my hair in his hand, he brought his face close so that our foreheads knocked together. My breathing was rough. My shoulders rose and fell and I was groaning. His finger continued to slam into me, creating sensations I'd never felt before.

I was barely standing up by myself, relying completely for support on Eric's big body.

With our foreheads pressed to each other's, Eric stared into my eyes. I stared back.

"Are you going to come for me?" he asked. It wasn't really a question. It was more like a command. Besides, he knew the answer to that already.

His middle finger joined his forefinger inside me now. I cried out his name and threw my head back. My body shuddered. I wouldn't be able to hold back much longer. I clutched his bulging biceps and my nails dug into his skin. When I opened my eyes and looked down, I saw his massive throbbing cock swinging between his legs. I smacked my mouth, imagining the feeling of having that cock inside and out between my lips.

The knots loosened in the pit of my stomach and I felt myself go.

"There's a good girl," Eric spoke softly in my ear, encouragingly. My hair covered his mouth, muffling his voice, but I heard him loud and clear. My orgasm took over my body in magnificent waves. I held on to Eric for support while I quaked and quivered. It was like we were stuck together while I felt the pleasure of coming in his arms.

I gave up all control of my body. I didn't care about that anymore. This feeling was the only thing that mattered. By the time it finally subsided, I was completely out of breath. I realized I was enclosed in Eric's arms.

He'd pushed me up against the wall while he'd wrapped his arms around me tightly. The top of my head was at level with his handsome, strong chin. He looked down at me with his clear blue eyes.

"That was insane," he mumbled, and I pulled myself up to reach his lips. Our mouths parted. He was ready for the kiss and I pushed my tongue into his mouth. I leaned on him, our bodies were still entwined.

I could feel the powerful throbbing sensation between my legs—*he* made me feel this way. I was on top of the world, and I was going to do everything in my power to return the favor.

"Your turn," I said in an excited voice, biting down on my lip.

Eric's fingers were in my hair and he was holding my face tightly, staring into my eyes.

"The sexiest two words in the English language," he replied and we both smiled at each other. He was right. A tingle had run down my spine as I thought of all the ways I could please him now.

My hand slid down his body until I cupped his cock again. He was ready for me. I stroked him, staring straight into his eyes so he knew I wasn't going to stop. His eyes darkened as he glared back. His jaws tightened. He was focused on me and nothing else. We were doing the right thing. What else could ever make us feel this way? It had to be the right thing.

"Eric...I..." I spoke softly. I wanted to tell him before this went any further. I wanted him to know I thought we were doing the right thing. Maybe he was about to smile. He had that eased look on his face, but before I could finish what I was about to say, there was a loud knock on the door.

Startled, I jumped away from him. We were still close to the door, right there in the corridor.

It was close to midnight. Was he expecting someone?

From the way Eric's brows crossed and he waited a few beats, it seemed like he definitely wasn't expecting anyone.

"Eric!" A woman's voice from the outside filled the corridor of the house. I moved further back from the door. My heart was beating out of my chest. What was going on? I started scrambling for my clothes. He wasn't even looking at me anymore.

"Eric! I know you're home. You have to let me in. It's the middle of the night!" Her voice was shrill and loud.

My breath was caught in my throat with panic while I started to put on my clothes. How could this be happening right now?

I watched Eric while he slowly began to put on his clothes too. He hadn't turned to meet my eyes or say anything to me.

"Eric. Come on. Don't do this. How long are you going to make me wait out here in the cold? It's Cynthia," she said.

## 12

# ERIC

*F uck, fuck, fuck!*

I was screwed.

Nina, my beautiful twenty-one-year-old babysitter, who I had very nearly just fucked, was standing half-naked in my corridor, while my ex-wife was banging on the door of the house.

I managed to get my clothes on without making eye contact with Nina. Cynthia knocking on my door had quickly brought me back to reality. I should have kept my hands to myself tonight.

"Eric!" She was relentless. It had been at least five minutes and she continued to bang on the door and call out to me. At this rate, she was going to end up waking up James.

"Maybe you should answer the door and I'll check on James." Nina spoke up in a whisper behind me. When I turned to look at her now, I saw that she was back to being fully dressed again.

"Yeah, okay," I mumbled.

She nodded and quickly started walking away from me. I waited a few more moments before finally opening the door.

Cynthia was on the other side, standing with her arms crossed over her breasts. Two bags were on the ground beside her and she had a sour look on her face.

"You took your time," she remarked and rolled her eyes.

"What the fuck are you doing here, Cynthia?" I demanded, standing guard at the door. I wasn't about to let her waltz into my house just because she'd shown up here in the middle of the night.

"I've come here for my son. I want to see James. You can't keep him away from me like this. It isn't right, Eric, and you know it!" She looked straight into my eyes threateningly, even though she didn't really have anything to threaten me with.

"How did you find us?"

"It wasn't that hard, Eric, your mother still cares about me, even if you don't."

I sighed. Mom. She was so weak.

A smile spread on Cynthia's face now. "We had a long chat over the phone. I was able to explain to her how much has changed for me. She thinks it's a brilliant idea and is in full support of it. She might call you in the morning and talk to you about it herself."

"What idea?" I growled. My poor gullible mother. She

hadn't been the same since Dad died. She barely listened when being spoken to.

Cynthia shrugged. "The idea of me coming to stay here with you two."

I gripped the open door tightly with my hand. "You've got to be kidding me."

She shook her head. "This isn't a joke, Eric. I don't take matters regarding my life lightly. This is about my son and his relationship with his mother."

I shook my head and raked a hand through my hair. "It's the middle of the night, Cynthia. How dare you show up here, banging on my door with this ridiculous plan?" I growled at her through gritted teeth. She looked at me like she wasn't completely sure of what I was capable of. But she was determined to push her way through.

"Exactly, it's the middle of the night. What are you going to do, Eric? Turn me away? Do you want me to tell James when he grows up that you wouldn't let me see him? Even though I tried my best."

I glared at her, with rage pouring out of my every cell. How dare she? How could she say anything about James?

Cynthia moved toward me. She was closing in on the door now. "We don't have to discuss it all now, we can talk about it in the morning once we've both slept on it. Yes?"

I couldn't stop her as she entered the house now. I wanted to. I wanted to just shove her back, push her back into the night, but I couldn't. Not after everything.

She stepped into the corridor and turned to give me a look.

"Would you mind bringing my bags in, babe?"

Her words were like bullets piercing my soul. I had to do everything in my power to not lash out at her. But I just did it silently, I brought her bags in and placed them by the door.

Cynthia looked around. "This is lovely. It's a big house too, isn't it? Just the two of you?" she asked. I had no intention of answering that question, but at this opportune moment, Nina stepped out of James's room and directly in our view.

She was wearing that sexy black dress she'd worn to her date. Her silky dark hair looked disheveled and she wasn't wearing any shoes.

Cynthia clamped her mouth shut when she saw Nina. Her eyes studied her but she said nothing for a few moments. Nina, on the other hand, had this deer-in-the-headlights look in her eyes.

"And who do we have here?" Cynthia said, with a strain in her voice. The two women stared at each other.

"Hi, I'm Nina. I work here. I'm James's babysitter." Nina acted quickly, rushing toward Cynthia to shake her hand. I stood back, not interfering in this. Although it wasn't a crime to employ a full-time babysitter for our son, the air in the house right now was thick with sexual tension. Could Cynthia feel it?

Instead of replying to Nina, she turned to glare at me now. "A babysitter? You hired a babysitter?"

I crossed my arms over my chest and held her gaze strongly. "I need the help. James needs it." I didn't owe her an explanation, but I felt guilty because of what had just happened between Nina and me. I couldn't even look at her now.

Cynthia rolled her eyes. "Well, you won't be needing her anymore. Not when he has his mother in the house," she said and finally gave Nina a smile. It was a quick fake smile, and it wasn't fooling anyone. There was no way that Nina couldn't feel the hostility emanating from Cynthia. Things were about to get a whole lot trickier around here, I knew.

There was another spare room in the house, apart from the one Nina was staying in. I deposited Cynthia's bags in there while she followed me to it.

"You can stay here tonight and we'll discuss this in the morning," I growled, turning to her. Cynthia was the one blocking the doorway now. She stood with a hand on her hip and her lips curling in a smile.

"We can talk now, if that's what you want, Eric. I'm all up for reminiscing about the old days."

I wasn't sure if she was kidding. I made to leave, pushing past her, but she placed a hand on my arm and held me back.

"Where are you going?"

"To sleep. It's past midnight. I have work in the morning."

Cynthia was pulling me back by the arm now. "C'mon, stay

here with me, just for a bit. Let's talk. We have so much to talk about…"

I pulled my arm away from her and stood there facing her with a grimace scarring my face. "I have nothing to talk to you about, Cynthia. I'm letting you stay here tonight because I won't allow you to roam the streets of Chicago at night with nowhere to go. And not because you think we share a special relationship or whatever the fuck, but because you are the mother of my child."

She tipped her head to one side and looked at me calmly. Nothing I said had any effect on her. She wasn't taking it seriously. "I knew you'd come through, Eric. I knew you wouldn't turn me away and we'd be able to work this out."

"Aren't you listening to me?" I growled again and took a threatening step in her direction. I needed her to understand this wasn't going anywhere.

Cynthia took a step toward me too. She tipped her head back and stared up at my face.

"I *am* listening to you, babe. I can hear you loud and clear." She reached out and placed a hand on my chest. "You can stay here tonight, cuddle up with me if you want. I won't tell anyone."

I grabbed her hand and pushed it off my chest. "One night. That's all you get. Only because you have nowhere else to go. You're leaving tomorrow."

I moved away from her and banged the door shut behind me. I wasn't about to lock it but I wished I would. I didn't want to have to see her or interact with her again. I knew she wasn't about to give up easily, especially not now that she was here, actually in our house.

I rubbed my face with a hand and took in a deep breath. How had this happened?

I needed to speak to my mother first thing in the morning. She had no right giving away my address to anyone—let alone Cynthia! I went back to the living room because I knew I wanted another drink, and when I got there, I saw Nina waiting there for me.

Of course, she wanted answers.

Nina was standing by the big window at the back of the room. She'd parted the curtains and was looking out into the backyard in silence.

I said nothing, just went up to the drinks cabinet and started pouring myself a whiskey. She turned when she likely heard the glasses tinkling.

"Who is she?" were her first words. There was a look of betrayal in her eyes. Was she upset? Was she angry?

I got that she wanted answers, but what was she angry about? It wasn't like I'd cheated on her. It wasn't like we were in a relationship.

"She's my ex-wife. James's mom," I replied and took a sip of my drink.

Nina was still in that damn black dress. She looked even sexier now that I could taste her mouth on my lips and feel the heat of her body.

Nina nodded and hung her head down.

"Yeah, okay. So does that mean you're going to let me go now? Like she said? You don't need me to look after James anymore." She spoke in a low quiet voice but firmly. Nina was not the kind of woman who would show her weakness to me, that much I'd figured about her.

"I'm not making any major decisions yet. It's going to be business as usual for now. Nothing has changed," I said.

"But she said…"

"It doesn't matter what she said. I'm your boss, remember? This is my house. James is my son and my responsibility."

She looked into my eyes and I held her gaze strongly. Then she nodded. "Okay, I just wanted some clarity on that."

We were silent for a little while. The truth was that I wanted to be left alone. Cynthia showing up like this here was a total game-changer. I didn't know what I was supposed to do next or how to deal with her. I didn't have the head-space to think about Nina right now.

"I just wanted to say…" She was beginning to speak again but I shot her a look of warning. If she wanted to talk about tonight, about what happened between us—this wasn't the time. I hoped she could see that in my eyes.

Maybe she did, because she clamped her mouth shut and took in a few quick breaths.

"It's getting late. I should go to sleep. James will be up early," she said and moved toward me. I turned from her to pour some more whiskey in my glass.

"Yes, goodnight. Sleep well." I said the words unthinkingly. I wasn't really paying attention anymore. Nina was a distraction and I didn't need that in my life right now. I kept my back turned to her and hoped she was gone.

Eventually, I heard her footsteps leave the room and the door slowly creak shut.

I was alone again. I needed this. I needed some peace.

## 13

### NINA

*I* woke up early the next morning, not that I'd slept much the previous night. I'd tossed and turned in bed, feeling embarrassed and like a fool. I should have known none of that was real. Eric's attraction to me was purely physical. I was a young babysitter, we were living under the same roof...I very clearly wanted him.

He would have been an idiot to not take the opportunity to sleep with me.

I was the one who shouldn't have slipped up...twice.

I should have known better than to assume a guy like Eric could actually want me. That this was anything more.

And now his beautiful ex-wife was here, and I didn't even want to compete. There was literally no competition. She was James's mother, they clearly had history.

I couldn't sleep.

I woke early and took a long shower. By the time I went to

the kitchen, it was nearly time for me to wake James up, but I decided to let him sleep in a little longer.

What I wasn't expecting to find in the kitchen was Cynthia. I thought she'd be sleeping, but here she was, in a beautiful silk kimono robe and what looked like just lingerie underneath. She was flipping pancakes and had the coffee machine going at the same time.

I stood there at the kitchen door, wondering if I should just turn around and run back to my room. But she saw me before I could decide anything.

"Ah, good! You're up. Pancakes?" She was in a chirpy mood, smiling and energetic. The previous night when we first met, she'd barely even looked at me. She'd dismissed my presence rudely.

"No, thanks," I murmured and walked over to the cupboard to grab a bowl of cereal instead. Even though I knew I had no reason to yet, I didn't like Cynthia.

And now she was prancing around the place, with her supermodel airs, and I hated her even more.

She shrugged when I started pouring milk into my cereal. She brought a plate of the pancakes over to the breakfast table and sat down.

"You must be surprised to see me, you poor thing," she said. I had no choice but to sit down at the table too.

"A little bit, but it's okay. This is just a job," I replied and tried to smile, but nothing came out. Cynthia took a large chunk of pancake and popped it in her mouth.

"I get the feeling Eric told you nothing about me."

"Why would he?"

"I'm James's mother," she remarked and narrowed her eyes at me. It was my turn to shrug.

"It's not like we share personal information with each other. He's told me whatever I need to know that'll help me take care of James."

There was a sour tone in my voice which I knew Cynthia must have heard. We ate our food in silence for a few moments and then I checked the clock. It was past James's wake-up time, but I wanted him to sleep a little longer.

"I just want you to know, dear Nina, that you'll probably have to look for a different job soon. Eric might not tell you this now, but I would hate for you to be left without work out of the blue."

Her words were sympathetic but her tone wasn't. This was a woman who was taking a lot of joy in the fact that she had some kind of an upper hand here.

"That's okay. I'm sure I'll figure it out if it comes to that," I replied and ate my cereal.

Cynthia sipped her coffee and smiled. "Of course it will. Eric is going to soon see that I'm not disposable like he thinks I am. James is going to want his mommy and everything will fall into place soon enough."

I stared at her, slipping the spoon back in my bowl again. I couldn't believe she was actually saying these things to me. They almost sounded like a threat. She stared back, enjoying herself.

"So you should prepare yourself for that," she added.

I could feel my nostrils flaring. I tried to keep my hands from shaking with anger. "Like I said, this is just a job. I'm sure I'll be able to move on easily if Eric decides to let me go."

"Eric?"

I stared at her blankly.

"You call him by his first name? Not Mr. Hall?" She had an accusatory tone in her voice.

"Mommy?" It was James. He was standing at the kitchen door now. He'd dragged his favorite bunny with him. He was still in his pajamas and his hair was all ruffled with sleep.

"Oh, baby! James, my darling!" Cynthia squealed. She jumped out of her chair and went running to her son and picked him up in her arms.

I stood up too, feeling a little protective of him. He looked surprised to see his mother. Even though he was in her arms now, it didn't seem like he wanted to be held by her. Cynthia showered him with kisses but he didn't reciprocate. He wasn't even smiling.

"Should we get you something to eat?" I asked him, directing his attention to me. James stretched his arms out toward me, like he wanted me to take him, but Cynthia kept a steady grip on him.

"Do you want me to make you something, baby? Mommy can make you pancakes?"

James looked at me, and now his eyes had a pleading look in them. He wanted to be in my arms instead and I was willing to forcibly pull him out of Cynthia's if I had to. I hated seeing him sad.

"What would you like to eat, baby?" She was ignoring me again, but James looked at her now and spoke in the firmest manner a kid could speak in.

"I want Nina to make me eggs."

## 14

### ERIC

*I* dialed my mother's number early the next morning. It took her several rings to answer the phone.

"Mom!"

"Eric, hi, honey, how are you? How is Chicago? How is my little grandson?"

"Well, Cynthia showed up here last night, and according to her, you're the one who gave her our address." I got straight to the point.

Mom was silent for a few moments while I paced around my bedroom with the phone stuck to my ear.

"She called me a few days ago, in tears. She was completely shattered, honey, I didn't know what to do." Mom sounded upset and I softened my voice. There was no point taking my frustration out on her.

"Yes, I know, she does that sometimes," I replied.

"Are you saying she was pretending?" Mom waited for me to answer.

I rubbed a hand over my face with frustration. "I don't know, Mom. I don't know what to believe anymore. I just wish you'd called me instead of just offering our address up to her."

She sighed. I could picture her sitting in the living room with a cup of tea in her hand, her nose pinched in confusion and sadness.

"Well, all I know, honey, is that a boy needs his mother. Who are we to stand in the way of that? Especially now that she is here and wants to be a part of James's life."

I couldn't contribute to this train of thought. I didn't have anything to say, so Mom sighed and continued.

"When this little boy grows up and wants to know what happened between his parents, you are going to have to truthfully explain everything to him. Will you be able to tell him that you turned his mother away when she wanted to be a part of his life? How will you explain that?" Mom spoke in a quiet voice, softly, kindly. She was doing her best to help me see things from her perspective and I had to admit there was no arguing that.

I sat down on the edge of my bed. "I understand what you're saying, Mom, but you don't know Cynthia the way I do. Nothing is permanent in her world. Pretty soon, she's going to get tired of this and move on."

Mom clucked her tongue. "But the Cynthia you're talking about is the *teenager* you knew and fell in love with. You were nothing but a kid then too."

"I've known her all my life, Mom, nothing has changed."

"But you haven't known her these past five years," she argued.

"And you have?" I snapped.

A few moments of silence passed between us.

"All I'm saying, honey, is that she deserves a chance. She is the mother of your child and she deserves the opportunity to prove herself worthy of being a part of your family. Don't you think your son deserves that too?"

She let me think about it for a few moments before she spoke again. "Eric, I know what you think has happened to me since your father died. You think I'm losing my marbles..."

"I've never said that, Mom."

"No, you haven't, but that's what you think of me. That I'm nothing but an old woman who is slowly losing her mind and her memory."

I remained silent because sometimes I did think that of her, I wasn't going to lie.

"Maybe that is true, but if there is one last piece of advice that you take from me before things really go south, it is that you give Cynthia another chance. For James's sake. Will you do that, Eric? All I want is for you to have a happy family. You deserve that, son."

Mom breathed softly into the phone while she waited for me to answer. I didn't know what to say. I hated hearing her talk like this. And maybe she was right about everything. I'd respected everything my parents said and believed in, all my life...so why not now? Why not respect my mother's wishes now?

"Of course, Mom. I'll give Cynthia another chance," I said.

"Oh, that's wonderful!" She was joyous and excited. "You are the best son a mother could ask for!"

"Okay, I should go now. James must be up and I think so is Cynthia and the...the babysitter. I should go check on them."

"Have a lovely day, honey. Tell James I'll call him in the evening."

"Okay, Mom. You take care of yourself."

"Love you, honey."

I ended the call and took in a deep breath. As if things couldn't get any more complicated than they already were. Now I was going to have to make nice with Cynthia.

In the kitchen, tensions were high. I could feel it in the air.

Nina was cooking eggs, but there was a mess everywhere. Someone had made pancakes, and I guessed it was Cynthia. She'd clearly not cleaned up after herself. Some things never changed.

She was now sitting at the breakfast table with James on her knee. He refused to look at her or speak to her.

"Where is Sarah? This place is a mess," I said.

"She said she'll be coming in late today. A dentist appointment," Nina answered.

"Daddy!" James tried to pull away from his mother and I helped him out by taking him into my arms, away from Cynthia.

"I hope you don't mind, I helped myself to some pancakes. I could make you some too if you like." She was speaking to me sweetly and the truth was, I had no reason to be rude with her, but I just couldn't bring myself to act normally around her anymore. Something had cracked between us.

"It's fine, I'm good," I replied.

"Nina is making me scrambled eggs. I love scrambled eggs," James said excitedly. I sat him down on a chair beside me and we sat facing Cynthia. She continued to make happy, smiling faces at her son. Nina came over with scrambled eggs and toast and a small glass of orange juice.

"If it's all right with you, I'll take James to kindergarten today," Cynthia said while James dug into his food.

"I'm not sure that's a good idea. Nina can take him," I said.

"Yes, I want to go with Nina," James chipped in.

"But I want to do it, now that I'm here. I think it would be good for James."

"Daddy, I want to go with Nina."

I shot a look at her. She was standing at the kitchen sink, washing up the dishes and pans that were used. She hadn't contributed to this conversation, and I guessed it was because of the coldness between us from the previous night. Things were obviously going to be awkward between us now. My fingers were inside her. I made her come. I was going to fuck her if Cynthia hadn't shown up when she did.

Cynthia now turned her attention to James.

"Baby, I'm going to take you to playschool today." Her tone was firm and James now looked at me questioningly.

"Daddy, do I have to?" he asked.

"James, don't be like that!" his mother snapped. When I looked at her sharply, she smiled sweetly and turned to James again. "This will be good for us, won't it, sweetie? I'll drop you off, then pick you up, and we can go get ice cream. Won't that be fun? Maybe you could introduce me to your friends?"

James got off his chair and walked over to where Nina was drying the dishes with a towel now. She gave him her hand and he held on to her finger tightly.

"Will you take me to kindergarten, Nina?" he asked her. She put down the plate in her other hand and turned to him, bending down so that her face was at level with his.

"I would love to, but I think maybe you should go with your mommy today," she said.

I gritted my teeth as I watched them. It was difficult for me to make a decision on what the right thing to do was. But then I remembered my promise to my own mother. That I was going to give Cynthia a chance.

I got up from my chair and went up to James.

"Nina is right. It would be best if you went with Mommy to kindergarten today. Ice cream would be nice later won't it, buddy?" I lifted him up in my arms and he held on to me tightly.

"I guess," he said, distractedly, still eyeing Nina.

"Nina will be right here waiting to play with you later," I added and threw her a look. I caught her gaze but she quickly looked away, like she was embarrassed.

"It'll be fine. Stop worrying! I'm his mom!" Cynthia jumped up now and she pulled James away from me and showered him with kisses. James, although not too appreciative of this display of affection, tolerated it.

I could sense Nina's eyes on me now, but I didn't want to meet them. Was she judging me? I knew I'd say something idiotic if I looked at her.

"Should we get you dressed for the day?" she spoke up. James took it as the perfect opportunity to hop away from his mother and back to Nina again. They left the room in each other's arms like old lovers. Cynthia and I were alone again.

She sat down at the table, crossing her legs. The robe she was wearing seemed to slither away from her body, revealing her long smooth legs. I knew those legs well. I turned away from her, focusing on making a cup of coffee for myself instead.

"Have you missed me, Eric? You look like you've missed me," she said. I kept my back turned to her.

"It's been a while, Cynthia. Let's get this over with and move on."

"It's just a simple question, darling. Have you missed me?"

I could sense that she'd moved closer to me, but I didn't want to turn or meet her eyes. As little contact with her as possible would be what I needed.

"Last night I told you it was going to be just one night for you in this house, but I've had a chance to think it through and I've changed my mind."

"Good, I'm so glad." She placed a hand on my shoulder, which made me whip around to face her.

"It means you have the chance to spend some time with James. To finally get to know him."

She was smiling brightly at me. "I know him very well, Eric. I carried him in my belly for close to ten months. And he knows me too. We have a connection."

Now would not be the time to mention that it didn't seem like James shared much of a connection with her, or point out that he seemed to prefer the babysitter over her. I wanted to avoid conflict as much as possible, wherever possible—for the sake of my son.

"Just go easy on him, will you? He's been having a tough time in a new city. I want to make him as comfortable as possible. He likes Nina."

"The babysitter?" There was a look of annoyance in Cynthia's eyes, but she blinked it away, smiling again. "The poor thing doesn't know any better. He needs his mommy."

"And whose fault is that?" I snapped.

She leaned toward me again, so close that I could smell the pancakes that she'd just eaten on her breath.

"Let's not stoop into the blame game again, Eric. Come on, you're better than that."

I banged the coffee mug down on the counter and stepped away from her. "I have work to do. Figure this out. Just remember, do not, under any circumstances, upset James."

I walked out of the kitchen, leaving Cynthia by herself. I had resolved to uphold the promise I made to my mother but I wasn't about to do any more than necessary.

As far as I was concerned, Cynthia and I had been over for a long time.

*I*t felt strange seeing James leave the house with Cynthia, *with someone else*. Even though it hadn't been long at all that I was taking him to playschool, somehow this just felt wrong. I felt responsible for him, and I could see he wasn't entirely comfortable with her, even though she was his mother.

Cynthia said she would meet me at the park later, after they got ice cream together, and I agreed. I told myself this free time would be the perfect opportunity for me to catch up on my own stuff, like studying in the college library.

I didn't bump into Eric after the morning's scene. He'd either left the house already or was locked up in his room, refusing to interact with any of us. The latter seemed more probable.

As per plan, I went to the college library. Karen had classes and said she wouldn't be able to see me, so I took the opportunity to catch up on course work. But it turned out that I wasn't being productive at all. I could barely concentrate on my books. I had too much on my mind and was unable to focus.

When my phone vibrated in my bag and I saw it was my brother, Corey, calling, I was relieved.

Rushing out of the library, I answered the phone. "Hey!"

"Where have you been?"

"I've been around. What's up with you?"

"Raina told me you're living with some guy now?"

"I'm not living with *some guy*...for fuck's sake, Corey! You make it sound like I'm shacking up with some stranger."

He laughed at that. "So, what's the deal with you?"

"I got a job as a full-time babysitter, or nanny, or whatever."

"One of Miles's rich pals?"

"Something like that."

"You doing it for the money?"

"And this way, I don't have to live in the dorm."

I wanted to convince my brother that there was nothing suspicious going on. He had his life and I had mine. Even though we were close, our lives never really crossed each other's. And the last thing I wanted was for him to find out about the man who'd been stalking me. I didn't want Corey getting into any trouble. If he found out someone had threatened me or our family, he would try and deal with it himself...and that could turn out to be a dangerous game.

"Yeah, okay, whatever. Sounds boring to me," he said after some thought.

"It's not so bad. The kid is actually great. It's not a difficult job," I said, defending my position. It was weird that I felt defensive of James and Eric. I could sense Corey rolling his eyes.

"You want to come hang with me sometime? We need to catch up. It's like I don't even know you anymore," he said. He was right, it did feel like that. We were twins. We were deeply important to each other. We were quite dissimilar, but that didn't mean we didn't care for each other.

"Yeah, we should hang out."

"Come party with me."

That made me laugh. In the twenty years that we'd known each other—the fact that we had shared a womb—didn't he know me by now?

"I'm serious, Nina, you need to get out there. You need to do things your peers are doing. Pretty soon, when you're older with a boring-ass job, you're going to feel like you missed out."

I listened carefully to what my brother was saying. As he spoke, I remembered the way Eric refused to meet my eyes this morning. We nearly had sex last night. I could still feel his fingers banging inside me. The thought of that orgasm sent shivers down my spine...and this morning. It was all forgotten. His ex-wife was back in his life and he hardly even knew I was living in his house.

"Yeah, sure, that's a good idea. We should do that sometime," I said to Corey.

"Good. I'm glad. I'll text you soon and you better show up," he said. We spoke for a few more minutes about nothing in particular. I didn't want him to hang up but my brother was a popular and busy guy.

I had to return to the library and now I was beginning to feel anxious.

I couldn't get anything done. The truth was that I missed James. Even though I knew he was in playschool for most of that time and then out with his mother getting ice cream, I still couldn't help but wish it was me he was spending time with. Had I really grown this attached to a little kid this quickly?

I left the library early to head out to the park where I'd agreed to meet Cynthia and James. I didn't want to waste a single moment when I could be spending time with him instead. I found myself worrying if he had a nice day, if he'd eaten well, if he made any new friends today.

I had to constantly remind myself that I wasn't his mother, I wasn't even family...I was nothing more than his babysitter. Someone who was being paid to look after him temporarily. Then why did I feel this way?

Was it purely because I was attracted to his dad?

I was filled with feelings of guilt and frustration. I was early, so I sat on one of the benches with a book in my hand, but I didn't really do any reading.

Then, fifteen minutes after we were supposed to meet, I finally saw Cynthia and James enter the park. I could see she was trying to hold on to his hand, but James broke away from her and came running toward me. He'd missed me too!

I stood up to greet him and take him into my arms and I realized I had some tears in my eyes that I tried to hurriedly blink away.

"Nina!" he yelped as he flung himself at me. I lifted him up in my arms and swung him around joyously. This was crazy! We'd only been apart for half the day. Most of which time he was in playschool. I hadn't even realized how much I cared about the welfare of this child.

"How are you doing, cutie? Did you have a fun day?" I asked him and he looked up at me with his bright blue eyes. His lips were downturned, and he didn't look happy.

"No. I hated today," James replied.

When Cynthia came over to us, it seemed like she was in as much of a bad mood as James was. She had a sour expression on her face and it seemed like she didn't even want to look at her son.

I was holding on to James, while she carried her handbag in the crook of her arm.

"Seriously badly behaved. It looks like I'm going to have to work extra hard to instill some manners in him," Cynthia complained sharply, speaking as though James wasn't there.

"What happened?" I asked. James seemed sad now. He turned away from his mother and rested his head on my shoulder. I patted his back gently. Even though this wasn't comfortable for me, carrying a five-year-old in my arms like this, I didn't want to put him down. I was here to fulfill whatever emotional needs he had.

Cynthia rolled her eyes as she stood there. Every aspect of her body language told me that she was in a bad mood.

"He made a scene when I was dropping him off at kindergarten. He refused to go in. His teachers and I literally had to force him to go!" she started to complain. I gulped but said nothing, not even to James. I'd have a conversation with him later, in private.

"And then his teacher told me he had a fight with some boy in his class. I was so embarrassed. He refused to apologize to anyone!"

I was sorry I even asked her about the day. I didn't want to put James through the trauma of listening to his mother complaining like this.

"I'm sure we can talk about it and get through this," I said, but Cynthia wasn't about to stop now.

"Then I had to take him for ice cream because I promised and I didn't want him throwing another fit...oh, my God! First, he couldn't decide which flavor he wanted, so I ordered chocolate and he didn't like it and we had to eventually throw it away. Not before he got ice cream all over his pants and hands. I didn't even have anything to clean him up with!"

I stroked James's hair in sympathy.

"It's okay. Do you want to go home, cutie?" I tried looking at him but he refused to lift his head off my shoulder and look at me. I could sense how upset he was.

Cynthia was still talking, still shaking her head like she was utterly disgusted. "I mean, he's not a baby anymore. He is five years old. You would think he'd know how to behave himself by now. And *I'm* the monster! He talks to me like I'm a complete stranger."

"He's just a kid," I said defensively and she shot me a look of warning.

"And who do you think *you* are?"

I didn't mind if she wanted to direct her anger at me instead of James. I was willing to take it if it meant he would be spared.

"I just think we should discuss this at home instead of at a park, and especially not in front of him," I tried.

Cynthia narrowed her eyes at me and placed her hands on her hips in a confrontational way. I had no idea what was going through her head, but I was sure they weren't nice thoughts about me.

"You think you're some angel sent from heaven, don't you? Just because James thinks you're hot stuff today. You do realize he's going to forget about you soon enough and discard you? You're nothing but a new toy to him." Her voice was hissy and threatening.

If I could, I would have hit her.

But what kind of lesson would that be teaching James? Besides, I'd never hit anyone in my life. But I was from south side Chicago. We weren't afraid to use our fists if the need arose.

"We should go home," was all I offered. My nonviolence and refusal to engage in an argument seemed to piss her off even more.

"What makes you think you know what is best for my kid?

You're not his mother."

"That's not what I said."

"And whatever plans you have with Eric...you can drop it. Do you hear me?" She was pointing a finger at my face now.

This was too much. All I could do was bounce James gently in my arms and try to keep him turned away from her. "I have no plans."

"Oh, please. Spare me the bullshit. You really think I haven't seen the way you look at him? With those puppy dog eyes. Sticking your tits out at him."

She disgusted me. "I'm going to go now. James doesn't need to hear this."

Cynthia rolled her eyes. "Eric isn't going to go for you. You aren't his type. He likes blondes," she continued, smirking now.

So this whole thing was about *him*, not about their son. It was becoming clearer now. I started walking away from her with James in tow. There was no way I was standing there listening to any more of this. Neither was James.

"Hey! Where do you think you're going?" she yelled at us, but she wasn't following us.

"Home," I said and kept walking.

James winced and I patted his back. "You don't have to worry about anything, sweetheart. It'll be fine. She's just confused about some things. None of this is your fault, okay?"

I hoped he believed me.

## 16

# ERIC

*I* came home after dinner that night. My business meeting with Miles had gone on longer than expected. We met up for dinner at a restaurant and stayed for a few drinks. Things were looking good. I was ready to invest. I had complete faith in Miles's idea and the success of the app.

For the first time since our move to Chicago, I was actually feeling confident about making this huge change in our lives. I knew I was making a good business decision—and something my father would have been proud of too.

When I arrived at the house, I hoped the others would all be asleep. I didn't want to have to deal with Cynthia or Nina right now. I hoped James would be asleep too and I could just check in on him asleep in his room.

The house seemed quiet, like maybe I was going to get what I wanted. I walked quietly through the house in the direction of the kitchen. I needed something to quench my thirst.

Cynthia was sitting at the kitchen table, flipping through a glossy magazine. It was highly possible she'd been waiting for me to show up.

"Busy evening?" she asked, flipping the magazine shut. I walked straight to the fridge and grabbed a bottle of orange juice.

"I had work," I replied and chugged some juice down my throat thirstily. This was exactly the kind of small-talk conversation I wanted to avoid with her.

She stood up now and came toward me. "You know what this reminds me of?" she asked and waited a few beats to give me a chance to respond.

I wasn't going to say anything.

"Of when we were married, and you were so busy at work, trying to manage your dad's business."

I put the bottle back in the fridge and turned to her, wiping my mouth with the back of my hand. "I don't remember you ever waiting for me in the kitchen to return home," I snapped. I didn't even try to hold my tongue. The whiskeys I drank tonight were making me speak my mind.

Cynthia smiled and put a hand on my shoulder. "But I'm here now, darling. Why don't we sit down and talk?" she asked.

I swayed from her so that her hand fell away from my shoulder. Firmly, I drove my hands into the pockets of my pants.

"Talk about what, Cynthia? There's nothing to talk about. I believe I've said everything I needed to say."

She ran a hand through her bouncing golden waves and

shook her hair out like she was in a celebrity photoshoot. I had to admit she was as beautiful as ever.

"We need to talk about our son."

"What about him?"

"We need to provide a safe and stable environment for him," she said, staring confidently into my eyes. I couldn't believe it. Had those words actually come out of *her* mouth?

"You can't be fucking serious about this."

"Serious about what? Wanting to make my son happy?"

"I really didn't want to go through the unpleasantness of reminding you what you did to us. Your family. Especially this son that you suddenly care about so much." I gritted my teeth. There was rage in my voice. I had to do everything I could to not break a few plates.

"You need to stop pointing to the past, Eric. It's over. We've gone through this already. I'm here now," she complained. We were standing at some distance from each other now, which was good. I *needed* to keep my distance from her.

"I am doing the best I can for my son."

"Oh, honey...I know that..." Cynthia's voice seemed to melt and she came rushing to me like I was some wounded soldier. She stroked my back even though I tried to move away from her and she looked up at me and smiled.

"It's going to be okay, honey, I'm here now. We don't have to pay money to a stranger to look after our son anymore," she said.

I rubbed a hand over my face in frustration. I knew Nina

was a stranger, technically, but that wasn't how I perceived her. Especially not after I'd nearly fucked her. Especially not since I couldn't get her out of my mind.

"I think it would be for the best if we didn't make any more sudden changes in James's life. He likes Nina and they get along," I said. I felt confused all of a sudden. Did I actually believe all these things Cynthia was telling me now? Was it possible that she had changed?

She nodded. She rarely ever agreed with me. "I guess you're right. She is good with him, for now. She's more like a companion, though. You know that, right? She's too young and naïve to actually take responsibility for his safety and wellbeing."

Cynthia looked and sounded serious, and I felt a headache coming on. It had to be the alcohol, I reminded myself.

"I can't make a decision right now. I need time and James needs time to settle with all this too," I said, rubbing my temples.

Cynthia smiled widely and stroked my left cheek with the back of her fingers. "My sweet, darling Eric Hall. You have grown up but just a little bit. You don't see it, do you? That girl is trying to take advantage of the situation. It's a good thing I got here when I did. James and you don't need that bullshit in your life, do you?" She sounded sweet and even wise, but I had no idea what she was talking about.

"I think I need to go to sleep, Cynthia."

She bit down on her lip and leaned toward me, close enough that I could feel her hot breath on my neck. "Yes, we both need to relax, and I know just the way to do that," she said and started to wrap her arms around my neck. She was going to kiss me. A few seconds more and Cynthia's mouth would be on mine.

I pushed her away. "Go to bed, Cynthia."

"Your bed?" she asked with a giggle and I stepped away from her.

"Goodnight, we'll talk tomorrow," I said dismissively.

She didn't seem to be offended and instead continued to smile mischievously like she had some plan up her sleeve. I needed to sleep on this. I didn't feel like my head was clear. Maybe what she was saying about Nina was right. Maybe my mother was right too.

It could be possible what James needed most right now was his mother. Was I too blinded by my attraction toward Nina to see the situation for what it really was?

I walked out of the kitchen with the full intention of going to my bedroom, but I found myself walking in the direction of the spare room. I wanted to see her, even if just for a few seconds. It felt like if I saw her, I'd be able to think straight again.

## 17

# NINA

*a*fter James went to sleep that night, I'd retreated to my room to try to study—but following the recent trend of the state of my mind, I couldn't focus on my essay.

I'd spent the entire evening trying to keep James away from Cynthia after she returned to the house. The last thing I wanted was for him to feel even worse than he already did. He had a tough day, and he needed to cope with his own emotions and experiences first before he could deal with the relationship with his mother.

I knew I needed to discuss all this with Eric, but I wasn't sure how receptive he would be. Would he even understand?

I heard his car pull up to the driveway a few hours later. I'd been sitting up in my bed with a book. No sleep in sight. I didn't even know if Cynthia was still in the house. Or had she gone out? I needed to get to him before she did. Someone had to defend James!

Rushing out of my room, I went to the kitchen where I could

see the lights switched on. I figured he was hungry and getting something to eat. When I treaded to the kitchen door, I saw Cynthia was there too. In one of her silk robes again, looking as beautiful as she did before with that perfect figure and her long legs.

I knew I was no match for her.

And now they were standing close together and talking in hushed tones. I could barely hear them.

I stepped back from the door because I didn't want to be seen. My cheeks burned up. Just the sight of them together seemed to give me a fever. The last thing I saw before I turned away was Cynthia leaning toward Eric and brushing her fingers on his cheek.

My heart was racing out of my chest. I felt faint. I clutched my stomach with both hands and ran back to my bedroom because I couldn't bear to see that scene anymore.

How could I have been so foolish?

I shut the door behind me and leaned the back of my head against it. I pressed my eyes closed and tried to erase the memory of that image—of how perfect Cynthia and Eric looked together.

What was I thinking?

I had no place in this household any longer.

I had no rights over James.

He was certainly not my responsibility.

Then there was a quiet knock on the door that startled me out of my thoughts.

I opened it slowly, suddenly afraid of who it could possibly be on the other side.

Eric was standing with his hands thrust in his pockets and his head hanging low. Even in the dimness of the light in the hallway, I could see how stormy blue his eyes were.

"I just wanted to make sure you were doing okay," he said in a low, deep voice. That caught my heart in my throat. I didn't know what he meant by it.

"I'm doing fine, I think, but we need to talk about James," I replied. I watched as Eric ran a hand through his closely cropped blond hair. It reminded me of what Cynthia had said earlier—that I wasn't Eric's 'type'. That he preferred blondes like her.

"I've been trying to raise this kid alone all these years, and now all of a sudden, everyone seems to have an opinion on what to do for him," he said. His voice sounded bitter. Had I overstepped my boundaries?

"I'm sorry if you think I've done or said anything wrong. I just think he's a sensitive child and he's been through a lot of—"

Eric cut me off. He shook his head and looked intently at me. "I don't want to talk about James right now."

I clamped my mouth shut. What *did* he want to talk about? Despite how foolish it made me feel, I couldn't help but hope he wanted to talk about *us*. About the way the air caught fire whenever he was around, whenever we simply looked at each other. Did he feel it too?

"Okay, we can discuss it later. Do you want to come in?"

I was taking a risk by suggesting that. I was forcing myself to be brave. But I wasn't prepared for the rejection I was going to be faced with now.

"No, Nina, I don't want to go into your bedroom," he said. Like he was putting me in my place.

I felt my soul shrivel up and hide inside me somewhere. I wanted to run away. I'd never felt this embarrassed before.

"Okay..." I said, nearly choking on my own voice.

"I just wanted to check in on you," Eric added and I nodded. Hot tears pricked the backs of my eyelids. I wanted to cry. I wanted Raina, my older sister to hug me. To rescue me from this moment.

Eric stepped away, still looking like he was mad at something.

"Goodnight, Nina. Sleep well," he said and then he was gone.

Didn't he know I was going to get no sleep tonight?

## 18

## ERIC

That night, I lay awake in bed, with a raging headache thumping in the back of my head. I couldn't sleep because all my thoughts were jumbled in my head. James, my mother, Cynthia, and Nina.

The only thing I knew with absolute certainty was that James's wellbeing was my first priority and nothing else. If I had to suck it up and deal with Cynthia being a part of our lives again—then so be it.

But the trouble was that I couldn't get Nina out of my head. I'd wound up at her door because I needed to see her again. She invited me in and at the last moment, I caught myself from doing something stupid. She deserved better than this. She deserved a better man. She was not the kind of girl who should be played around with.

I wracked my brain now, staring up at the ceiling, trying to decide if I had ever felt that way toward Cynthia.

The truth was that I'd known her all my life, and I'd wanted her all my teenage years. Cynthia was the *popular girl* in school...with her long blonde, shining hair and the crop tops that showed off her flat, perfect belly. She was a cheerleader and a party girl. I wanted her like every other guy in school did, and she strung me along for years.

We were 'friends', she claimed, and yet, she kissed me when she got drunk at parties. For years, I couldn't make a move on any other girl because I clung to the hope that one day Cynthia would be mine. I truly believed that we would end up together.

But did I feel a burning passion for her? The way I felt for Nina now? Like my own body would consume me in a fire if I couldn't have her? If I even saw her again? With Nina, somehow it was different. I was hard just thinking about her.

As far as I remembered it, Cynthia was a force of habit. I wanted her because everyone else did, because she was the most desirable girl in school, and because I was lucky enough to get some of her attention.

Years went by and I waited for her to make up her mind, and eventually, I decided it was time for me to move on.

I signed up for the Marines. This would keep me distracted. I'd be serving my country and live far away from Cynthia. I'd hoped I'd begin to forget her.

The night before I left town was the first time we had sex. Cynthia was drunk and so was I. She said she was sorry to see me go, that she would miss me, that she'd always hoped we'd be together. When she took off her clothes and smiled at me, I couldn't believe my luck. It was like a dream come true for me.

In the morning when I woke up, the bed was empty where she'd fallen asleep. She hadn't left a note or got in touch, and in a few hours, I was on a bus, waving goodbye to my parents.

It felt like it was finally over. Like sleeping with Cynthia that night was the closure I needed.

And I was happy.

I was good at my job. I made good friends. I felt proud and capable. I was a good Marine.

But then I got that phone call from Cynthia. Eight months after I'd left town. She asked my mother for my contact details and I couldn't believe it when I heard her voice on the line.

She told me she was pregnant. She was crying and unhappy. She was going to have the baby in a few weeks' time and wished she hadn't kept it. I was stunned to cold silence as she spoke and cried and blamed me. In the end, she said she was going to give the baby away but her guilty conscience had forced her to call me and let me know.

I didn't miss a beat. I knew what needed to be done.

"I'm coming home, Cynthia. Marry me. Let's raise this baby together. Don't give him away."

I remembered my voice clearly. I knew she'd heard me, but she remained silent for a few minutes. I couldn't say any more.

"Okay," she'd replied in a small voice and as soon as the call ended, I wrote a letter to my Commanding Officer. My life in the Marines was over. I was going home on an early retirement. I wanted to be honorably discharged. Even though I didn't know what I would do next, the one thing I did know was I would do my best to be a good father.

I was back home in time for James's birth. I was there in the hospital, holding Cynthia's hand as she delivered our child. She seemed happy at first and we got married the next week at City Hall. Technically, I did end up getting what I wanted. Cynthia and I were going to be together now. We were going to raise a child together and make a life.

But then she started sleeping with Rick Meyers and everything changed. Just within a few months of the birth of our son, Cynthia decided this life wasn't for her and she would rather run away with Rick, the jock from our school, than look after our son.

·

## 19

## NINA

*I*t made me sick to my stomach to recall the way Eric rejected me last night. How stupid was I? What was I thinking? Why had I even put myself in a position where he could just turn me down so bluntly?

What did I think was going to happen minutes after he was cozying up with his ex-wife? That he was going to come into my room and we'd make love?

I stayed up all night thinking about it. I considered quitting the job because I couldn't bear to face Eric anymore. But I couldn't do it to James. Now more than ever, he needed me. This was going to be a complicated phase of his life. He told me I was his best friend. Best friends weren't supposed to treat each other this way.

And this job had so far kept me safely out of *the man's* reach. He hadn't contacted me yet or threatened anyone.

So when I got out of bed the next morning, I was a wreck. I hadn't slept, I was agitated and upset with myself, and I couldn't remember the last time I'd eaten properly.

I took a shower and tried to look presentable, but when I saw myself in the mirror, all I saw were dark circles under my eyes and sunken cheeks. There was no way that Eric would even want to look at me anymore. There was nothing attractive about me. All I could do now was blame myself for all my problems.

I went to James's room and knocked on his door before entering.

It was Saturday, which meant he didn't have to go to playschool and we could have the whole day to ourselves. As long as Cynthia didn't interfere.

I stood over James's bed, watching him sleep, and I could feel my heart melting. He looked so peaceful under the covers, breathing easily, clutching one of his teddy bears.

I could have stood there watching him all day. It was a blessing to have him in my life, I was realizing that now. His innocence and his honesty were exactly what I needed. Even though he was just five years old, it was true that he was probably my best friend too.

"Cute, isn't he?"

Cynthia's voice startled me. I whipped around to see her standing at the door. I felt miserable the moment I saw her. I should have closed the door on my way in.

She must have just woken up too, but she looked fresh and ready for the day. She stepped in closer to the bed where I was standing.

"The moment he was born and I looked into his face, I knew he was going to be a little heartbreaker. He has my good genes," she continued with a laugh in her voice.

I took in a deep breath and nodded. "He *is* very cute," I said. It was the truth and I wanted to remain civil with Cynthia.

She watched him in silence for a few moments before she looked up at me. There was a smile on her face. I could see the makeup she'd adorned on her face already, this early in the morning. I got the sense that she was the kind of woman who was always ready to impress.

"I want you to know one thing, Nina, dear," she began and when she crossed her arms defensively over her chest, I knew what she was about to say wasn't going to be good.

"Look, Cynthia, whatever you think you have to say, you really don't have to—"

I'd had enough of these people putting me in my place. She cut me off though, as she continued, "It would be better and easier for you if you just left now."

I glared at her with my nostrils flaring in anger. She smiled, like she knew her words were affecting me.

"You know, for your own sake and your dignity, just to save yourself from getting fired. Wouldn't it be better if you just quit on your own accord?"

"And why would I want to do that?" I asked, turning to her fully now. It wasn't ideal, having this conversation in front of James even though he was asleep. But I wasn't about to run away from her.

"Because we are a family now. Don't you see that?"

"Just yesterday, you were complaining about how unhappy you were with his behavior."

"Sure, and as his mother, I have the right to be able to discipline him. Which I will. He needs to learn."

I licked my lips. James was moving in his bed now. He may have heard our voices and was starting to wake up.

"I will do whatever Eric...Mr. Hall wants me to do. If he wants me to leave, I will do that. I'll wait for his orders."

Cynthia's brow furrowed as she glared at me. "Suit yourself. I was just trying to do you a favor and give you a chance to leave."

"Thank you for your consideration, but I'd prefer to stick it out 'til I'm *asked* to leave," I replied.

James opened his eyes then and looked a little surprised to find both of us standing over him.

"Good morning, my darling!" Cynthia exclaimed. She lunged forward to give him a hug, but James shifted back, digging himself further in his bed. He swung his face to look at me like he needed my help.

"What do you want to do for the day, sweetheart?" Cynthia continued, forcibly ruffling his hair now. James looked like he was about to break into tears.

"I want to be with Nina," he said and my heart immediately warmed. Cynthia was his mother, sure, and maybe I was overstepping my boundaries, but I wasn't going to let her force herself on a little five-year-old boy.

I pushed past her and went to him, gently pulling him out of the bed and into my arms.

"Why don't we plan out our day over breakfast?" I suggested and he was smiling again.

James said he wanted to go to the Chicago Children's Museum today and I was more than happy to take him. He was smiling and in a good mood, and I just wanted to make the day nice for him. Over breakfast, we discussed what all we would see and the treats we might get for lunch.

Cynthia seemed to be lurking in the background. She made her coffee and drank it at the counter in the kitchen. It was obvious that she was listening in on the conversation, but she didn't participate. I didn't care about being polite to her anymore. She had been outrightly threatening towards me.

Eric hadn't emerged out of his room yet. He was either still asleep or in hiding. It was probably for the best. I didn't want to face him yet. I was sure I wouldn't be able to look at him today after last night's rejection.

After breakfast, I asked James to go wash his face and get changed. I was going to get ready too and then we'd leave. He was excited to spend the day with me and I looked forward to it just as much.

In the kitchen, I helped Sarah clear up the plates and do the dishes before I went to get changed and ready for the day. Cynthia had disappeared somewhere, and she was nowhere in sight.

As I washed my face and brushed my hair, I tried to be as positive as I possibly could. This was a job. I was here for James. I was here for the money. What happened with Eric was unhealthy, anyway. It was for the best if we kept out of each other's way, if I saw him as little as possible.

I changed into a pair of tight blue jeans and a stretchy blue vest for the day. A thin navy jacket hung from my arm as I went looking for James. He said he would get dressed himself for the day, but I was sure I'd have to help him, at least brush his hair a bit and tie his shoelaces.

I knocked on his door and entered and saw he wasn't there. "James?" I called out to him and then went to check the bathroom attached to his room. That was empty too.

"Hey, kiddo?" I left his room and went checking in the other rooms. He wasn't in the living room, nor in the other bathrooms. In the kitchen, Sarah was starting to bake a pie for dessert later in the day.

"Did you see James?" I asked her, a little breathlessly.

"Not since breakfast. Have you checked his room?" Sarah asked. I didn't bother answering. I had this bad feeling that Cynthia was forcing him to spend time with her again.

I rushed in the direction of the spare room she was occupying.

"James? Cynthia?" I called out loudly at the door. When there was no response, I opened the door because I had no other choice.

That room was empty too. I stood there at the door, looking around. I couldn't even see her bags there, or any stray bits of clothing or her belongings on the dresser. Had she left?

The thought entered my brain, followed by the shocking realization that she might have taken James with her.

"James!" I screeched his name and went running out of the room. I was at Eric's door, banging on it. There was no answer from in there either.

"Eric!" I kept banging on his door, until I finally pushed that open too. Again. Empty.

This was quickly beginning to feel like some kind of horror film. Was this really happening? Why did it feel like I was the only person here? Like I was part of some cruel prank.

"Nina, what's going on?" Sarah had appeared at the end of the hallway, wiping her hands on her apron.

"Eric. Where is he?" I asked, my eyes seemed to be popping out of my sockets.

"He left for the gym earlier, at his usual time."

"And Cynthia? Did you see her leaving?"

Sarah shook her head and came toward me. "No, but she might have stepped out for a coffee or something, no?"

"With James. I think she's taken James with her," I said. My voice was shaky. Sarah was looking at me now like I was crazy...deranged.

"Maybe she did. I'm sure he's fine," she said and came toward me and put a hand on my shoulder.

I couldn't get that image out of my mind; of Cynthia lurking in the kitchen, listening in on our conversation while James and I planned our day. Did she look jealous? Would she have done something as extreme as...kidnap him?

"But all her stuff is gone from her bedroom. She didn't tell me or you that she was taking James..."

Sarah gulped. There was worry marking her face too now. "You think maybe she's..." She didn't finish that sentence.

"I don't know what to think," I said.

Sarah and I were holding each other now. She'd obviously sensed the tension in the house too. Maybe Eric hadn't explicitly told her who Cynthia was, but Sarah had guessed the connection.

"Maybe we should wait for Mr. Hall to return, and then he can decide what to do," she suggested.

I was afraid, my heart was racing. Just the thought that James might have been forcibly taken from the house was distressing. I wanted him back.

"It might be too late. The more time we waste, the more difficult it might be to find him," I said.

Sarah rubbed a hand over her forehead. "So what do we do?" she asked.

## 20

## ERIC

*T*o my surprise, there was a cop car in my driveway when I returned from the gym.

"What the hell," I murmured under my breath as I rushed up the steps. The front door was wide open.

There were two uniformed officers in the hallway. Nina and Sarah were standing there speaking to them.

"What is going on? Where is James?" I growled at them. They all turned to face me.

"Are you Mr. Hall?" one of the cops asked me.

"Yes, care to explain what's going on?"

I looked at Nina then. I could see the anxiety in her eyes. Something had happened. I wanted to pull her into my arms and tell her I'd take care of it.

"Cynthia...she took him," Nina said, struggling with her words.

"What did you say?" I snapped. She looked into my eyes. Her hands were clasped together.

"I was getting changed. We were supposed to go to the museum. When I went to look for James, he was gone. So was Cynthia. All her stuff from her room is gone too."

I could sense all eyes on me. Her words hadn't even started to sink in yet. They sounded like gibberish to me because I didn't want to believe them.

"No," I blurted. This couldn't actually be happening.

"Mr. Hall, we understand that Mrs. Cynthia Hall is your wife?"

"My ex-wife," I snapped and turned to the cop who was talking to me. "James is gone?" I looked at Nina again.

Her face was a deathly pale and now there were tears brimming in her eyes.

"I'm sorry, I should have kept a better eye on him. I shouldn't have left him alone." She was full of apology and I could see she meant every word of it. This wasn't her fault. How was she supposed to know that she'd have to keep James safe from his own mother?

"This is a complicated situation, Mr. Hall. I'm sure you understand. We can't issue this as a kidnapping since the person he's with is his own mother," the cop continued.

"The woman is crazy, do you fuckin' hear me?" I raged at the cops. Something suddenly snapped in my head.

James could be in danger.

"I have no idea where she could be or what she could be planning to do with my son," I growled. My hands were fists on my sides. I wanted to hit something, punch the wall. Anything.

"But she was living in this house with you," the other cop said, almost like he was making fun of the situation.

"I was giving her a fucking chance."

"What can we do now?" Nina stepped in. I looked at her. She had her face firmly planted toward the cops.

"Protocol is to give it a few hours and then issue an alert. It's only been an hour, ma'am. They might have gone for breakfast or something. They might be back."

I wanted to punch this guy in the face. Wasn't he hearing what we were saying? Cynthia was crazy. She'd disappeared with James with the full intention of not being found. Why else would she take her stuff? Why wouldn't she leave a note?

I took a threatening step toward the cops. Did they really expect us to sit around and do nothing?

I felt Nina's hand in mine. She gently tugged me back, pulling me away from the cops before I did any damage.

"Okay, thank you, officers. We'll wait," she said.

I glared at her and she blinked her eyes rapidly. What the fuck was that supposed to mean?

Sarah showed the cops out to the door. They promised to check in on us in a few hours and then they left.

Nina quickly drew her hand away from me once they were

gone, like she didn't need to worry about me acting out anymore.

"What the actual fuck!" I growled. Sarah rushed to the kitchen, like she didn't want to be associated with this. Nina ran a hand through her dark sleek hair.

"Maybe they're right, maybe we should wait. Maybe we're overreacting. Do you have her phone number?"

"No!" I growled and then turned from her and pushed my fist into the wall. I needed to do that. Get it out of my system.

It made Nina gasp and take a few steps back. My knuckles throbbed, but I felt better.

"I shouldn't have trusted her. I should have trusted my own gut instincts. Cynthia hasn't changed. She will do anything to get her way."

"Maybe one hour. Let's give it one more hour," Nina said, looking pleadingly at me. It was like neither of us was really listening to each other.

"She left us. She left her three-month-old son and ran away with some guy. Rick Meyers. She decided she was done being a mom." I spoke in a low mumbling voice.

I'd never spoken about Cynthia like this aloud. I'd always kept my problems to myself, but now she'd taken my kid. She'd gone too far. I was prepared to kill her if I had to.

Maybe Nina saw that look in my eyes, so she came toward me.

"We'll find him. She won't be able to do it. James will be back home in no time," she spoke softly.

I held her gaze, her beautiful green eyes. She had no idea how much I needed her. "You don't know Cynthia like I do," I said and she gulped. "She isn't a monster but she can do monstrous things."

Nina licked her lips nervously and nodded her head. "One hour. If they're not back in one hour then we go looking for them. Fuck the cops. I know people. My brother and his friends. They'll bring James back. They won't let her leave this city."

Nina sounded confident. Her words reminded me of how little I knew about her. What did her brother and his friends do? I didn't care. I was just glad she was here because if I was alone, I knew I'd go insane. I'd bring this house down. I'd be roaming the streets looking for my son.

"So we just wait now?"

Nina nodded. Then she checked her wristwatch. "Fifty-five minutes to go."

There was a lot to say, but neither of us spoke while we waited. Sarah was still in the house, cleaning and cooking, but neither of us seemed to notice her. Nina and I remained in the hallway, pacing it up and down, eyeing each other from time to time with worry.

The only thing I cared about right now was the ticking clock. Thirty minutes more, fifteen, ten…five.

When we were three minutes away, I looked at Nina and she looked at me.

"I need to find my son," I growled. I was pissed with her now because her plan hadn't worked. We'd wasted an hour when I could have been out there looking for James.

"I'm going to call Corey and tell him to gather a team."

I was barely listening to what she had to say. I didn't trust anyone right now, especially not a gang of people I'd never met. I didn't know where to even start looking for them. For all I knew, they were already on a flight somewhere out of Chicago.

The doorbell rang. We exchanged looks and then we both rushed to open the door.

Cynthia was standing outside, holding James's hand, but he was crying.

"Buddy!"

He broke away from his mother and pounced at me. I lifted him up in my arms and brought him inside the house.

Cynthia was standing at the door with her bags on her side. Her brows were crossed and she looked upset.

"Where did you take him?" Nina raged at her. I didn't even know she was capable of this kind of rage. She'd seemed pretty calm to me until now.

"I don't need to answer any of your questions," Cynthia snapped at her and stepped in, just at the door. From the body language between the two women, it seemed that they might have already exchanged words earlier.

"Answer the fucking question, Cynthia. Where did you take James?" I growled.

My son had buried his face in my shoulders and I clung to him tightly. I could still feel him sobbing lightly against my clothes.

Cynthia rolled her eyes. "He is such a little cry baby. I mean, seriously, I'm his mother. He should have some respect!" Cynthia was mad at our boy and she had no right to be.

"You're a mother he barely knows. I'm surprised he even remembers you. His attitude toward you isn't his fault. You keep abandoning him," I said. I realized I didn't need to shout at Cynthia, the weight of my words would be enough to bring her down.

She sighed aloud and stared at me holding James in my arms. "The truth is, Eric, you don't know the first thing about raising a child."

"I was willing to give it a shot, instead of giving him up."

Cynthia snorted amusedly. "You think you've done him a favor? He is a spoiled brat with no manners."

"He is not!" Nina screeched. We both looked at her, and she seemed like she was ready to break into tears.

"He is five years old. He's having a hard time adjusting to a new city and a new kindergarten and no friends. And I'm pretty sure he's getting bullied in class. The least you can do, as his mother, is show him some compassion!"

Nina stepped toward me and opened her arms wide so I'd let her take James from me. "You both can sort this out between yourselves. James doesn't need to hear it."

My son was more than happy to go to Nina, who held him

close. She threw me a look of warning—and I knew exactly what she was trying to say—*keep him out of it.*

And then she walked away with him. I assumed she took him to his room. Once again, I was left alone with Cynthia and this time I was sure I would kill her.

She stood leaning against the door now, looking like nothing Nina had said affected her.

"You've given your babysitter too much free rein around this house," she complained.

"Are you fucking serious? Are you still criticizing me after you just tried to kidnap our son?" I growled.

Cynthia grinned and at that moment, I hated her more than I'd ever hated her before. "I was just trying to do something nice for him."

"Where were you taking him?"

"I thought we could go to New York. See Times Square, go to Central Park..."

"Are you kidding me? He's five. He has a home here. He has kindergarten. You can't just take him anywhere you want without a plan. Without letting me know. Without asking my permission." I knew she could see just how red my face had turned. How close I was to bursting my lid.

Cynthia took in a deep breath and stared at me from under her long thick lashes. "See that's the problem with you, Eric. You take things a little too seriously. You always have."

I clenched my jaws in anger. She had never made me this mad at her before. Not even when she decided to leave

James and run away with another man. Not even when I decided that the best thing for us would be to get a divorce.

"Yeah, I was totally serious about looking after our son. Something you could never get serious about."

She straightened herself up and took a few steps toward me. "You've spent half your life being in love with me, Eric. What makes you think you'll ever be completely rid of me?" She was proud. She thought she had me wrapped around her little finger. She was trying to seduce me. I could see it in her eyes, the way she licked her lower lip thickly, how she fluttered her long lashes.

I knew her too well. I knew exactly what she was doing and I wasn't going to fall for it. "I was a kid, I was an idiot. I was never in love with you, Cynthia. I wanted to fuck you, which I did, and now I don't want you anymore."

I saw the way the words stung her. She jerked away from me, and the grin seemed to droop on her face. She gulped once and then tried to hide her nerves. "Sure, tell yourself what you need to sleep at night."

"Get out of my house, Cynthia, and don't ever think about getting in touch with me. Don't ever contact James."

She crossed her arms over her breasts and glared at me. Her cheeks had turned pink, which meant she was embarrassed. I was winning this battle.

"You don't know what you're doing. My son needs me."

"Is that why he couldn't stop crying when you tried to take him to New York? Tell me, Cynthia, did he cry so much that you had to turn around and cancel your plans? Because you knew you wouldn't be able to deal with it for the whole trip?"

She was speechless. I knew I was right.

She had a romantic notion of going on an exciting adventure with her son. But he was five. She didn't know him well enough. She had no realistic idea of how to look after a kid. She had no choice but to change her mind.

"I could get to know him…" she began to say and I took one threatening step toward her and looked deep into her eyes. I wanted her to know that I meant business.

"Listen to me carefully, Cynthia, because I'm not going to repeat myself. You need to leave now and if you ever pull a stunt like this again, if you even try and talk to my son without my permission, I'll get a restraining order against you. I'll pull every string available to me and I'll have you arrested if I have to. You'll regret ever knowing me."

From the way her shoulders quaked, I got the sense that she knew she was defeated. There was no way I'd let her put James through this experience again.

She opened her mouth to say more, but I put my hands on her shoulders and spun her around. "Have a good life, Cynthia, just leave us out of it."

I pushed her out of the door and banged it shut behind her.

She was gone. She was never coming back. The one thing I knew about her was that she was a coward. The spell was broken. Now she knew she had no control over me.

Nothing was more important in my life than my son.

## 21

# NINA

*J*ames was too upset to go to the museum after the ordeal he had that morning. He told me how his mother had forcibly dragged him out of the house and into a cab. He said he couldn't stop crying in the car and wanted his dad or me, and Cynthia continued to scold him for it.

All I could do was hold him as he cried and related the story. Cynthia had gone as far as taking him to the airport where he kicked up a fuss by pushing her luggage and kicking her. She called another cab and they got back to the house after that.

A part of me was proud of him. Despite how horrific the whole situation must have been for him, it seemed like he knew exactly what to do. He wasn't going to go down quietly.

After he was done with the story, I held him and reassured him and tried to distract him with games.

Eric joined us some time later. I didn't have to ask him if Cynthia was gone. I could see it in his eyes that she was and she wasn't coming back.

Eric said he wanted to spend the day with us and James was excited. His mood changed instantly. I was relieved too because I knew he needed it today.

We spent the day in the house, playing with his toys and playing the games James wanted to play. Despite how taxing the morning had been, Eric and I, together, were able to help James forget about it for most of the time.

He had moments when he stopped playing and he'd look at his father or at me and ask if his mother was coming back. We always reassured him that it was over, that she wasn't staying in the house anymore. Eric told him that he wouldn't have to see her again if he didn't want to. James didn't want to.

I knew I was dangerously attached to him. I could feel it in my bones. It had been such a short time, but I'd never felt this protective about someone before. It was like I could see the kindness in James's soul and I knew him for the sweet innocent boy that he was. I would do anything to make sure he was safe and happy, even though he wasn't my son.

Didn't Eric want the same things for him?

What was going to happen between us?

The drama of the day had shifted the focus away from my feelings about him, but now that the day had calmed down and we were all laughing and playing and enjoying ourselves—I couldn't help but think about *us* again.

Last night, when he came knocking on my door and then rejected me, he made it very clear what he really thought of me. That I was nothing more than a one-night thing. A passing phase. I was much more useful to him as his son's babysitter.

After dinner, Eric suggested he would put James to sleep tonight and I agreed it was for the best. I left the two of them alone together for some much-needed father-son time and went to my own room.

I needed to think things through. I needed to prioritize. If I was going to continue working in this house, I needed to follow some ground rules concerning Eric. Under no circumstances could I develop feelings for this man. That was the number one rule.

I kept myself busy in my room while James and Eric spent time together. I vowed that I would stick to my own rules, starting tonight. But then there was a knock on my door a few hours later and even though I knew who it was, I couldn't hold myself back.

I could have simply pretended that I was already asleep, but I didn't. I went over and opened the door to find Eric on the other side. He had a glass of whiskey in his hand already, although he didn't look like he'd been drinking for long.

"How is he?" I asked. If I hadn't said something we'd just be standing there staring at each other in silence. The feverish attraction between us was palpable, and tonight, I felt like I needed him.

Eric ran a hand through his hair and sighed aloud. "He's fine. He went to sleep easily and I sat with him a while longer. He's doing a lot better because of you."

I blushed. I was never one for taking compliments easily, and I definitely couldn't handle them from Eric. I looked down at my feet awkwardly and tried to steady my breathing.

"It's strange, but I really do care about James. I know it's only been a few days."

"I can see that," he said promptly and our eyes met again.

"I just wanted to come by to say how much I appreciate the work you are doing with my son. You have made a real difference in our lives and for that, I will always be grateful to you." Even though Eric's words were kind and gentle, that wasn't the way he was looking at me. There was a dark glare in his eyes. I didn't have to take a wild guess to know what he was thinking.

He was undressing me with my eyes.

But after the way he rejected me the previous night, I wasn't going to make the first move tonight. I couldn't put myself through that again.

"I'm just doing my job," I replied.

He shook his head.

"No, you're doing more than that. You're going above and beyond to help James feel better about our lives here in Chicago. He was doing much worse before you came into the picture. I...was doing much worse."

I licked my bottom lip nervously. I hadn't expected him to make this about himself. A thrill ran through my body. What was he saying? I made him happy? What did that mean?

I'd never had a conversation like this with a man before.

These were never the emotions exchanged.

Eric seemed to be watching me closely and then he took a large sip of the whiskey and breathed heavily into his glass.

"And I'm going to take your advice and look into the situation at his playschool."

I was relieved to hear that, and it made me smile.

"That would be a huge help. I'm fairly certain James isn't happy in that place for a particular reason."

"I'll speak to the teachers and see what they have to say."

I nodded. I couldn't believe he actually respected my opinion and took it seriously.

"You're doing an excellent job here, Nina."

My smile grew wider. I was blushing too, and there was a tightness in my belly I couldn't explain. Eric stood before me, tall and muscular. His black t-shirt taut against his strong torso. I knew what his body felt like, I could never forget it. I wanted more...but how? If it wasn't what he wanted, then why was he here?

"Were you going to bed?" he asked, making me nearly jump. I didn't realize I was lost in my thoughts.

"Umm, no, not yet," I said, fumbling with my words a little.

"Do you want to talk some more?" he asked, staring right into my eyes. There was that thrill running down my spine again. I didn't know what that was supposed to mean, but I sure as hell wanted to find out.

I stepped out of my room and followed him to the living room where I now saw he'd gotten a fire going. I hadn't even noticed the fireplace before this. Eric sat down on a chair and I took the armchair across from him. Once more, he didn't offer me a drink.

I didn't want one.

Being in his presence like this, alone with him in this cozy room by a fireplace, was intoxicating enough. Could he see it in my eyes?

"I figured we should get to know each other a little better, now that we're living together, don't you think?"

"Yes, that's true."

"So you and Miles are related."

"He is married to my sister, well, my half-sister, but she is more like a mother to me. She raised me, us. I have a twin brother." I'd never revealed so much about myself so quickly, and especially to somebody I didn't really know. I was breathless by the end of that, like I had no control over my emotions.

Eric was watching me closely. "A twin, huh?"

"Do you have siblings?"

"No, I'm the only child."

I twiddled with my fingers in my lap. The fire blazed beside us and I was filled with warmth. There was a fire burning in the pit of my stomach, too, but all I could do was try to suppress it.

"Are you guys close? Your brother and you?"

I couldn't remember the last time someone had asked me that question. "We used to be. When we were kids, it felt like he was a part of me. I don't know how else to explain it. We were the same person. We wanted the same things at the same time."

"And now?" he asked in a low voice.

"He has his life and I have mine." I knew I said that with some sadness in my voice. I hadn't realized until now how much I really missed Corey. I hadn't thought about him that way.

Eric nodded. "As a twin, I'm sure you share a special bond with him that can never be replaced by anyone."

"I guess not."

"Maybe you both should make an effort to reconnect. I'm sure it'll make a huge difference in your life."

Even though I wasn't expecting this tone of conversation from him tonight, there was something warm and nice about it. I didn't want him to stop. I wanted him to continue. I looked at him like I wanted to hear more and Eric smiled.

"Maybe I shouldn't be the one dishing out relationship advice," he said with a grin. A handsome grin. Did he even know how damn sexy he was? I could feel the moisture between my legs, in that secret spot between my thighs. No matter how much we talked, he wouldn't know how wet I was unless he actually touched me there.

"You think you aren't qualified to talk to me about my sibling because you're divorced? Do you know how many marriages don't work out in this country?"

Eric laughed and shook his head. "I stopped comparing myself with other people a long time ago. My situation is rather unique. Cynthia is unique."

I couldn't help but smile at that.

She tried to kidnap her son today...*unique* was an under-statement! I said nothing, but Eric was watching me again. Like really studying me. A part of me wanted to hide from his solid gaze, and another part of me was proud of revealing myself to him. He could have asked me anything and I would have answered him with all honesty.

"I really just want to do what is right by my son," he continued.

"And you're doing a good job."

"What is this? A mutual appreciation society?" he said with a laugh, and that made me laugh too.

"I have nothing to fault you with. You are a good dad. You are doing the best you can, given the circumstances. I can see the bond you share with James. He's lucky to have you."

Eric drank some more and then looked into the fire. "Honestly, I don't know what I'm doing."

"Parenting doesn't come with a manual," I said and he shook his head.

"Yeah, but it does come with a lot of unsolicited advice. Pretty much any decision I make for my son is met with criticism and advice."

"From your parents? Family?"

"Well, my dad died, so yeah, from my mom, and just people in general. From his playschool, from friends...a single dad is not really considered to be the best decision-maker."

"I disagree with that. James is a good kid, and yeah, sure, he's going to take some time to adjust to life in Chicago, but you are doing the best you can and he'll get there soon enough. And dealing with your ex-wife mustn't be easy."

Eric held my gaze after I spoke, and it seemed like he was considering my words. We remained silent for some time, just staring at each other.

"I'm glad you decided to stick around, after..." His voice seemed to fade and I felt a prickly sensation on my skin. I craved his touch. Would he touch me? He seemed pretty determined not to.

I knew what he was referring to and it made my cheeks burn. I looked away from him and nodded.

"This job is important to me, and I care about James. I don't want to abandon him."

Eric still looked at me. I could feel his eyes on me.

"Good, that's what I want to hear. He told me tonight that he loves you and you are his best friend."

We stared at each other as he spoke and I could feel my whole body charging up.

I felt grateful to hear that James spoke that way about me, and Eric saying it was even more magical. What was it about this man that made me feel like I was on fire? It had to be more than his incredible good looks, right? More than how sexy he looked under those clothes? Was I really that shallow?

"I don't mean to embarrass you."

I shook my head. "I'm just happy to be working here, to help James," I replied quickly and Eric started to stand up from his chair.

"Well, I hope you continue to work with us as long as you can. I promise not to do anything that'll make it awkward for you. Whatever happened between us—"

I cut him off because I didn't want him to actually say the words. *That it meant nothing to him*. That would literally break my heart. I knew it.

"It's forgotten. It's a thing of the past. You don't need to worry about it."

"Okay, good," he said and I smiled weakly at him.

He stood up and then he went to his drinks cabinet. I thought he was going to pour himself another whiskey, but Eric seemed to change his mind at the last minute. He just stood there, staring at the cabinet. I could see he was thinking about something. What? What did he want to say? What was on his mind?

"Maybe I should go back to my room." I started to stand up too. Maybe he wanted to be alone again and just didn't want to be rude and say it directly to me.

"No, you don't have to go."

I stopped in my tracks and turned to him.

I could see he had his palms fisted tightly on his sides. Was he angry about something?

"You're right, it's in the past. It was a mistake, and we should forget about it."

I nodded. My breathing was starting to quicken because he walked toward me now.

Eric loomed over me, his jaw clenched, his body inches away from me. I tipped my head back so I could look up at him.

"Then why do I want to push you up against the wall right now and fuck you?"

His voice was a low, deep, guttural growl. At first, I thought I hadn't heard him correctly, but I knew I had. I was never going to forget those words for as long as I lived. They sent electric waves pulsating through my body. I was in shock.

Was he waiting for me to say something? Because he was looking down at me with his blue eyes stormy dark.

"Because it isn't over," I replied.

It was the truth. It wasn't over between us. Not until we saw this through.

He took another step toward me and I felt like my body was swinging backward. I was breathless, and my body was awakened. It was like he was torturing me. His eyes never left my body, like burning a hole through my skin.

"You're very perceptive, Nina Jones," he commented and his eyes traveled down.

I wasn't sexily dressed like Cynthia always was. I was in my usual pair of ripped jeans and a stretchy camisole with thin spaghetti sleeves. I knew my breasts stuck out in this top. Could he see my nipples? Did he have any idea how he could turn me on by just looking at me like that?

I gulped, suddenly feeling my throat go dry. Eric watched me closely, studying every part of me.

"Please...don't..." I managed to get the words out and it sounded like I was pleading.

"Don't what?"

"Don't look at me like that if you're not going to do anything about it."

He seemed to clench his jaw harder. "Patience, Nina. All you have to do is have patience," he said.

My body was on fire. I couldn't be patient anymore. My shoulders heaved as I watched him. Couldn't he hear how raspy my breathing had become?

"Do you feel it? Do you feel you?" he asked. At first, I was confused by what he was asking and then I gulped and nodded. Of course, I felt it. The throbbing wet sensation between my legs. It was spreading everywhere.

"I want to see you feel yourself. Can you do that for me?"

Eric spoke in a low, gentle voice, and I would have done anything he asked me to do right now.

My fingers worked on the buttons and zip of my jeans and

then I pushed it down to my ankles. I slipped my hand into my black lace panties while Eric watched me. It looked like his deep-blue eyes got wider.

"Nina," he said my name firmly, just as fingers grazed my swollen throbbing clit. "I said I want to see you."

I gulped again, but I followed his command. I stripped my panties down and now I stood before him in nothing but the camisole that stretched over my heaving breasts. I'd taken my bra off hours before.

When I touched myself again this time, Eric smiled. My clit was swollen and thirsty for his touch, so I rubbed myself harder. He stared at me from under his heavy eyelids. I could see his cock growing and getting harder in his pants.

Slowly, while I continued touching myself, Eric began to touch himself too.

He took off his jeans and I saw his cock. Big and strong, throbbing in his hand. He stroked himself slowly until he started matching the rhythm with which I was rubbing myself.

We were still at a distance from each other, but somehow we'd managed to make each other breathless. I moaned, shaking slightly as I hung from the edge of my sanity.

"I want to watch you make yourself come. Do it. Now."

His voice was a command. Like a military command. I had no choice but to follow those orders.

My fingers slipped in between my folds until I could feel them deep inside me. With my thumb, I continued to rub my clit...until I knew I was going to come. Eric glared at me darkly, his hand moving up and down his big cock. I salivated just thinking about what it would feel like to have him inside me, and that was enough to make me combust.

I fell backward and my back met the wall. It was the support I needed while my orgasm took control of my body. I could feel every cell and nerve of my body charged and on fire. This wasn't the first time I was making myself come, but it was certainly the first time it felt like this. Like I had no control over myself.

Eric's stroking became harder and stronger. His face had turned even darker now and I didn't know what he was going to do next. But he stopped just as my orgasm began to fade.

I was breathing hard, out of breath, and he came closer to me. His tall hulking body guarded me to the wall. He lowered his face down toward me and I could feel his hot breath on my nose.

"You have any idea how fucking sexy you are?" he growled in a low wild voice. I had the courage to meet his eyes and I looked into them deeply.

"Why aren't you doing something about it then?" I challenged him. He could see it in my eyes, and I knew from the expression on his face that he wasn't about to walk away from this unscathed. Not this time.

I reached for his cock and he took in a deep breath. I held him in my right hand and started to stroke. He leaned closer to me until our lips met.

And then Eric was kissing me. Slowly at first, almost sweetly, then wildly like he couldn't control himself. He used his tongue to push my lips apart and he dove into me. With one hand, I clung to his shoulder, while I used the other to continue stroking him.

His tongue explored my mouth while I brought him to the brink of his orgasm. He growled and raged like a caged animal, tasting my mouth, diving deep down my throat until he finally peeled himself away from me.

I glared at him some more. Challenging him again.

*Was this all he had?*

Eric missed a few beats. It was the time he was taking to steady himself. Then he lunged at me again, grabbing my bare waist and spinning me around to face the wall.

I knew what he was about to do, but I wasn't prepared for it. He pushed me further so that my breasts squeezed up against the wall. He stood behind me, and my butt grazed his strong muscular thighs. They were like solid trunks of trees. Above, his throbbing erect cock hung and within a few moments, he was going to be inside me.

First, he put on a condom. I heard the wrapper rip and the smack of latex against that angry cock. Then his hands were on mine, pinning them to the wall. Didn't he know I was going nowhere? I wanted to savor and experience every part of this.

He kissed the back of my neck, then the top of my shoulders —sending electric waves running down my spine until it felt like I had no control over my body or my mind.

"I've wanted you since the first moment I saw you." I heard him speak and the words were like magic. Enough to make me come, but I held back.

He moved his hands away from mine while I stared at the wall hungrily. He massaged my shoulders, just for a quick hot second and then he was traveling down my back, stroking my hips, and then he grabbed my butt and squeezed.

I leaned forward, biting down hard on my bottom lip because I felt like I couldn't take it anymore. I could feel the heat emanating from his cock. A few more seconds and we'd both explode.

He held my butt and then without warning, thrust himself inside me. I cried out and then tried to muffle my own voice.

Oh. My. God.

I'd never experienced anything this sexy before.

This man knew what he wanted and he wasn't afraid of just taking it. I clung to the wall while he drove into me with a loud grunt. I could feel the thickness and length of his cock —it reached deep inside me. Enough to make my body rise and fall and quake.

Then Eric started thrusting; in and out, and we both moaned along with the motion. He clutched my hips while I shook against the wall.

He was bigger than me, much bigger and finally, I felt fulfilled. Like someone had just filled up the empty hole in me.

He leaned over my back so his mouth was by my right ear. His breath was hot, and I could feel the strong iron grip of his hands on my hips.

"I'm going to come inside you, Nina."

"I want you to come inside me."

"You feel so fucking good."

"Come inside me, Eric."

Saying his name seemed to be some kind of trigger. He growled and then came with a jerk. I let go at the same time. Feeling him come inside me was all I needed to push me over the edge.

I cried out, chewing my lip so I wasn't loud, while Eric growled with no concern of who heard him. We shook and swayed together, and it felt like our orgasms were going to last forever.

I was stuck to the wall and he seemed stuck to my back. We were still slowly moving together and then I felt him starting to pull himself out of me. I wanted to hold on to him, the feeling, for as long as I could, but then we were separated and I felt empty again.

I couldn't face him. Not now, not yet. All I could do was stare at the wall and try to catch my breath. Behind me, I could hear Eric starting to pull up his pants. Do up his zip and belt.

I pressed my eyes closed, trying to magically make myself disappear. I wasn't sure what he was going to say. Now that it was over, was it his turn to reject me again? Or did it mean something to him this time? Would it ever mean anything to him, other than fucking his babysitter?

"Your phone is buzzing."

That was what he said to me. Those were his first words to me after we just had sex.

"What?" I whipped around. Still completely naked from the waist down.

"Your phone," he repeated himself. I looked down and saw what he was talking about. My phone was blinking and vibrating on the floor. It had slipped out of the pocket of my jeans.

"Oh..."

Instantly, I felt relief. This was what I needed to help me disappear.

I picked it up and saw it was Corey calling. "Sorry, it's my brother. I should take this."

"Sure, yeah."

Eric was fully dressed by now and he turned away from me. I rushed to put on my panties and jeans and even though the call ended, I decided I was going to call Corey back.

Eric threw me one look over his shoulder while he returned to the drinks cabinet.

Was he going to stay up? Was he going to wait for me?

I didn't even know what the dynamic between us was going to be from now. What did the sex mean? There were so many questions, but I didn't want to ask him any of them. I was too embarrassed. I'd never made myself emotionally vulnerable like that before, and I wasn't about to start now.

Eric was unavailable. He had other, more important priorities in his life and he'd made himself very clear on that.

I left the room in a hurry, without saying anything more to

him. My body still tingled from the memory of having him inside me. He came inside me. We came together.

Outside, in the hallway near the kitchen, I dialed Corey's number in the dark. He answered on the first ring.

"Nina?"

"Hi, I'm glad you called. Where are you?" I said.

*I* put on my clothes as quickly as possible and decided to pour myself another whiskey. I definitely needed it. What happened today between the two of us was totally unacceptable.

I was lost in the moment. The whole episode with Cynthia, the near-kidnapping, then getting James back home safely —were all an adrenaline rush in my brain. And then we got talking. I hadn't realized how nice it was to just talk to a woman who was intelligent and smart. I felt warm talking to Nina tonight. I felt a connection with her.

But what did that connection mean? Nothing.

She was doing a job here.

We happened to be two healthy, attractive adults living under the same roof. There was a sexual connection between us, sure, but that was where it ended. Besides, she was more than a decade younger than me. It was starting to feel a hell of a lot like I was taking advantage of her.

I could hear the low hum of her voice in the kitchen now. She'd said it was her brother calling and she'd rushed away. It seemed like she was relieved someone was calling her, so she didn't have to actually face me after we had sex.

Was she embarrassed or angry? Or was it worse? Did she regret it? Was she going to quit her job? Why hadn't I thought of all this before making a move on her? Before suggesting that I wanted to fuck her.

In all the situations where honesty was important in life, this was definitely not one of them.

I'd just taken a sip of my drink when I heard her return to the room. At least she didn't sneak away and make things even more awkward between us.

"Hey, is it all right if I go out now?"

I turned to her, clutching the whiskey glass tightly in my hand. My first instinct was to look at the time, but I stopped myself. I wasn't her guardian. I wasn't her boyfriend. How did it matter what time it was?

"Sure, yeah. You have a key, right?"

Nina nodded.

Her usually shiny straight dark hair was a little disheveled in places now. I could see her nipples through that thin top she was wearing without a bra. I wanted to tell her just how jealous it made me—to know that if she went out now, there would be other men who'd see her like this.

I had no right over her. I had no right to tell her any of this.

"Yeah, I hope I'm not too late returning. My brother is at some party. I haven't been out with him in ages."

I remembered our conversation from earlier. She wanted to fix her relationship with her brother.

"This will be good for you guys," I replied. I didn't know what to say. Was I supposed to stop her? Was I supposed to ask her questions about where she was going?

Nina just stood there, staring at me like she expected me to say something more.

"Have fun," I added and then I gulped down the rest of the drink from my glass. When I looked back at her, Nina's expression had turned sour somehow.

"Yeah, sure, I think I will," she replied and then she was gone.

I wished I could chase after her, hold her back, tell her I wanted to spend the night with her—that I didn't want any other man looking at her right now. But she was gone and I knew I couldn't do that.

I heard the front door open and shut, and for the first time since Nina had started working for us a few days ago, I was alone in the house with James again. But it didn't feel like the old times. Something had changed inside me. I felt like a different person tonight. Being with Nina had made a difference that I couldn't explain.

## 23

## NINA

*I* wanted to get out of the house and put some distance between Eric and me, but at the same time, I couldn't help but wish that he had tried to stop me. Or at least asked me where I was going. Or *something*...I didn't know what. I wished he'd shown a little interest in me after we just had sex.

I was rushing to take the L now and I realized I was severely underdressed. It was cold and I was in nothing but a camisole and jeans. I checked to make sure I had my phone and wallet with me, at least. I was in such a hurry to leave the house that I hadn't prepared for anything.

And now, in my mind, I could see Eric's face in the dim light of the living room. His handsome, chiseled face, those sharp blue eyes and his muscular shoulders rising and falling.

He seemed pleased I was going out. He wanted to put some distance between us too. Didn't he have anything to say? No explanation?

This was no ordinary one-night stand. This was going to actually affect our daily lives. Didn't he see it that way? He just seemed so calm and casual about the whole thing. Like it didn't make an ounce of difference to him at all. Was I really that insignificant to him? Were women in general insignificant to him?

I sat in the L, shivering a little as it lurched forward toward town. I'd practically all but begged Corey to let me join him wherever he was. We hadn't seen each other in months. He was the one who'd suggested the last time we spoke that we should hang out more—well, I wanted to hang out tonight.

He said he was at a friend's house. Some of them were high. He said it as a warning because he knew how I didn't approve of drugs of any kind. I barely ever had a drink. But I didn't care tonight. I just wanted to see him. I just wanted to get away from these feelings I thought I was feeling for Eric.

*Feelings*...I didn't want to think about that tonight.

Corey was waiting for me outside his friend's apartment, standing in the dark with his hoodie up. I rushed to him, still shivering and yet so glad to finally see him.

"Hey, you! You look cold," he said, throwing an arm around me. We were like two pieces of a puzzle. He was my twin. All this time, I hadn't thought about how much I actually missed him, but now I could feel it.

I buried my face in his shoulder and he held me tight.

We'd never been the kind of family that hugged and kissed and exchanged I-love-yous, but I really needed to be held by my brother today.

"Hey, you okay? What's going on with you?" he asked when I was finally done with hugging him.

I pulled myself away and looked up at the apartment building. "Should we go inside?"

Corey held on to my left elbow, keeping me back. Of course he'd sensed something was wrong.

"Not before you tell me what's going on. Something is up. Is everything okay?" He was concerned. I looked into my brother's eyes and sighed.

"Nothing, nothing is up. I'm just tired...you know, with college and my job."

"Then quit. Why do you need to work? I'm sure Raina will be able to help you out for a few months. How much do you need? What do you even need it for? It's not like you party or anything."

I nodded. There were so many things I hadn't told Corey about in the past few months, that I wouldn't know where to even begin.

"Yeah, maybe I will talk to Raina. Can we please just go inside for now?" I asked.

He was still eyeing me suspiciously, like he knew I was hiding more from him. "Sure, yeah, we can go inside."

I smiled weakly at him and started walking toward the door of the building, but he held me back again.

"Hey, Nina, you'd tell me, right? If something was wrong?"

I stopped to look at him and then I nodded. "I would, and there's nothing wrong. I'm exhausted. I could use a chair," I replied with a grin but my brother wasn't smiling. He seemed to want to say something more, but then he put an arm around me and led me to the building.

I was glad he'd called. I was glad I had his arm holding me up. All my life, I'd underestimated how much I actually needed my brother and sister, how much I would miss them if I didn't see them every day.

Corey wasn't exaggerating when he told me over the phone this was not 'my kinda scene'. It definitely wasn't. This was exactly the kind of lifestyle I'd tried to get away from on the south side.

There were at least a handful of people in this tiny apartment and all of them seemed stoned. There were pizza boxes and clothes everywhere on the floor of this place. Some guy was asleep on the couch and the others had piled more takeout boxes on top of him.

The TV screen was big and bright in the darkness of the apartment. Two guys were playing video games. There was only one other girl here and she was passed out in the kitchen on a chair, clutching a bottle of beer.

When Corey first brought me in here, I threw him a look of shock and he shrugged. He did warn me.

"You want something to drink?" he offered and I nodded. I definitely needed a drink tonight of all nights. A drink to forget.

"Hey, guys, this is my sister Nina. Nina, these are the guys," Corey offered before he disappeared somewhere to presumably get me a drink. I smiled and waved at the handful of guys who'd looked up when Corey spoke. Most of them returned to what they were doing within moments—it probably hadn't even registered in them that there was a new person in their midst.

One guy stood up, though, and came toward me. I noticed he had a friendly face and he was smiling.

"You're Corey's twin? You guys do look alike," he said. He had a bottle of beer in one hand but it seemed like he hadn't been drinking it. I smiled at him, still on edge a little. I wasn't here to make friends. I was here to get away from Eric and hopefully spend some time with Corey.

"I'm Gareth," he said and held out his hand.

"Hello, Gareth."

"If you're waiting for your brother to show up with a drink, you'll be waiting a long time."

"Why, where has he gone?"

Gareth shrugged.

I was confused. "What, he's just disappeared? He wouldn't do that to me."

"I saw him go into one of the bedrooms with the phone stuck to his ear. Once he does that, it means we've lost Corey for an hour at least."

"Who is he talking to?"

Gareth's brow furrowed and he looked at me intently—like he was trying to figure out something important.

"Is something going on with my brother?" I asked him.

"I'm sure he'll tell you himself when he wants to."

I felt a wave of anger and worry. But did I really have a right to be upset with him when I was hiding so many secrets from him myself?

Gareth was smiling now. "It's not life-threatening. Don't worry about it."

"Is it about a girl? Is Corey seeing someone who's making him miserable?"

Gareth sighed. "Sure, yeah, something like that."

I glanced around the apartment and sighed. Coming here tonight wasn't a good idea. Corey wasn't even available for me to talk to. What was I supposed to do now?

It was like Gareth had read my mind. "Why don't I get you that drink and maybe *we* can chill?" he suggested.

I didn't respond, but he walked away and returned moments later with another beer in his hand. He handed it to me and the condensation on the bottle felt cool in my hand. It calmed me a little. This apartment was too warm and stuffy, despite it being so chilly outside.

"Is there a window here we can open?" I asked Gareth and he smiled.

"There's a balcony we can go to. Once you spend a few hours in here, you start forgetting what fresh air feels like."

I followed him out to a small balcony, big enough for two. Gareth was right; when we stepped out of the smoke, haze, and warmth of the apartment, the air was nippy and fresh.

We stood side by side, facing out, taking quiet sips of our beers.

"So, how do you know Corey?" I asked him. It was kind of nice that he wasn't too concerned with the conversation either. He allowed me to remain with my thoughts.

Gareth shrugged. "I don't actually remember. I guess we hung out with the same crowd and just ended up in a lot of the same places."

I looked at him more closely now. Was he good looking? It was hard to tell. He had a bushy beard and a long, smiling face. He wasn't too tall, but seemed to have an athletic, well-looked-after body. He looked nothing like Eric. But why was I comparing the two of them, anyway? Not every guy had to match up to him.

"You're thinking about something," Gareth interrupted my thoughts.

I took a swing of beer to flush away those thoughts of Eric.

"Just trying to convince myself I should get out more. I'm too caught up with college and work at the moment."

"What are you studying?"

"Philosophy and political theory," I replied, rolling my eyes. Gareth made this face like he was impressed, but maybe he wasn't.

"So what kind of a job do you have?"

"Totally unrelated. I'm a full-time babysitter to this five-year-old kid. He's adorable. Single dad."

He smiled. "Wow. I don't think I would ever be able to take on that kind of responsibility."

He was right. I hadn't thought about how much of a responsibility it was. It was all about being responsible for another human being.

"I enjoy the work, he's a good kid..."

Gareth nodded. "And what about...are you...you know? Seeing somebody?"

That took me by surprise. I didn't realize he would be interested. I was terrible at reading these cues. I wished Karen was around so she could have pointed it out to me. Had I strung Gareth along? Did I make him think I was interested in him?

"Not really. Not seriously," I replied, blushing. The answer should have been a hard no. The thing with Eric was nothing. It was over and it was a mistake.

"Okay, that's exactly what I wanted to hear. I mean, I'm sure you didn't come here looking to be hit on and trust me, that's not what I'm doing. In fact, I'm not even going to ask you out or anything."

Even though Gareth seemed to be struggling to get the words right, he didn't appear to be nervous. I liked that. I appreciated his confidence. I also appreciated the fact that he was being honest about what he wanted.

"Okay, so what are you saying?"

We smiled at each other. Gareth took in a deep breath.

"I'm saying that we should hang out, like outside this dismal setting. We should party. You were just saying how you wish you'd go out more. Well, come out with me."

I raised my eyebrows high on my forehead. "And what about Corey?"

"What about him?"

"He is not going to like the fact that I'm hanging out with one of his friends."

"We'll invite him too, if you want. Like I said, I'm not asking you out on a date. Not yet."

Again, my cheeks were flushed. Did I *want* Gareth to ask me on a date? No, I was relieved that he hadn't because I would've had to turn him down. But I did like talking to him.

"Sure, yeah. I'd like to hang out with you," I said.

"Great, that's awesome. I know some places around town I think you'd like. And maybe sometime in the future, when we've gotten to know each other a little better, we could maybe, I don't know, go out. Just the two of us. On an official date or whatever. You don't have to decide right now."

This was unconventional. No other guy had ever asked me out like this, but something was trusting and friendly about this. Gareth wasn't pushing me to make a decision. He wasn't giving me an ultimatum. He wanted to be my friend first, before anything else, and I liked that.

I stretched my hand out at him and we shook on it. I was glad Corey called and I came here and met Gareth. I desperately needed someone positive and honest in my life right now, and it was even better that it happened to be a fairly decent-looking guy.

For a few minutes there, I'd completely forgotten about Eric and what happened between us. Maybe if I hung out more with Gareth, I'd be able to forget about Eric completely?

"Should we go look for your brother?" he asked and I nodded.

I didn't feel so bad anymore.

## 24

# ERIC

*I* met Miles the next day at the café he liked to conduct his meetings at. I was early and he was late, but I spent the time going through the accounts and files he'd left with me before, not that I could really focus on anything.

My brain was still replaying every moment from the previous day. Cynthia disappearing with James. How upset and afraid my boy looked when they returned to the house.

Nina in that top...her nipples erect, her body luscious, pinned to the wall. The warmth of her.

"Hey, man. You waiting long?" Miles showed up and sat down across from me with a thump. His interruption of my thoughts was much needed. I definitely needed the distraction.

All he had to do was look in the direction of the baristas and they seemed to know exactly what his order was.

"Not long. Twenty minutes maybe."

"Sorry, the meeting ran long."

"I'd love to sit in with you for any meeting coming up," I offered.

"Great, we could use the help. Especially *your* help, with your boardroom experience," Miles replied.

We talked shop for a few more minutes. Miles had a lot of information to share about the other investors who were looking into the business. Although I was the top investor and more hands-on with the company, other people were going to be involved too. That was the only way this company could grow at the rate we wanted it to.

Miles was passionate about his work, and his passion rubbed off on me too. This was good. This was great. This was exactly the kind of reason I was looking for to move to Chicago. It made everything worth it.

When there was a lull in our conversation, he took a sip of his coffee and sat back, sighing.

"How is everything else? How are James and Nina getting on?"

It was a casual question. I knew he meant nothing by it, but I couldn't look Miles in the eye. I slept with his sister-in-law. He trusted me with her and now I felt like I'd betrayed him.

I ran a hand through my hair and nodded. "It's going great. James loves her, she's fit in very well into the household. Although you should probably ask *her* how she feels about the job."

Miles grinned and stirred his coffee. "If Nina had any

complaints, she would have let us know already. She isn't the kind of girl to keep her thoughts to herself," he said.

In the short time that I knew her, I knew that about her already. I nodded. "I'm glad to hear it. Thanks for recommending her, Miles. James and I would've been lost without her."

"Frankly, I'm a little surprised. Nina was never the type to be good with kids or even be interested in babysitting." He shrugged. "But if she's happy with this job, it makes Raina happy and that's all that matters to me."

I nodded. I didn't know what to say. I didn't want to consider the possibility that maybe Nina was staying in this job because of me. Because I'd led her on somehow. The last thing I wanted to do was give her any false hope. I didn't want to string her along.

"You okay, man?" Miles was watching me closely.

"Yeah, all good, I just remembered I need to go for a run."

Miles seemed confused at first but then he shrugged it off.

"You know, I get that things are finally starting to look good for you here, you guys are settling in...but I was throwing this idea around in my head the other day and wanted to bring it up with you."

I crossed my arms on the table and leaned toward him. "What idea?"

"Shoot it down if you think this is nonsense."

"What is it?"

"What do you think of utilizing your boardroom skills in Washington?"

"DC?"

"The very one," Miles replied, smiling now.

I sat back in my chair...not quite sure yet of where he was going with this. Miles tapped a pen on the table, and he had that look on his face like he had a great idea.

"What are you thinking?" I asked.

"Lobbying. I think you'd be great at it. I've seen you at meetings. You know how to work people, how to make a presentation. We need representation in DC. For our veterans, people who would benefit from our app."

"And you want me to lobby to the government?"

"Why not?"

"Because I have no experience with government policies or agencies."

Miles shrugged. "So? Educate yourself in it. You want to be involved in the business, right? You don't want to be a silent investor?"

I clenched my jaw. This sounded crazy to me, and at the same time, my blood was pumping frantically in my veins at the thought of a new, exciting opportunity.

"Yeah, I want to do something, help somehow."

"Well, you are the most appropriate person to do this," Miles said. "I can't think of anyone else who would fit this role. You're a former Marine. You're an investor in this company. You genuinely want to do what is best for our veterans. You want to do what is right by them. So represent them."

I nodded. Things were starting to become clearer now. Miles let out a deep sigh at the end of that. "But this would mean that you'll have to move to DC. Move James out of Chicago."

I stared at my friend. He was right. I couldn't work in DC and make James live here. If we lived apart, it would mean we couldn't share the same relationship as we did now.

"You don't have to decide right away, man. Take your time," Miles spoke up again and I nodded.

"Yeah, I guess I need to think about this. It'll be a huge decision for me," I replied, but tossing the idea around in my head was enough to make me realize how good it'd be for me. It was exactly the kind of role I'd been looking for all these days.

I stayed out that day because I didn't know what I'd say if I saw Nina again. I'd barely seen her at all since the previous night when she walked out of the house after we had sex.

When I returned after dinner, James was nearly ready to go to bed and I offered to take him. Nina almost seemed glad about my offer and she barely met my eyes. It was evident that she would have preferred if we didn't see much of each other too.

I read two of James's favorite books to him, then we talked a little about his day at playschool, and soon enough, he'd drifted off to sleep. I watched him for a little while, then stroked his forehead while he slept and stepped out of his room. In the hallway, I saw Nina again.

She looked ready to go out. I'd never seen her this dressed up before.

Her hair looked shiny and sleek. She was in a low-cut blouse with her breasts spilling out and a pair of tight jeans that made her butt look scrumptious.

I'd never seen her in makeup before either, but tonight she had pink lipstick on and her eyes looked darker and brighter at the same time.

A surge of jealousy ran through me.

I wanted to command her to stay here, with me, so I could look at her a little longer. So I could admire her.

But Nina barely even smiled at me and then tucked some loose strands behind her ear. "I'm going out. Not sure when I'll be back, but I have a key."

She didn't wait for a response but just walked past me. It was like I was dumbstruck and kept standing there. I watched as she went to the door, stepped out, and didn't even turn to give me another glance. She was gone, and I had nothing to do but wait for her to come back.

Maybe I shouldn't have waited for her to return. I had no reason to do that. No responsibility and no right. But I couldn't sleep until I knew she was back in the house. I couldn't get the image out of my head—of the way she looked at me, like she was bored and annoyed. That bright pink lipstick which made her lips look even more delicious than before.

I had this desperation to find out where she'd gone. Who she was with. Was any other guy touching her?

I turned the TV on. I drank a little. I paced around the living room and kept checking the clock on the wall.

What the fuck was happening to me?

Was I her dad? Her boyfriend? Her husband? Her keeper?

I was none of those things.

It was close to one in the morning and I thought I was on the brink of madness when I heard the key rattle in the front door.

I stood in the middle of the living room, nearly holding my breath, my hands clenched into fists on my sides.

I could hear her heels in the hallway, slowly approaching the living room door now. She was going to walk past but stopped when she saw the light, then me just standing there.

It must have been a bizarre scene to come home to but I didn't care what she thought of me right now.

"Where were you?" I growled.

Her brows crossed in confusion at first. "Excuse me?"

"You heard what I said. I asked you where you were."

I took a step in her direction and Nina straightened her back, holding her head up higher so she could look me in the eyes.

"I went out with my friends and my brother. Anyway, why do I need to tell you where I was?"

She was challenging me with her eyes. I'd walked up close to her, breathing down harshly on her face now. I wanted to taste her again, feel the creaminess of her lipstick on my mouth, feel the softness of her nipples between my fingers. I could feel my cock throbbing in my pants.

"It's fuckin' late," I growled and slowly, she nodded.

"So?"

Exactly. So what?

I had no answer to that. She was totally right. She wasn't even on working hours. James was asleep. I was at home. Technically, in these hours, she could do whatever she wanted.

I gritted my jaw, slowly nodded my head, and then stepped back. I needed to put some distance between us. "Nothing. Go ahead. Go to your room if you want to. I have nothing more to say to you."

Despite the fiery look in her eyes, Nina seemed to gulp. I saw that hazy gaze, like she was trying to decide what she would do next. Then she licked her lips and took in a deep breath. "Goodnight, Eric," she said and then turned away from me.

I shut the living room door behind her because I needed to fuckin' breathe. I could have driven my fist through the wall but I held myself back. What was she doing to me? Who had I become?

Why did I obsess about her whereabouts all evening?

She was nothing more than my babysitter. My employee.

I poured myself another drink and washed it down my

throat in a desperate attempt to feel anything other than what I was feeling right now. I just needed to think clearly. I needed to get Nina out of my head.

Another shot of whiskey went down my throat and my need for her seemed to intensify. Drinking definitely wasn't working, but I had nothing else to do.

I was fuckin' losing my mind over this girl.

## 25

# NINA

*I*'d invited Karen to join us at the nightclub. Gareth suggested this place and Corey had texted to say he'd be there too. This was my second time going out with Gareth, and this time I didn't even ask Eric before leaving the house. I just walked out and left a note for him to find in the kitchen.

I was one of the first to arrive at the club so I hung about outside, waiting for someone to show up and checked my phone every two minutes. I was nervous because I hadn't actually been in a nightclub many times before. This was going to be my second time and I wasn't sure if I'd like it.

But that wasn't the only reason my nerves were frayed. Eric had a big part to play in it too.

I was never going to forget the way he looked at me the other night when he asked me where I'd been. How stony and dark his face had turned when he glared at me, expecting answers. I'd stood up to him, instead of melting to a puddle at my feet. It was one of the hardest things I'd ever done because all I really wanted to do was fall into him and beg him to spend the night with me.

I was here now, standing outside a club and waiting for somebody to show up and rescue me, but I still couldn't get Eric out of my mind. Was he jealous? Was he trying to be my boss and set some ground rules? What did he want from me?

Did he *want* me?

I had so many questions and no answers.

I could have burst into tears right there and then, but I felt a tap on my shoulder at that moment. I whipped around to see Karen standing there, beaming from ear to ear.

"I don't freakin' believe this!" she exclaimed and drew me into a tight hug. "Nina Jones at the door of a club. With makeup on!"

She was smiling and seemed to not have picked up on my mood yet. I wanted to tell her what was going on. I *needed* to tell her what was going on with Eric. I needed to get it out of my system. But before I could say anything, I saw Gareth approaching us. He had two other guys with him. Like he promised, this was not a date.

"Hey, you," he said and hugged me before I could stop him, but I sank into him, a little relieved to feel his arms around me. It was a friendly and warm hug. Karen was close to giggles beside us.

"These are my pals, Jordan and Mark. Guys, this is Nina, Corey's sister."

"I'm Karen, her best friend."

The introductions were complete and it seemed like everyone was going to get along with everyone. I looked around for my brother, but I couldn't see him anywhere yet.

Gareth led us into the club and soon enough, the music was too loud in my ear and the lights were strobing and bright and dull all at the same time. It was an assault on my senses, and for a few moments, I felt like I couldn't hear or feel anything.

The only thing I was starkly conscious of was Gareth's hand firmly resting on my waist. When I looked up at him, he was smiling.

"How are you doing?" He leaned in to shout in my ear over all the noise of the club. How was I supposed to tell him the truth?

"I'm good. I'm great," I lied. I looked for Karen. She was sandwiched between Gareth's two friends and it seemed like they were flirting with each other. If I knew anything about Karen, by the end of the night, those two guys were going to be fighting each other for her attention.

I looked back at Gareth.

"Don't worry about them, would you like a drink?"

I nodded like my life depended on it. Gareth went away and suddenly I felt all alone in this crowd of people who were dancing and pulsating to the rhythm of the club. The floor was shaking. The air was suffocating in here. I wanted to cry out for Karen, but she was lost in her world, already gyrating with those two guys.

Gareth returned just in time, right when I thought I would explode into smithereens.

"You okay? You look a little worked up," he asked me.

"I...I don't come to these places too often."

"I can tell. We can go somewhere else if you're not comfortable."

"No, this is great. I need this," I said and tipped the glass of alcohol over my mouth. I'd poured most of it down my throat in a hurry and the liquid burned. I didn't even know what I was drinking.

"Whoa! Slow down there. The night's just starting," Gareth said and I wiped my mouth with the back of my hand.

"Yeah, but I want to party," I said.

I felt like a wave was crashing into me. I needed to get out of this skin. I needed to do something different tonight. Be someone else.

The person I truly was would never get Eric. He didn't want *me*. So I didn't want to be me either.

I grabbed Gareth's hand and even though he looked shocked, I started dragging him in the direction of where the pulsating dancing was going on. I'd never done this, but then again, I'd never felt like this before either.

Gareth pulled me into his arms and I fell on his chest. Our faces were close to each other's and we started moving together, matching the rhythm and beat of the shrill electronic music.

"Wow. You're something else," he said, grinning at me while

we swayed. I stared up at his face and I didn't know what else to do. What to say. All I could think about was Eric, Eric, and Eric. Why could nobody else make me feel the way he did? What was I going to do with the rest of my life?

So I said nothing to Gareth. Tonight, all I could do was dance.

## 26

## ERIC

*T*he next morning, I checked in on James before leaving the house to go to the gym. It was past eight already and Sarah was seeing herself into the house. I knew her routine; she'd clean around the house first, waiting for Nina to wake up James...then she'd help with the breakfast.

Sarah and I exchanged our good mornings and then I left the house, not sure of when Nina had returned to the house the previous night. She'd gone out late at night on two consecutive nights. Even though it wasn't my place to dictate where she could and couldn't go and at what time, I still couldn't help but be curious about it.

Who was I kidding?

She was a twenty-one-year-old college student. Of course she was going to party. What else did I expect?

I made sure to run harder this morning, to pump more, and sweat more. So that by the time I hit the showers, I could feel every muscle aching in my body. My hands shook slightly as I scrubbed my skin. It was only ten in the morning and I was already tired.

This was what I needed. I *needed* to feel tired so I wouldn't obsess over Nina so much. I planned on spending the rest of the day working on Miles's proposal. I had a lot of research to conduct.

When I returned to the house, I wasn't expecting James or Nina to be there. Usually, they left by now on their way to James's kindergarten. But when I walked into the kitchen, I saw my son sitting at the breakfast table in his pajamas with a big bowl of scrambled eggs in front of him.

Sarah was trying to get him to eat his eggs and James was in a particularly bad mood.

He seemed to brighten up a little when he saw me, though.

"Hey, buddy, what are you doing here?" I asked, pulling him into my arms when he jumped toward me.

"We don't know where Nina is. Daddy, has she gone away?" James asked. I was confused by this.

"What do you mean? Isn't she in her room? Didn't she come to get you?"

I glanced at Sarah, who shook her head glumly.

"She forgot about me, Daddy, and she's not answering the door," James said and he sounded genuinely sad. I felt anger sweep through me again. Her going out at night gave me a bad feeling.

I put James down and left him in the kitchen to walk over to

Nina's room. I knocked on it repeatedly. There was no answer. I didn't think she was in there. And now I was starting to worry.

Where did she go last night? I found her note sometime after she'd already left. Was she safe? Should I get in touch with Miles? Or was she just staying over with somebody and I was overreacting. Was she at some guy's place?

I was just about to turn the knob on her door when it opened.

Nina was on the other side, her makeup smudged all over her face, her hair disheveled madly. She was still in going-out clothes, so it seemed like she hadn't changed. Had she just crashed into bed?

She was blinking blindly now, barely even looking at me as she stood there in her tight black skirt that had ridden all the way up her legs.

"What time is it?" she asked hoarsely.

"Ten thirty."

"Shit!" she exclaimed and rushed back into the room. The door was left open but I didn't follow her inside. Of course I was going to give her privacy.

"Is James up? Shit. He's going to be late for kindergarten!"

I stood at the door with my hands in my pockets, watching her as she tried to hurriedly brush her hair in front of the mirror.

"Yes, he's up and yes, he's going to be late."

"Oh, God, I'm so sorry. I must have missed the alarms. I slept right through them."

She was now scrubbing her face like she was trying to take off her makeup, but it wasn't working.

I said nothing to her. I didn't know what to say.

I was disappointed, angry, and jealous. I had no handle on my own emotions.

"I'm sorry...Eric. I don't know what to do here. I can't take James to his playschool looking like this." She whipped around to me and I glared at her. Her shoulders heaved and her nostrils were flared. She looked desperate and a part of me was glad. I was glad she was having a rough morning even though she might have had a good night.

"I'll take him."

"Thank you." She was waiting to hear that.

"Take the morning off and gather yourself," I said.

She approached the door again, nodding quietly. "I'm really sorry, Eric. I shouldn't have put you or James in this situation."

I looked her up and down. A part of me was trying to figure out if she'd been with someone else last night. The jealous part of me. The one I was ashamed of and hoped Nina would never have to see.

"Once you've freshened up and taken some rest, we need to talk," I told her. Nina looked away from me, hanging her head low now as we stood there in front of each other.

Before she could say anything, I turned from her and walked away.

James and Sarah were both waiting in the kitchen.

"Nina is fine. She's just feeling a little unwell so she's going to rest, okay, bud? I'll take you to playschool instead," I told him. James seemed pleased with that suggestion but worried about Nina at the same time.

I would feel like shit if I had to break his heart over her.

I dropped James off at the kindergarten, got a coffee, and returned to the house at eleven-thirty. Sarah had left by now and the house was quiet. Nina still seemed to be either asleep or resting. The one thing I was sure of was that she was hungover.

I'd told her we needed to talk, but the truth was that I didn't really know what I wanted to speak to her about.

I sat down at the kitchen table with my laptop to research the things I was going to, and fifteen minutes later, I heard her footsteps approaching.

She'd showered and changed into fresh clothes. All her smudged makeup had come off and her hair was damp and clean. She walked past me to pour herself some coffee. I continued to stare at the screen, trying to ignore her for as long as I could. Finally, she cleared her throat to draw my attention.

"I'm so sorry about this morning."

"James was late was for school, but they took him in," I replied.

I watched her sipping her coffee and tried to gather my thoughts. I knew I had to say something. "I'm not going to ask you where you were last night because it's none of my business," I began.

Nina put down her mug and stared at me with her green eyes widened. "But what happened this morning is not acceptable."

She nodded. "I know that. I feel horrible about it."

"I don't need you to feel horrible. I just want you to understand why my son can't be exposed to this kind of behavior."

She stood listening to me in silence. Her face looked pale and she appeared to be sad.

"James is five years old. He is at his most impressionable age, and he adores you. He looks up to you. I want him to be around people who will set the right example."

Nina's nostrils flared. I could see I'd touched a nerve. "I have been nothing but consistent and supportive toward him," she spoke up.

"And yet the last few nights, you've been going out and returning late. This morning, you didn't even answer the door when James knocked on it to wake you up. It was probably for the best because it wouldn't have helped him to see you in that state."

I could see Nina blushing. She looked away from me and gulped. "I told you it's never going to happen again."

"I should have known better than to hire a twenty-one-year-old college student for the job," I continued. I was fueled by my jealousy and I wanted her to think that I didn't give a shit what she did outside this house, but I did.

"Are you saying I'm fired?"

"That is not what I'm saying," I replied and she approached me.

"Then why are you standing here lecturing me?" There was fire in her eyes. Nina was challenging me again, like she had that night I asked her where she'd been.

"I'm warning you. Not lecturing you. Have you forgotten I'm your boss? I hand you a paycheck at the end of every week."

Nina stood close to me. I was sitting back in my chair, looking at her intently. I got a whiff of the scent of her shampoo. Her hair was still damp and had left little wet patches on the shoulders of her gray shirt. I wanted to feel the squeaky cleanness of her pale skin. I wanted to taste the minty freshness of her mouth.

Did she know how much I wanted her? Was she playing a game with me?

"No, I haven't forgotten, Eric. I remember exactly who you are. You're my boss and you're telling me that I've been a bad girl."

Her voice was low and hoarse, but there was no mistaking the seduction. Her eyelids were heavy and the tops of her cheeks were red. I could feel my cock throbbing in my pants.

I couldn't help it, my eyes washed over her body. Her breasts, her small waist, her curves and hips. There were so many things I wanted to do to her right now. None of them were right.

"What are you doing, Nina?" I growled.

I needed her to stop before things got out of hand.

*Focus!*

"I'm just saying what is on your mind. You want to discipline me, don't you? You want me to face the consequences of my actions?"

She approached the kitchen table and stood at the edge, biting down on her lip. My cock was hard. My fists were clenched. I wanted her to just disappear so I could stop feeling like this.

"We need to fuckin' stop this," I said, slowly standing up. But we both knew I didn't mean it.

"Now is your chance, Mr. Hall. Show me what you really think of me," she continued, and slowly pulling her gaze away from me, she turned and bent over the edge of the table.

I hadn't noticed the skirt she was wearing, but now I did. It was short and lacey, but now it had ridden right up her butt so I could see the pink panties she had underneath.

She stretched herself so her arms were on either side of her, up the table. Her cheek was pressed down on it and her delicious naughty ass was up in the air.

I stood behind her. I knew exactly what needed to be done.

So I grabbed her butt with both hands at first, feeling their perfect roundness in my palms. Nina didn't look at me, but I could hear her breathing heavily, almost panting.

"I'm sorry I've been bad. I promise I won't do it again," she said in a small voice.

"Are you sure about that?" I asked in a deep, wild, animal-istic growl before I slapped my hand hard against her butt. It made her jump but then she moaned with delight and I knew I wasn't going to last long against her.

## 27

# NINA

*H*is hand clapped down on my butt and I felt the pinch of the slap on my skin. I bit down on my lip, pressing my face down hard on the table. It gave me intense pleasure. Nothing like anything I'd experienced before. I didn't even know I wanted it like this until it just happened.

"I promise not to be a bad girl again, Mr. Hall," I said in a low voice. I wasn't sure if he'd even heard me. I could feel him moving behind me and I dared not look at him. His hand came down on my butt again.

"Your promises mean nothing to me."

This time, he'd spanked me harder. It was a delicious feeling, knowing he had complete control over me. I wanted to surrender to him, to push out any other thoughts from my head.

I moaned and purred, and then felt his fingers snapping my panties away. He pushed my skirt further up and my panties were down at my ankles so that now I was completely exposed. Bent over his kitchen table, breathless and hungry for more.

I'd never imagined myself in a situation like this before but I wasn't ashamed. I was finally claiming what I always wanted.

Eric got down on his knees behind me and his hands were on my thighs, holding me in place. I tensed up in anticipation, but only for a moment.

"Eric..." I moaned his name softly and then I felt his tongue on me. He was tasting me, tasting my pussy with his mouth. I thought I would be nervous and self-conscious about this, but I loved it. Maybe it was because he knew exactly what to do, how to touch me like that.

His tongue stroked my wet pussy folds at first. Repeatedly, softly. I shuddered while he did that. I could feel these waves of pleasure taking over my body, like I was ready to crash. Then I heard him groan with approval, like he loved how I tasted. I couldn't contain it...I knew I would come any moment now.

Then his tongue found my swollen, sensitive clit and he started sucking on it, teasing it with the tip of his tongue. His forefinger entered me at the same time and I knew I would explode.

"Oh, my God!" I cried out with pleasure and surprise. I tried to hold on to something on the table for support, but I could feel my body sliding. Eric's thick finger thrust in and out of me while he continued to stroke and suck my clit with his mouth. All I could do was cry out repeatedly. I didn't want him to stop, but I wanted to freeze this moment in time.

I wanted to be able to feel this forever.

"Please..." I cried. I didn't know what to say. He groaned again like he was giving me his approval. When his fingers tightened on my thigh and he banged my pussy even harder, I couldn't hold it back any longer.

I came hard. I cried out and my body shook while he drilled his finger into me and sucked my clit. My legs were parted wide and my torso was stretched out over the kitchen table. I literally had no control over myself, but I didn't care. All I cared about was feeling the power of my orgasm.

No other guy had ever made me feel this way. None of them were men like Eric. I moaned and cried while he took over my body, and it felt like hours after which I finally started to descend from the orgasm.

He could feel it too and slowly, he slid his finger out of me. He straightened up behind me. It was over.

But I wasn't going to let him end it like this. Not this time. I wanted more and I was determined to get it.

Eric had stood up by now, and I turned to face him. I was breathing hard, I was naked from my waist down, and I looked up at him with obvious desire in my eyes.

His blue eyes were dark with desire too. It was his turn, but it seemed like he didn't know what I wanted. Did he really think I was that selfish? That I wasn't prepared to give him what he wanted after how he'd just made me feel?

"Sit down, Eric," I said in a low, seductive voice. He stared at me for a moment before he did what I wanted him to do.

He sat back down on the chair, facing me sideways. He

studied me, looking at my body. I just had to take a few steps and I was in front of him now.

Without a word, I weaved my fingers through his thick blond hair, pulling his head backward. He let me do it, like he was a puppet in my hands. I felt powerful, like it was me with the control now.

I looked into his eyes, and my stomach seemed to somersault with more desire. His handsome face was sharp and chiseled, and I knew I would never be able to forget him. Or the way he was looking at me now.

Was there anything in this world I wanted more than to wake up every morning to this face beside me?

I lowered myself slowly, with my legs parted wide. I lowered myself right on to his lap. My pussy rubbed against the fabric of his pants and I rolled my hips so I could give him a preview of what it would be like once I was riding him.

I wrapped my arms around his neck, and now our faces were aligned.

"It's not over yet, Eric. I want more," I whispered. He reached up and grabbed the back of my head, bunching a fistful of my hair in his hand.

"No, it's not," he growled and then leaned forward so that our mouths met. His tongue slid straight into my mouth and my body sizzled. This kiss was strong. With just a kiss, he was taking over my body and I was ready to give it up to him.

With one hand in my hair and the other on my waist, he held me in place while he kissed me. While his tongue explored my mouth, I moved, rubbing myself on his leg and rolling my hips. The kiss was beautiful and sexy at the same time and I wished I could tell him just how unique this was. How I'd never experienced something like this before. I wanted to keep kissing him forever.

And I let him decide when he thought the kiss was over. Slowly, when he started to pull away from me, I leaned back to look at his handsome face again. He was watching me too, like he was trying to learn my face.

With his eyes still on me, he started to unzip his pants. I had to move just a little bit to give him the wiggle room he needed to pull down his pants and his underwear.

Now he was sitting on the chair with his big throbbing cock in his hand. I lowered myself down on his thigh again, keeping a steady watch on his face. Little shocks of electricity were running through my body already in anticipation of what was about to come.

"Are you ready for this, Nina?" he asked in a low, hoarse voice. All I could do was nod.

From the pocket of his pants, he pulled out a condom which he ripped open. I sat holding my breath, watching him closely as he unrolled the condom over his big cock. It was alive and erect, and it looked rock-hard and ready. My pussy throbbed for it too.

Then he pulled me toward him, angling me by my waist. I moved toward his cock, holding his gaze until I adjusted myself just over it. We were staring into each other's eyes when my pussy met his cock. I was wet, warm, and pulsating with my need for him.

Slowly, I guided him in and sat on his legs so that his cock was deep inside me. He held on to my waist tightly and I wrapped myself around his neck. I saw the exact moment when his cock reached me there, deep down where I wanted him to be.

"You are so fuckin' beautiful, Nina," he said in a low grunt. I started moving while he sat there, grunting. I wanted to feel every inch of him and his cock. It reached deep inside me and I moved, so he moved too.

It was so hard, so big, and it took some time before I could start to feel the absolute pleasure I was supposed to feel. I felt beautiful and desired...I couldn't believe a man like Eric would want this with me. But it seemed like he did because he was groaning with pleasure too, just like I was.

In and out, his cock filled me up and then slid out of me. I moved and rolled my hips, biting down on my lip as I watched his handsome face. I believed him when he told me I was beautiful. I wouldn't have believed anyone else, but him, I trusted.

We both groaned from time to time as we moved together. I was taking it slow this time. There was no rush, there was no animalistic need to possess. I just wanted to enjoy it, and it seemed like he wanted the same.

When the pressure started to build up in me, Eric leaned in and started moving, bouncing me up and down his legs. We'd been entwined like this for probably fifteen minutes, maybe more, just slowly moving together like waves on an ocean.

And now it was time to crash.

My bouncing got faster and I could feel those knots in my belly beginning to tighten up. He was going to loosen them. He held me close to him now. My breasts pressed against his chest while we moved and I bounced and his cock filled me up...and finally, I was coming again.

This time Eric was too.

We held each other like there was nobody else in the world to hold. I couldn't help it, I was smiling as I came because nothing could ever feel this way again. I didn't want to stop coming for him, *with* him.

I could feel him shooting into the condom, filling it up inside me. He grunted and roared as he came and then it was over.

We were both panting, exhausted and out of breath. Eric glared at me with his mouth open and that soft look of surrender had left his eyes. It was replaced with the stoniness I saw in those eyes so often.

I knew it was over now. That was it.

I slowly stood up, moving away from him. He remained sitting on the chair, watching me.

I was in a hurry to dress up because I was afraid of another rejection, but he just sat there, staring at me with his pants still down.

I pulled up my panties, pulled up my skirt, and ran a hand through my hair until I was ready to walk out of the room if needed.

"Will you slow down there for a minute, Nina?" he said, startling me.

I looked up at him, waiting for him to say something more but he just stared at me, so I stared back.

"Okay," I murmured.

"Sit down, finish your coffee, eat something if you're hungry. We still haven't talked," he said and never before in my life had I felt this confused.

It seemed like he had something important to tell me. Earlier, when he said we needed to talk, I assumed he was talking about the conversation we had already. I was still embarrassed by it. He'd called me out on my blossoming nightlife and of course, I wasn't proud of what happened this morning.

I grabbed the mug of coffee from the counter again. It was barely warm anymore but I still sipped it. Eric sat at the table. He'd pulled his pants up now and his hands were on his knees. He looked at me like I was still undressed.

"What did you want to say to me?" I asked. I tried not to be meek, but I couldn't help but be intimidated when he looked at me that way.

"Firstly, I want you to know that despite everything that happened today, you are very good at your job. James is lucky and happy to have someone like you to look after him."

Even though this was a compliment, I couldn't help but wonder what else was on the way. It didn't sound like it was going to be positive, whatever he had to say.

"Thank you, and I am truly sorry about today. I'm going to make sure he never has to think I'm missing again," I replied, to which Eric cleared his throat forcibly.

"And about this thing between us..." he began to say but I interrupted him.

"You don't have to talk about that, it's forgotten already—"

"Maybe we *should* discuss it."

"Why?"

A flicker of hope cropped up in me. What did he want to discuss?

"Because your brother-in-law is my friend and someone I'm in business with," he replied firmly.

So all this was about his work. He didn't want this thing between us interfering with his business. I had a lump in my throat which I tried to push down.

"You don't have to worry about Miles. I'm not going to tell him. He's not going to find out."

"Maybe we should tell him. Maybe I should," he said and I stared at him in surprise.

"Excuse me?"

"The last thing I want in my business relationships is dishonesty. So maybe I should tell him what's been happening between us."

My heart was thudding against my chest. At first, I panicked. What did it mean? Then I was hopeful again—maybe he wanted to come clean with Miles because he saw us as more than just a casual fling. Maybe he wanted to do things properly with me. Was he going to ask me out?

I licked my lips nervously. "If you think it would be a good idea, then maybe yes, you should speak to him. Not that Miles should care what's going on in either of our personal lives."

Eric took in a deep breath. "No, he shouldn't, but if I was in his place I would have wanted to know. He is the one who set you up for this job after all."

I nodded.

*This* was the brave thing to do. Eric was a brave man.

I clutched the coffee cup tightly and took a sip. It was cold but I didn't care. I just wanted to hide my flushed cheeks from him so he wouldn't see how excited I was by all this.

"And now that our circumstances are changing, even if Miles is upset by all this, it wouldn't matter anymore," Eric continued.

I brought the mug down, my brow furrowed.

"Circumstances are changing?" My heart was in my hand because I was so sure he was going to officially ask me out. That he was going to tell me he wanted more from me than just casual sex.

"I've accepted Miles's suggestion to move to Washington," Eric replied.

My grip on the mug loosened and it slipped out of my hand, but I intercepted it before it hit the floor. The cooled-down coffee was everywhere and before I knew it, I was on my hands and knees on the floor.

Eric stood up and rushed toward me.

"It's okay, I can manage," I said, fumbling a little. I reached for the bottom drawer at the counter and pulled out a tea towel to mop the coffee.

"Nina...I'm sorry if this is coming as a shock to you." Eric stood over me and was still talking. I didn't want to look up at him, I couldn't bear to do it.

"It's fine, it's your life. I'm sure you'll do what is best for James."

"Yes, I'm trying to. I want to set the right example for him. I want to make this company a success and DC is where I'll be of most use to Miles and the rest of the business."

I mopped the floor until the towel was drenched and soggy. Then I had no choice but to stand up and wring it out in the sink. I still refused to look at Eric even though he was standing directly behind me.

"I'm sure you'll find another job easily. I'll give you all the good references you need," he continued.

I nodded, washing the towel out under the faucet.

"And Miles, I guess he should know, and once James and I leave, it won't matter because we won't be seeing each other." Eric's voice was strong and firm. How could he be this cold-hearted? This aloof?

"No. I don't want him to know. I don't want anyone to know," I snapped. The last thing I wanted right now was my family finding out how badly I'd fucked up. If he was going to leave, I would have to move on and I preferred to do it alone.

Before he could say anything more, I walked away, leaving

the towel on the draining board. I didn't want him to look at me.

## 28

# ERIC

*I* had to take up Miles's offer of moving to DC because if I didn't—this thing with Nina would spiral out of control. I could feel it happening already. It was like she was taking over my life and I had no way of stopping it.

Every time we were alone, every time I looked at her—the only thing I could think about was being inside her. At night, I had restless fantasies of having her in my bed, waking up to see her face, burying my face in her breasts.

For the sake of my son and my own sanity, I needed to put some distance between us.

She walked out of the kitchen when I told her what was going to happen. Was she mad at me? But fuck that. I needed to take back control.

I texted Miles and told him I wanted to meet him today. He agreed and I left the house in a hurry to go to the coffee shop. I didn't see Nina again. She'd clearly locked herself in her room and that was okay.

Miles was late again and I had to wait for close to an hour before he finally showed up.

"Hey, sorry, man. Had a meeting."

"Yeah, fine, no problem. Just sit down."

Maybe he could see the anxiety on my face because he sat down with his brows crossed, leaning toward me over the table.

"What is up with you, man?" he asked and I glared at him angrily. I wanted to tell him about Nina. It was the right thing to do. We'd been friends for years and we trusted each other. We were brothers in arms. We were now in business together and this was one of my father's top rules— complete honesty in a partnership.

But Nina told me she didn't want Miles to know. I didn't know why, but I guessed it was because she wanted to keep her personal life personal. And maybe that was fair. I was going to leave, and I wouldn't have to face Miles on a daily basis. Maybe Nina didn't want to have to deal with that and it was my duty to respect that. As shitty as it made me feel to keep a secret like that from a man I considered to be as good as a brother.

"Is there something you want to tell me?" Miles asked and I drank my coffee.

"Yeah, well, I've looked into it and decided I'm willing to make the move to Washington."

At first, it looked like he didn't believe what he was hearing but then he jerked up off his chair and lunged at me. He slapped my back and shook my hand.

"That is great news, man. Absolutely great! I'm glad you made that decision. I'm sure it wasn't easy."

"It was easy enough. It makes sense."

"No, I mean with James and just hiring Nina and you said they're doing so well together."

"He'll just have to get over it," I replied and Miles looked at me closely.

"There's no rush. If you think your kid needs some time, take a few months to make the move, if you have to. It's not like we have anything set up there."

"I think the best thing to do would be to rip it off like a Band-Aid. James will learn."

"The hard way, you mean?"

"He'll learn," I insisted and looked around the coffee shop to distract myself. I heard Miles sigh.

"Is there something going on with you, man?"

"What are you talking about?"

"You seem different."

"Today?"

"These days," Miles replied.

I shrugged, trying to quickly come up with a believable response.

"Cynthia found us here in Chicago. She tried to take James with her to New York without telling me."

"Shit."

"Yeah."

"Fuck. Why didn't you tell me? Why didn't you call? I could have tried to help."

"How? Things with her have been fucked-up for a while."

Miles sat back. I knew I'd diverted his attention. He ran a hand through his hair. "I'm sorry you had to deal with this shit, man. Are you sure you don't need our help with anything? With James?"

"Nina has been able to keep him calm. She's been a big help. I'll be disappointed to let her go."

"Have you told her about your plans yet?"

"This morning. I haven't given her a date because I don't know it yet, but I guess she's expecting it to be soon. I told her I'll give any reference she wants."

Miles nodded and shrugged. "Well, man, you gotta do what you gotta do. Maybe Cynthia coming here has ruined Chicago for you a little too, eh?"

"Yeah, maybe it has."

"Don't worry about it. Take as much time as you need with this thing, but moving to Washington is probably the best decision at the moment. You're going to do great," Miles said.

We spoke a little longer about the work that needed to be done in DC, then Miles had to leave for another meeting.

I sat at the table, drinking my coffee for a little longer. I couldn't wait to dive into work, to keep busy the way Miles did. DC was going to give me all that. A renewed sense of purpose, a new life for James, some distance from Nina. It was the whole package.

I tried not to think about it, but the truth was that I would miss her. I'd miss seeing her in the kitchen in the mornings, or watch her playing with my son. I'd miss hearing her singing with James while she gave him a bath. And more than anything, I'd crave for our stolen moments together.

The sex was good. It was great. She was beautiful—but there was more to it than that. I was dangerously close to developing feelings for this girl and no way was I going to let myself do that.

Once in a lifetime; having my heart trampled the way Cynthia did was enough. I'd be a fool to let it happen to me twice.

## 29

## NINA

To say I was shattered would have been an understatement. I didn't know what I was going to do once Eric left, once he took James away from me. Yes, that was how it felt to me, like he was snatching this kid away. This kid I had formed a special bond with.

It wasn't just Eric I was developing feelings for, it was like I was falling in love with them both at the same time. And now it was all over.

I had driven them away.

It had to be me, right?

Why else would Eric decide to leave Chicago and move to a completely different part of the country?

I couldn't leave my room all morning. I just stayed in bed, still recovering from the hangover that felt devastating, and also this physical pain I was experiencing from the news Eric had given me.

I knew he'd left the house, so I was aware that at some point

I would have to get out and go pick up James from his playschool. But as simple a task as that felt like a huge burden.

I didn't know how to face him with a straight face. How to not break into tears the moment I saw him. I knew he trusted me and relied on me. He considered me his best friend and now we were going to part ways forever.

Eventually, I had no choice but to go meet him at his playschool.

I was forlorn and the moment James saw me at his playschool gate, it was like he knew instantly that something was wrong.

He came rushing to me and I took him into my arms.

"Where have you been, Nina? Daddy said you were sickly."

I ruffled his hair and looked at him carefully, like I was trying to memorize his face. "Yes, kid, I'm sorry about this morning. I wasn't feeling too well so I couldn't take you to kindergarten."

"That's okay, Nina. Daddy brought me. We played a game on the way." James was back to being happy and cheerful. He clung on to my hand as we walked to the bus stop and I could feel that lump in my throat.

How long would we prolong this? When was Eric going to tell him? I knew James wasn't going to take the news well and it was all my fault.

We took the bus back to the house and he sat close to me. We sang a few songs on the way to keep him distracted, and then he told me all about playschool. From what I could tell, whatever problems he had with bullying and not being able to make friends things had improved. Maybe Eric had spoken to his teachers and they'd looked into the matter.

Either way, James was a much happier kid after kindergarten these days and I was relieved to see that.

Although now that they were moving again, who knew what kind of new problems would crop up for him in the new playschool. Who would look out for him there? Why was I so worried?

James was carefree and he couldn't sense how worried I was. We walked hand-in-hand back to the house from the bus stop. Eric's car was in the driveway, so he had to be back from wherever he'd disappeared to in the morning.

"Daddy!" James exclaimed when he rushed into the house to find Eric in the living room.

"Hey, bud, how was playschool?" Eric took his son into his arms. It literally hurt me to even look at them together because I knew how short-lived this whole thing was.

Father and son were exchanging notes on the day, and then finally Eric was able to convince James to go to his room and that I'd go and find him there in a bit.

Clearly, he had something he wanted to tell me in private.

I wasn't looking forward to hearing it. It seemed like the only thing Eric had to tell me could be bad news.

When James finally left, Eric turned to me quickly—almost like he was worried I would try to leave the room too.

"I met up with Miles this morning. I didn't tell him about us so you don't have anything to worry about."

He held my gaze and I kept my chin up.

"Did you tell him you're going to DC?" I asked.

"Yeah, I did. It was on the table already. Miles knew I was thinking about it."

I gulped but hoped he wouldn't notice how pale my face had gotten. "Okay, then I want to hand in my notice."

"That is not necessary, Nina. I don't know when we're leaving. Nothing is planned yet."

"I don't care. I want to leave. Ten days. That is how long I can keep working here. At some point, James has to find out and it should be sooner rather than later."

I glared at him defiantly and knew Eric could see the fury in my eyes.

Who did he think he was? Was he really going to make a huge life decision such as this and expect me to just hang about, waiting for him to leave?

"Okay," he replied, after a few moments of silence had passed between us.

"Okay. Ten days, and I'm gone," I said firmly and then I walked out of the room. James was waiting for me and I didn't want him to get lonely. Besides, there really was nothing to say between Eric and me. We'd said all that needed to be said. Decisions had been made. It was time for me to return to reality.

I had no idea how I got through the rest of the day. James

was full of energy and he wanted to be engaged in a lot of physical activity which involved running around the house and playing catch.

It was hard for me to keep up with him because I had so much on my mind, because it made me sad to see him this happy and satisfied. I felt physically sick and tired. Thankfully, Eric kept to himself and out of my way.

Once James had eaten, I helped him to sleep and then returned to my room for the night. It was obvious Eric was avoiding me because he was purposely keeping out of my way.

In my room, I lay flat on the bed, staring up at the ceiling and wishing I was somewhere else. Anywhere but here tonight. I felt alone and disappointed with myself.

He was an older man. A successful man with more romantic experience. Of course, he wanted to be with a woman who could give him what he needed. I couldn't. Like he said, I was nothing more than a twenty-something college student who didn't know what she was doing.

I reached for my phone and called Karen. I knew I needed to talk to her, just to ease my mind.

"Where are you? Aren't you meeting us at L'Orange tonight?" It sounded like Karen was out. I'd forgotten we'd made plans to meet up again tonight. The whole thing was a mistake. I was still ashamed of how drunk and hungover I was this morning. This nightlife scene wasn't for me, and Gareth was nice and handsome, but he wasn't for me.

I was mistaken to think I could use him to forget about Eric. If anything, spending time with another guy had driven me straight into Eric's arms because I had seen firsthand how much sexier he was than anyone else I could possibly meet.

"No, I can't come, I have to work," I replied to Karen.

"Right now?"

"No, but I need to keep myself together for the morning, which I won't be if I'm partying all night with you guys."

"Hmm…okay, if you say so, but you've been so fun these last few nights."

"Karen, I can't. Don't make me," I said.

She paused for a bit, but I knew she was trying to figure out what was happening.

"Are you okay, Nina?"

"I guess I am."

"You don't sound okay. You sound…I don't know…distracted or something. All good with work?"

I sighed aloud.

"So it *is* about work…"

"Yeah, kind of. I'm going to have to find new work," I admitted.

"Why? What happened with the family you're at?"

"They're moving to DC."

"The father?"

"Yeah, and the kid obviously."

"You sound really unhappy."

"I guess I am…"

She was silent again. I could almost hear the cogs in her brain moving as she tried to do the math.

"Okay, Nina, I'm going to ask you a serious question now and I want you to answer truthfully."

I knew what she was going to ask but I didn't want to have to answer it. But what choice did I have? I was the one who'd called her.

"Nina, are you sleeping with this man?"

I remained silent. I couldn't speak. I hadn't expected her to be this direct with me. Neither had I actually been honest about what was going on with Eric.

But my silence was all the answer that Karen needed.

"Oh, my God," she said in a low voice.

"It isn't what you think it is."

"How old is this guy?"

"He's in his thirties," I replied.

"Oh, my God!" she exclaimed louder this time, like she was midway between a shriek and a laugh.

"Keep your voice down, Karen. Who are you with?"

"You don't have to worry. I'm not going to tell."

"You really shouldn't, especially not Corey if you're out with them He's a family friend, you know, my brother-in-law's friend and business partner."

"And you're sleeping with him? What is the sex like? Tell me everything!" Karen was ready for gossip, but I just wasn't in the mood to talk about it.

Besides, how was I supposed to even begin to explain how Eric made me feel? Would Karen understand how transcendental the experience was?

"It doesn't matter, it's over, anyway."

"Wait a minute. Nina, are you sad about this? About him leaving?"

"It's just that I'll have to look for another job."

Karen saw right through that, of course.

"Why are you sad about this? What's going on? Is it more than sex? Do you have feelings for him or something?"

"I don't know," I replied.

I had my eyes pressed closed as I spoke to Karen. Even though I had her voice in my ear, I kept picturing Eric out there in the living room. What was he doing now? Pouring himself a shot of whiskey? What would happen if I walked over there and asked him to fuck me again? Would he refuse? Would he do the right thing and tell me to return to my room?

"It sounds an awful lot like you do have feelings for him, Nina," Karen continued.

"I don't know what I have. It's not like I actually know him either. Not like we've shown our souls to each other or anything."

Karen sighed. "It doesn't matter. When you like someone and you want something, it happens regardless of how much you know. That's what chemistry is all about."

It wasn't what I wanted to hear. I wished she told me I'd get over it in a few days. That I was just being foolish and child-ish. Instead, Karen was a romantic and sentimental.

"I don't think it's like that. I just like working here that's all," I said.

"Don't kid yourself, Nina. You need to come to terms with what you're feeling, as painful as it might be now."

"I've gotta go," I said.

"Nina! Come on. I'm trying to help."

"I need to make another call. Have a nice night out," I said hurriedly.

"Nina!" Karen was still scolding but I ended the call. I didn't want to hear anything else that she had to say because it was only making me sadder.

I needed to do something more drastic to get over this.

I called *him*.

I hadn't seen or heard from him in nearly a month, and I should have let it stay that way. Maybe he'd lost track of me, maybe he couldn't find me. Why hadn't he called me? He'd harassed me over the phone multiple times in the past. Had he finally given up? Was he going to let my family and me off the hook?

Whatever the circumstances with him were, I knew I was

making a mistake by calling him myself, with no provocation. In fact, I was the one provoking this time, but there was nothing else I wanted to do right now. I felt like I was on an unstoppable path to self-destruction, and it felt like the right direction to be on.

I was angry with myself for falling for a man like Eric. A part of me wanted to be punished. Another part of me wanted to do something rash, something high stakes—just to feel something.

He answered after the phone had been ringing for some time.

"Well, well, well," he said and his voice dragged on slowly. Just hearing him speak sent a shiver down my spine. Once again, I was reminded of the kind of risk I was taking by calling him. But now the deed was done.

"Look who's calling me. Do you have something for me, sweet bird?"

"No, I don't."

"Did you miss me, then? Is that what it is?" There was a laugh in his voice. He was thoroughly amused.

In reality, I didn't know why I was calling him. I was going to have to make it up along the way.

"I want to work for you, at the club, or wherever it is you wanted me to work."

I didn't think before I spoke. The words just tumbled out of me without restraint. What was I saying? It sounded ridiculous. Me? Working at a club? What kind of joint was it, anyway?

Again, he laughed. Then he stopped and breathed heavily into the phone.

"Sure, yeah. I can picture you in a short dress. You have those long legs of yours that could be great for this business."

"What business?" I snapped.

"Don't worry, bird, you're not going to do anything that'd be disrespectful to your daddy's memory. I wouldn't expect that of you," he said and again he laughed.

"I don't think so. Scratch that. I'm not doing it," I said hurriedly.

"Oh, no, did I scare you, sweetheart? There's nothing to be scared of. You just come over here, dolled up, and I'll put you to work. Don't worry. It's just a club. You don't have to do anything, just serve the drinks."

I listened to him quietly. I didn't know what to believe.

"Make sure you get a lot of tips because I'll be keeping all of it."

"I am not working for you for free. I need money. I need a new place to live."

"I'll pay you for the job. Don't worry, sweetheart. But I keep the tips. Do you remember what you owe me? Make enough tips working this job and it will all be forgotten. I won't bother you or your family again."

My heart was racing. This was the kind of world Raina worked so hard to take Corey and me out of. She'd given us an education, she made us see what a clean and good life could do for us...and now I was knowingly returning to the south side, to work at a sleazy cheap club.

"Agreed?" I heard him say.

I couldn't decide. My hand shook as I held on to the phone at my ear.

"Do you fuckin' agree?" he growled this time. It was a quick reminder of who he was. What he was capable of. I should have just hung up the phone right then. I should have told Eric what was going on...no, Corey. And Karen. Raina needed to know, maybe Miles could have helped. I should have told somebody.

Instead, I decided that I could handle it.

That it was my penance.

It was what I deserved for being an idiot. For thinking I could ever have something serious with Eric.

"Fine," I replied slowly.

He was laughing again. "Good. This Saturday night. Like I said, doll up for me, sweetheart. Show up at eight and I'll put you to work. It'll feel good to earn your own money through hard work and dedication." This was funny to him and he laughed again. He obviously didn't take any of it seriously. It was a joke.

I ended the call then because I just couldn't bear to hear him laughing anymore. It made my blood curdle and my stomach tighten with sickness. I threw my phone to the floor and just lay there in bed.

I felt self-destructive. That was the reason I'd called him. It was the reason why I decided I needed to work there. I wanted to feel something, even if it meant feeling sick and angry. I just wanted to find an outlet out of Eric's world, as far away from here as possible.

Very soon, James and Eric would be gone, and then what would I do? I needed to start now. I needed to find a way out, *now*.

I spent the rest of the night awake and fretting in bed.

I was nervous and excited about the new job. Maybe it was where I belonged, I told myself. Maybe I never should have left the south side. I didn't deserve to be here, in this house. I definitely didn't deserve to be in Eric's bed. I knew that now.

## 30

## ERIC

knew things had taken a bad turn when I saw Nina the next morning and she refused to even look at me.

I'd considered the possibility of her taking the news badly. I'd seen firsthand how close she and James had gotten in this short period. Did she think that I made the decision to leave because of *her*?

She *was* partly the reason for it.

In fact, she was one of the main reasons for it.

I didn't want to put myself in a position of weakness.

I was not in a position to date. I didn't want to be in a relationship. And I couldn't continue to have a casual sexual relationship with my son's babysitter. Especially not one who was also my friend's sister-in-law.

The only way to break this cycle was to move away.

It was the only way I could get her to stop working for me, because I wasn't going to fire her. Nina didn't deserve that.

Besides, I needed to move on from Chicago. Cynthia's presence here and the stunt she'd pulled—had spoiled it for me.

But now Nina told me she was only going to work for ten more days here before leaving. I needed to prepare James for it. I needed to find an alternative solution for James being looked after while I worked.

And even though I could have used Nina's insight because I respected her thoughts—she was refusing to talk to me.

I knew I had well and truly fucked it up this time.

When my mother called me in the morning, I was watching Nina getting James to eat his breakfast. I was in the hallway...spying on them because I didn't want to interrupt their smiles and giggles...and my phone buzzed.

I answered the call because I was relieved to be distracted. I could have stood there all day staring at that girl's body and made a fool of myself.

"Eric, my darling, how are you coping?"

I'd spoken to Mom briefly before, to tell her she was wrong about Cynthia.

"I'm fine, Mom. How are you?"

"Are you really fine? How is my grandson?"

"We are both doing good. It's forgotten, that thing with Cynthia," I said.

Mom sighed and I could picture her shaking her head now. "I'm so sorry you had to go through that, honey. I wish I could have helped you in some way, but you're all the way over there and I'm over here," she continued.

"It's fine, Mom, I don't need your help. We're managing just fine. We have a housekeeper and a babysitter, remember?" I tried to sound casual, so she wouldn't pick up on how I felt about the babysitter.

"Sure, honey, I'm glad you have help, but what about family? James needs family, the boy needs stability. He needs a father *and* a mother."

"Well, tough luck for him, but I am not exposing him to Cynthia again. His safety and his sanity are more important to me than some Hallmark-card family moment, which is all fake anyway."

"Ah, Eric! So cynical. Anyway, I didn't mean Cynthia. I'm talking about maybe finding somebody who can be a permanent part of the family. You know? Maybe it's time for that, son."

It took me a moment to respond because I couldn't believe she was bringing this up again.

"Are you seriously suggesting what I think you're suggesting, Mom?"

"Eric, son, you need to date."

I rubbed a hand over my face. "This isn't a good time."

"Are you hearing what I'm saying?"

"Yes, Mom, I heard you loud and clear, but I am not in a position to do that right now. I can't explain it to you."

"I don't need an explanation. You're not getting any younger and James is getting older. What he needs is a strong female presence in his life. Someone he can rely on for mothering. You need to find that woman."

I knocked my forehead against the wall in frustration, closing my eyes tightly because this wasn't the conversation I was hoping to have with my mother.

"Mom, things are on the move right now. Things are changing. The last thing I want to do right now is introduce another variable in James's life."

"What do you mean things are changing?"

"We're moving to Washington DC. Something's come up at work."

Mom gasped, rather dramatically, which made me roll my eyes.

"Not again, Eric. When will you stop putting that poor child through all this?"

"It is not a big deal. He'll get used to it soon. I need to get my work done and James is still discovering himself. It's not like he's overly attached to Chicago, anyway."

"That's it. I'm coming over," Mom said.

"That will not be necessary, Mom."

"I don't care what you think is necessary, son. You're clearly way in over your head. This is what your father would have wanted. He would have wanted me to step in and make sure you're doing it right."

"Mom!" I growled.

Nina and James shuffled past me in the hallway and I turned away from them.

"I don't need your help. I can handle this!" I hissed into the phone, just a few heartbeats away from cursing out loud.

Mom sighed. "Oh, honey, you don't even know that you do. I wish things didn't come to this, but I want what is best for my grandson and I think right now it would be best if I came over there and made sure he is doing okay."

"Mom. Do not come to Chicago," I growled. I didn't want her seeing Nina and me in close proximity. She'd see right through us in an instant. It was like she had X-Ray vision.

"We'll see," she replied and I already knew what I had to do.

James and I needed to get out of here as soon as possible. Before my mother arrived in Chicago unannounced.

## 31

# NINA

*I* went shopping for my job on Saturday. Not that I was excited about this new gig and neither did I want to impress. But what I did know I had to do, whether I liked it or not—was follow his instructions. He told me to wear a short dress, to 'doll up', and I knew him enough to know that I would have to do exactly that.

I was walking straight into his lair. I couldn't upset him or make him think he needed to discipline me in any way.

I'd never worked in a club before, I'd never waited tables... and now, as I stared at myself in the mirror; I knew I'd never looked like this either.

I maybe should have asked for Karen's help in getting ready for tonight, but I didn't want her asking questions which she would have if she saw me like this. I didn't know what I was doing. I didn't even know how to put on all this makeup I'd bought that afternoon while James was in playschool.

The only way I could help myself was by watching a dozen

tutorials online and hoping I didn't end up looking like a clown.

The dress I'd bought was a tight black thing that barely covered my butt. I'd considered wearing stockings underneath but decided against it. My heels were high too. Stilettos with pointy heels that I had to practice walking on.

I left my hair loose. I barely even combed through it because I liked the way it looked disheveled and unruly like this.

I used a shimmery copper eyeshadow and worked the rest of my makeup look around that. The end result was that my face looked glittery all over, including the lipstick I'd chosen. I knew it was too much, I'd gone all out—but this felt more like a costume than actual attire. I didn't care anymore if I was making a fool of myself. I just wanted to do something drastic.

I hadn't even told Eric I would be going out.

I knew he was in the house, even though we hadn't spoken to each other all day. He'd been avoiding me like the plague since I told him I would only work here for ten more days.

Now I found him sitting at his desk in the study. It was a large rarely used room, but it seemed like Eric had wound up there just to escape from me.

I knocked on the door and stood there until he looked up from his computer.

I saw the look of shock on his face immediately. He couldn't hide it.

"Oh..." he said, alarmed. Maybe this was the reaction I

*wanted* from him. I wanted him to feel like he had lost control of everything, just like I did.

"I'm going out," I said and he furrowed his brow. I was waiting for him to ask me where. Who with. Why was I dressed like that.

Eric stood up. His face had darkened. It looked like there was a storm brewing inside him. "I wasn't informed you would be taking off tonight," he said and stood behind his desk with his arms crossed tightly over his wide expansive chest. The chest I wanted to run my fingertips over.

"I'm not taking off, I *am* off. Once James is asleep, I've done my job for the day. I don't need to watch him twenty-four-seven even while he's asleep and you're at home." I was rude. There was a strain in my voice. The truth was that I didn't care about this job anymore. I also didn't want to care about Eric or what he thought of me.

Eric just stood there, glaring at me. The air between us had changed. We were both aware of the feeling of hostility that existed between us now.

"Of course, you are your own person, you can do what you want to do. I'm not trying to keep you confined in my home, Nina," he said firmly. As brave as I was trying to be, I gulped nervously.

If he asked me to stay right now, I would have. I was too weak. I would gladly spend the rest of the night here. All he had to do was ask.

Eric's eyes roamed over me. He was taking in the length of my dress, my makeup...by the look on his face, he wasn't impressed.

"You are free to do what you want. I would just like to be informed in advance the next time."

My throat had gone dry. I was so close to backing out, if he could give me one clue that he didn't want me to go. Instead, he sat back down on his chair with a thump. He focused back on his computer screen.

"You can leave when you want. I don't need you here tonight, I can watch James." His voice conveyed no emotion. He didn't give a fuck.

A jolt of electricity ran through my body as I realized how much I craved for him. That I'd gone through all this effort of dressing up and presenting myself in front of him just to make him jealous. But he wasn't. He only cared about his convenience.

I whipped around and ran down the hallway to the front door. I didn't even check in on James like I'd intended to. I just wanted to get out of here. I wanted to start a new life. I was sick of feeling like I didn't matter to the man I was ready to give my heart to.

I felt pathetic.

I needed to cure myself.

I wanted to feel desired again.

It would have been as easy as calling Gareth and asking him if he wanted to hang out. I knew he wanted me even though he hadn't officially asked me out on a date yet. But he was always looking at me, constantly flirting, and the truth was that he was a nice guy. He would make a good boyfriend. I really should have called him instead of coming here.

But I didn't care about Gareth. I didn't want to care about Eric either. I just wanted to be by myself somewhere where nobody knew me.

I stood at the entrance of the club and called him on his phone. I had to do everything to keep myself from shaking. I was cold and nervous. I was very close to changing my mind but it was too late. He'd seen me already. He was walking out of the club with a fat cigar between his lips.

"Wow! You really do know how to doll up. I was worried you'd need some help from one of my girls," he said. He had his arms thrown open and directed at me like he was expecting a hug. Like we were long-lost pals.

I kept my arms firmly on my sides.

"Hello, Jim."

I'd never said his name aloud. It was an ordinary name, but it made me feel sick to even say it. He used to work with my father. I'd seen him around when we were kids. They were friends. And now he was tarnishing the memory of my dad by coming after our family. By asking me to dress up provocatively. By putting me to work in a place like this. By ransacking my college dorm and threatening me.

It wasn't difficult to guess. I knew exactly the kind of man he was. Only now, I wasn't afraid of him anymore, I just hated him.

He came closer to me, plucking the cigar out of his mouth. It burned between his fingers and I followed the way the fumes rose from its end. I just wanted to avoid looking at him.

"You'll do great in there, little bird," he said. I could sense him eyeing me up and down, taking in every curve of my body. His gaze was different. It wasn't the way Eric looked at me.

Eric. Eric again! Why couldn't I stop thinking about him? Not even here.

"What do I have to do?" I snapped at Jim, interrupting his survey of my body. He grinned like it was a silly question.

"Not much, honey. Serve the drinks. Sell cigarettes. Smile often. Collect tips." He said it like it was the most obvious thing in the world. I tried looking into his eyes now.

"I've never done it before. I've never waitressed."

"There isn't much to it, don't worry. My girl Suzy will show you around." He came closer and threw an arm over my shoulder. My body froze from his sleazy touch. I wanted to pull away but he was dragging me in the direction of the entrance. It was too late now, I was going nowhere.

"Suzy!" he yelled out her name as soon as we entered. Supposedly, she was somewhere nearby.

I looked around the place. It was a lot like I'd always imagined a place like this to be. Just a few rungs away from being a strip club. The place was packed with men. The only women here were the servers or the ones the men had brought with them.

There were gambling tables everywhere and the music thumped loud and strong in my ears. The lights were dim, and it was too dark and smoky in here. I didn't know how people could see anything, but my eyes were already beginning to adjust to the low light.

It wasn't a big place. It was small and packed tight. As far as I could tell, it wasn't one of those places anyone could walk into at any time. It was probably invite-only. Maybe only open to members who were willing to pay for it. And they were guaranteed the best service.

I was still looking around, amazed and afraid at the same time of this place. All my life, I'd made the conscious decision to stay out of joints like these. The south side was filled with them and Raina had instilled in us the importance of staying away from them. And now I was here. I was going to *work* here.

"Take care of her. This is the little bird I was telling you about." Jim was speaking to another woman now. I turned to find her standing behind me, looking at me like she was assessing my worth. I felt judged and scrutinized. Was she trying to decide if I 'would do'?

Jim reached over and stroked my chin lightly before retreating. "I'm waiting to hear good things. All you have to do is impress Suzy," he said, walking away. I could feel an icy coldness filling my body and my stomach.

Suzy had thick blonde hair which could have been a wig. Her lipstick was bright pink to the point of being nearly fluorescent. It matched the color of her long fake nails.

She stood staring at me, still scrutinizing. Her dress was as short as mine but shinier, more eye-catching. Her big breasts seemed to spill out on purpose.

"You're not from around here, are ya?" she asked. I noticed she was chewing gum.

"I grew up here, Pike Avenue," I replied. I figured the only way I was going to make it through the night safely was by making sure these people knew I belonged to the south side as much as they did.

Suzy's brows arched on her forehead and it looked like she didn't believe me. "The first night is always the hardest," she said and her expression seemed to soften a little. "It'll be easier tomorrow and in a month, you wouldn't want to be anywhere else," she said with a grin. Suzy reached for my hand and then she was whisking me away somewhere to the back of the club and I allowed myself to be dragged away by her.

I had no choice. I'd already decided to be here and try out a new life.

Like I told Jim, I knew nothing about waitressing or working in a place like this. Besides, this club wasn't exactly an atmosphere I was comfortable in. So I knew from the outset that this job wasn't going to be easy.

Nonetheless, I followed Suzy around for the first hour like a baby chick followed its mother.

She took me to the back where the rest of the staff hung out and introduced me to the others. All women, all dressed similarly. They all had a dazed and bored look on their faces and they barely even looked at me when we walked in.

"Don't mind them, hun. We're all here to get the job done

and leave. Nobody's here to make friends. You'll get it eventually."

I nodded.

She got busy showing me where all the things were. Cleaning equipment and stuff like trays and glassware. There was even a small staff changing room where some of the women were putting on more makeup and fixing their clothes.

Suzy caught me staring at them and smiled.

"This will have to do for tonight but if you're going to work here, you'll have to try harder with what you got on." She looked me up and down and I could feel my cheeks flushing.

All this time, I'd convinced myself that I did a good job with my get-up, but clearly I had not. At least not a good enough job for this place.

Then Suzy showed me how it worked with the orders. Two women were working behind the bar and I was introduced to them too and taught how to place orders.

"It isn't much else I can teach you, hun. You just carry the drinks to the table and look as sweet as can be. The wider you smile and the more you swing your hips, the fatter the tip will be. Remember that."

I nodded. "Got it. Smile and swing."

That seemed to make Suzy grin.

"You'll do all right, hun. Jim sure knows how to pick 'em. You're real sweet and pretty, got that innocent thing going for you."

I was blushing again. I wasn't sure whether to feel flattered by that.

But my hour of training was over and Suzy said she had a ton of work to do. It was time for me to start working on my own, despite how unprepared I felt. I wasn't ready to do this, but I had no choice.

All of a sudden, I found myself standing alone by the bar, staring at the people around me and feeling sick to my stomach.

"Hey, new girl! Table sixteen." The woman named Candy who was working the bar was shouting at me over the thumping music.

Suzy had said something about table numbers but I had no idea what they were. I just looked around the place and saw a table with three burly men who were looking in my direction. I assumed they were who Candy was talking about.

I walked slowly up to them while each of them grinned at me wide like they knew something I didn't.

"Hi," I said meekly. It wasn't like Suzy had told me what I was supposed to say in a situation like this. I just had to go with the flow. "What can I get you?"

The man who was sitting closest to where I was standing leaned sideways in his chair. It took me several moments to realize what he was doing. He was checking out my butt. In full view of everyone. His pals continued to grin while I turned the color of a tomato.

"What's the matter, sweetheart? Cat got your tongue?" one of them asked while the others erupted in laughter.

"Just waiting for your order," I snapped. I was embarrassed and angry. They didn't stop checking me out with those same greedy, beady eyes. Their gazes were all over my body. I felt naked. I felt this incredible urge to pull down my dress. I could sense others at other tables turning to look at me.

"Watch that tone, sweetheart. We're friends of Jim's."

I gulped, remembering what Suzy had told me. Smile and swing. I couldn't do either.

"I'm sorry. I'm new here. What can I get you?" I said, hoping to appeal to their better side. Little did I know that they didn't have 'better sides'. Men like them never did.

"New meat!" one of them yelled. Men at other tables cheered at that, turning to me and thumping their drinks on their tables. I didn't realize this was some kind of a ritual here.

I wanted the ground to open up and swallow me whole. Never before in my life had I been stared at like this. I didn't know where to look. My voice was shaky. I tried to focus on the job.

"Should I come back for your orders?" I asked.

One of them, the first one who was staring at me, pulled me to him before I could stop him. I lost balance and fell on him. Within moments, I was sitting on his lap and another round of laughter erupted.

"She wants to come back for my order!" he exclaimed, laughing. I tried to get up and leave but he had a tight hold on me. I wasn't going anywhere. "No, sweetheart, you stay right here and tell me your name." He continued to speak to me, right in my ear now, while I squirmed in his lap. Apparently, nobody was going to come to my rescue. I couldn't see Suzy anywhere now.

"What is your name?" the man repeated.

I felt like the room was spinning. I was stuck to him, his breath was in my ear...in my face. I couldn't separate reality from my version of a nightmare.

"Nina," I squeaked.

"Nina!" the man growled aloud for all his friends to hear. More cheers rang out. Was I just imagining this or were they chanting my name now?

"Please...let me go...I have to get back to work." I continued to struggle in his arms, but he kept laughing. This was a big fat joke to him, to all of them.

I thought I was going to cry. I could feel a cry rising up in my throat. What would Jim say? What would Jim do?

"Oh, c'mon, Saul!" It was Suzy. She had finally shown up. She was standing over us with her hands on her hips and a big grin on her face. "Leave the poor girl alone, will ya?"

She was making light of the situation. She wasn't trying to be aggressive.

"We're just having a little fun," Saul said. I could feel his fingers creeping all over my body. I was frozen to his lap. I wasn't even struggling anymore. It was like my body was beginning to shut down.

"Sure, but you've scared the girl shitless!" Suzy laughed and so did a few others around us. She reached for me, gently prying me out of Saul's grasp. He let go and I stood up like a spring. Finally, I felt like I could breathe again.

I would surely have collapsed to the ground if it wasn't for Suzy holding me up. "Now, take their orders and do your job," Suzy said to me in a low voice. Her eyes were narrowed tight and all I could do was nod.

"You boys be good and maybe I'll pay you a visit later," she turned to them again and said it with a wink.

"We're always good, Suzy," one of the other guys said. Saul still had his eyes on me.

"What can I get you?" I asked once again, this time in the lowest, weakest voice I'd heard myself use.

They gave me their drink orders, it wasn't hard to remember. What was hard to do was walk away from the table with my head held high. I didn't know if I'd be able to do it without breaking down.

"Thanks, I'll be back," I replied. I was about to walk away when I felt the slap of his hand on my butt. It was Saul. I didn't have to turn to know it was him who did it. I was jerked forward from the force of it and I gasped, biting down on my lip when I heard their laugh breaking out. I wanted to cry.

Instead, I didn't turn around or look at them. I just walked directly to the counter and placed their order.

"Took you long enough," Candy muttered under her breath. I walked away from that too. I went directly to the staff room at the back.

I wanted to scrub the makeup off my face. I wanted to get out of this dress. I was wrong about all this. I couldn't do it. I couldn't survive the night.

I heard the door swinging open just when I'd walked through it.

"What do you think you're doing?" It was Suzy. She sounded angry.

I stood in front of the small mirror, staring at myself. I looked afraid. I glared over my shoulder at her reflection. She stood with her hands on her hips again.

"I can't do this. I'm going to go," I said.

She rolled her eyes.

"I told you it was going to be hard tonight."

"I wasn't expecting this. I'm sorry. I don't mean to disrespect you or any of the other girls who work here. It's just that this job isn't for me."

She raised her eyebrows like I was being a fool. She came closer to me and spun me around. Now I had no choice but to look up into her face. Was she taller than me, or was that just her heels?

"You will be fine. That was your first table. You really going to give up after the first one?"

"I can't do it. I feel degraded and humiliated."

Suzy crossed her brows like she was confused. Maybe she didn't know the meaning of those words. I hung my head down and gulped.

"You just gotta give it a few more shots. You'll be fine. Smile and swing, remember? None of these guys can actually do anything to you. Jim will break their legs if they try anything more. They're just playing. It's all just harmless fun, you understand?"

I looked up at her again. I was finding it hard to believe that this could be just harmless. It wasn't fun in any way, that much was for sure.

Suzy smiled now.

"Besides, you're on the clock tonight. Jim isn't going to let you just quit and walk away. You'll owe him for tonight if you don't do the hours."

What had I gotten myself into? How was I going to get out of it? I realized then that I didn't need to be afraid of the other men out there. Jim was the one I needed to watch out for.

"You're gonna be okay. Yes? Go out there and do your job. Don't be so sensitive."

Suzy looked over me at the mirror and fixed a few stray strands of hair before smiling at me again and then walking away.

"You got two minutes to pull yourself together, then I need you out there."

I was alone in the small staff room with my back to the mirror now. I wanted to cry. I wanted to scream. I had made a huge mistake and now I didn't know how to get out of it. If I could *ever* get out of it. Would Jim let me go?

But for now, I had no choice but to do my job like Suzy said. I just had to suck it up.

*I* didn't intend to stay up that night again, but I couldn't fall asleep.

I was in my study, researching and working on my computer for the new role in Washington. When I looked at the clock again, I saw it was nearly two in the morning and I hadn't heard Nina come in yet.

Tonight, I was shocked to see her dressed that way.

It wasn't just a regular 'going-out' get-up. It seemed like it was definitely something else. Where had she gone? Who did she go with? Who could she have been with who would expect her to dress like this?

She was always in the back of my mind. I couldn't help the fact that I felt protective of her. I knew she was capable of looking after herself. She was a strong and independent young woman, but I wanted to keep her safe. I wanted to make sure she was all right tonight.

I pulled out my cell phone and toyed with it. I was tempted

to text her. Just to ask if she was okay. I'd never texted her such a thing before and a part of me knew it was inappropriate. I was her boss, not her keeper. We had sex, but I wasn't her lover or partner. The truth was that I had no rights over her.

I put my cell phone away. It would be out of line for me to text her. Surely, if she needed help, she could text her brother or Miles or any of her friends. I'd probably be the last person she'd turn to for help.

I turned off my computer and rubbed a hand over my face. This late at night and I still couldn't sleep. But I didn't want Nina to think I was waiting up for her again, so I got up from my chair and decided to go to my room.

That was when I heard the front door open and shut. I breathed a sigh of relief. Nina was home.

I stepped out of my study into the hallway. She was at the end of it, softly making her way toward her bedroom. I saw she was carrying her shoes in her hands. There was even a limp. Had she hurt herself, or were those shoes uncomfortable for her tonight?

She looked up when she heard me and stopped in her path.

"Nice night?" I asked. I shouldn't have said anything. I should have kept my mouth shut, and now I sounded sarcastic. Like I was jealous.

She stopped in her path and sighed. "I wouldn't know how to describe it," she replied.

I leaned on the doorframe, crossing my arms over my chest. "I thought you weren't the type to party hard," I continued and Nina licked her lips and shrugged.

"That's what I thought too."

"You decided to try it out?"

"I guess I did. Gives me something to do at night. I'm not a great sleeper."

"Fair enough. I hope you have fun and stay safe."

There was a silence between us. Nina took a few steps toward me. It seemed like she was trying to study my face. Find out what I was thinking somehow.

"Eric, do you really have to go? Do you really have to uproot James again?"

I didn't expect her to say something like this, to be this direct. I thought she would keep her real thoughts bottled up. I looked straight at her so she would see the seriousness of my response.

"Yes, I have to go. This city doesn't have anything for me anymore. It might be tough for James now, but he'll learn eventually. It's just what life is."

Nina gulped and looked down at her feet. "If it's about...us... if you're uncomfortable or feeling guilty. You don't have to." She looked up at me again. "Is it so wrong for me to admit that I really want you to stay?"

The tip of Nina's nose had turned red. I couldn't tell if she'd been crying or if she was about to cry. Neither of those ideas appealed to me. I knew I wouldn't be able to deal with her crying. I needed to distance myself from this as quickly as possible.

"I have to go. It's for the sake of our lives. Both James's and mine. He'll understand it and I expect you to understand it too. This thing between us was messed-up and had to come to an end soon enough."

Nina gulped. Her nostrils were flared. She had her fingers clasped together, knotted up. Now, she nodded. "Yeah, of course. I understand."

"And I can see that this arrangement is hard and complicated for you. I think you shouldn't need to spend any more time here than necessary. And James and I should get out of here soon too. The quicker we get him used to the idea, the less complicated it will be."

Nina's eyes grew wide. I was thinking about my mother's suggestion of visiting us. I needed to avoid that at all cost. The last thing I wanted was the additional burden of having to deal with Mom.

"What are you saying, Eric?" Nina asked. When I looked into her eyes, I knew I'd hurt her with this. I had no choice. One of us needed to do this. It had to be me for both our sakes. For our sanity.

"I'm saying that you can leave sooner. Maybe stay another day. Two days if you want to. I don't expect you to work here any longer than that."

Her mouth opened in surprise at first and then she clamped it shut like she had nothing more to say.

I was about to call her name but she turned from me and walked away in silence to her room.

That was probably one of the hardest moments of my life. That image would be stuck in my head forever, of Nina walking away from me in silence.

## 33

## NINA

*I* woke up the next morning lying on the floor rather than the bed. I couldn't remember how I got there. Had I slid off the bed at some time or did I purposely lie down on the floor last night?

I was curled up in a ball, still in the disgusting dress from the previous night. I hadn't even bothered to take my makeup off. I just wanted to sleep. Just to shut out the rest of the world.

I woke up early and took a shower. I could still hear Eric's voice in my ears. He wanted me to leave the job sooner than the ten days' notice I gave him. Another day or two, he said.

I would barely have any time left with James. Just the thought of it broke my heart. I wanted to maximize on that time as much as possible.

I woke him up as soon as I was ready. I wasn't going to take him to playschool. That wasn't how I wanted him to remember his last few days with me. Instead, we were going to explore Chicago and eat candy and cakes all day.

James was thrilled about not having to go to kindergarten and he didn't care about the reason why. He was just happy to spend the day with me, to eat whatever he wanted. I wished for his innocence and his excitement to never leave. If only we could remain this joyous forever. What a wonderful world this would be...

Spending the day with James successfully kept my mind off Eric and my new job. I wasn't even sure if I'd return to the club. If Jim or Suzy even wanted me back on their staff. I knew I wasn't exactly the perfect waitress to be working in a place like that.

It got me worried, because I didn't know how I'd make the money to pay Jim now. Surely, he'd come looking for me and the cash. But I didn't want to think about that now, not when I was busy having fun with James.

I didn't want to tell James about the impending change in our situations because I figured it was his father's job to do it. Eric hadn't discussed it with me either so I didn't know how he wanted to go about it. The last thing I wanted was to step on his shoes.

Eric had made it very clear to me last night that I was nothing more than a fleeting affair to him. He was willing to change his whole life and uproot his family just to get away from me. That was how little I meant to him.

It broke my heart. I knew I would never feel this way about a man again. No other man would be capable of breaking my heart like this. I was in love with him and now it was over. He never had any feelings for me.

Late in the evening, James and I returned to the house together. James had balloons and stuffed animals and toy cars he was carrying. Gifts I'd showered on him today because I wanted him to remember me. At least have a vague recollection of me as he grew up.

Eric was in the house when we got home. He was in the living room, sitting on the couch with some files and papers spread out around him. It was obvious that he was keeping himself busy with work. Good for him, I thought. He was distracted. I wasn't on his mind.

James went running to his dad to show him all the stuff we'd bought today.

"You didn't have to do all this," Eric said to me but tried to put on a show of excitement for his son.

"It's nothing. I wanted him to have a fun day." I stood at the door, skeptical about entering the room because the truth was that I didn't belong in this household.

"Maybe it's time for bed now, buddy? Have you eaten dinner?" Eric got up and pulled his son up in his arms.

"We ate a pizza for dinner!" James exclaimed excitedly.

I just stood there, not able to move or say anything more. It was like I was taking snapshots of these moments so I could remember them like photographs.

James laughing and giggling in his father's arms.

Eric carrying his son out of the room in his big strong arms.

Both of them smiling at me handsomely...I was going to hold these moments close to me. They had no idea how much they meant to me.

"Say goodnight to Nina," Eric said.

"Goodnight, Nina!" James declared while he was carried out of the room like an airplane by Eric.

Once again, I was alone. I could have gone to my room but I stayed here. The room was warm. It was filled with the scent of Eric. I could feel his presence here even though he was gone.

I sat down on the couch where he had been sitting. Across the house, I could hear the faint murmur of their voices. Eric was trying to put James to bed but he'd have to read him a few of his storybooks first. I smiled at that—at the thought of James in his dinosaur pajamas, tucked into bed now. Eric sitting in the chair beside the bed and reading a book aloud.

I was sad today.

I didn't have the space in my heart to be angry or embarrassed. All I could feel today was a sense of loss, and I wasn't sure how to deal with it.

It felt like hours went by and I'd been sitting there on the couch forever. In silence. Just soaking it all in. I'd accepted the fact that Eric and James were going to leave. That I'd be alone again. I'd be heartbroken and in love with somebody I couldn't have.

By now, I was ready to begin the healing process. I just wanted to get over this. Being in love with somebody was a miserable feeling and I was right to stay away from it for so long. Now all I had to do was forget about him and I hoped I could return to feeling like myself again.

∾

I wasn't sure if Eric was even coming here after putting James down to sleep. I'd lost track of how much time I'd spent in the living room just sitting on the couch thinking about them.

When Eric returned, at first he seemed surprised to see me, like he wasn't expecting to see me there.

"Aren't you going out tonight?" he asked, walking straight to his bar so he could pour himself a drink. Was that a taunt?

"No. I'm not. I have to pack instead, among other things."

Eric had a glass of whiskey held up to his lips and now he looked at me with his blue eyes pinched and darkened. "You're packing already?"

"I'm going to leave tomorrow."

"Are you sure?"

"Isn't that what you want me to do? What you said I should do."

He took a large sip of his whiskey and I didn't move. I was sitting on the couch with my feet underneath my curled legs. To be fair, I was quite comfortable here despite the awkward tension in the room.

Eric stepped toward me and nodded his head.

"Yeah, I guess that would be for the best. There is no point prolonging this, for James's sake," he added.

"I haven't said anything to him. He doesn't know about DC or the fact that I'm leaving tomorrow."

He nodded again. "That is not your problem to deal with.

Once you're gone, I'll speak to him. It won't go down well, but I'll manage."

He was standing in front of me now and I couldn't help but admire his body—one last time. Those wide shoulders and the chiseled torso underneath his t-shirt. His narrow waist, muscular thighs. A wave of desire washed over me and I had to do everything I could to suppress it.

"And what about you, Eric? Will it be easy for you?" I asked.

He glared into my eyes and took a few extra moments to respond to me.

"What do you think?" he asked.

"I think you can't wait for me to leave. You can't wait for me to walk out that door and never return. You want to wash your hands of me because it is too beneath you to sleep with the *babysitter*."

Why was I saying this to him? I should have kept my mouth shut and made the parting easier. Instead, now I was complicating everything. I thought it would make him mad, but Eric came closer to me.

He stood directly above me now. I had to tip my head back to look up at him.

"Don't make up things you don't understand," he said in a low, growling voice.

"Am I wrong?"

"You don't know what you're talking about."

"Won't you be relieved to see me go?" I asked in a snappy voice.

Eric took another long sip of his drink while I waited for his response. "Relieved, probably, yes. It will be a relief to see you go. I won't have to worry about you all the time."

"Worry?" I was surprised by his choice of words.

"Worry about whether I'll accidentally end up fucking you again."

I gulped. My lips parted while I stared up at him. Did he *have* to speak this way? Why did everything Eric do drip with sexuality?

With his glass still in his hand, he leaned toward me. My neck stretched, my head tipped back. He placed his other hand on the back of the couch behind me. Now his body was like a canopy over my head. Our faces were inches away from each other's.

If I moved just a little bit, if I made the right motions now—our lips would graze.

My mind was filled with thoughts of kissing Eric, and then he kissed me. He pressed his lips to mine, his tongue slipped into my mouth. I gasped and moaned with desire while he tried to fill me up. I reached up and clutched his biceps. His strong, bulging muscles. I clung to him while our mouths fused.

I could have kissed him forever. I could have moved this forward. I wanted to. The wetness in my panties was proof that I wanted so much more than just a kiss. One last time, for old time's sake!

But I pulled away from him. Eric's eyes were filled with shock when I did that.

How weak did he think I was under his spell? Was the spell broken now? He had no choice but to straighten himself up.

"Goodnight, Eric. Tomorrow is a big day. I'll be leaving the house early, before James wakes up."

With that, I stood up from the couch while he stood back, watching me.

"You should do what you need to do," he grumbled. I nodded.

"Yes, I intend to," I said.

"Goodnight, Nina."

"Yep, goodnight."

It was like two friends, or rather, *acquaintances* exchanging hurried goodnights. I rushed out of the room before he could stop me or before I changed my mind.

I was going to sleep poorly tonight, I knew that already. Then I would wake early in the morning and go to James and kiss his forehead and leave the house before anyone else woke up.

It was the only way I knew how to say goodbye to the kid. I didn't want to make a scene. It wasn't my place to explain my departure to him. I wasn't his parent.

And that last kiss with Eric was the best goodbye I could have hoped for. I never wanted to see him again.

## 34

## ERIC

*N*ina was gone and now I was left to deal with a crying, angry five-year-old who couldn't understand why his best friend would just disappear on him.

It had been three days since Nina left the house and James was still refusing to go to kindergarten or say goodbye to his friends or help me pack. Most of the time, he refused to even leave his room.

I realized now that I'd probably burdened him with too much in one go. I told him Nina was gone and in the same breath told him we were moving cities at the end of the week.

The thought of changing kindergartens again, trying to make new friends, the absence of Nina from his life—everything was too overwhelming for his tiny brain and his big emotions.

While James stayed in his room, roaring or crying and refusing to come out, all I could do was sit outside his door and wonder how many more bad parenting decisions I was going to end up making in this lifetime.

In this situation, there was nobody else to blame but myself.

I was the one who slept with Nina.

I was the one who accepted the DC job idea.

I was the one who decided it was a good plan to put some distance between Nina and us.

It was all my fault, and my bad decisions were now going to have a lifelong impact on my son.

Sarah cleaned around the house. She cooked and packed up the kitchen and tried to get James to eat his meals. He was never a good eater but had made huge improvements in his eating habits when Nina was around. Now I was worried that he was forcibly starving himself.

Did he need to see a therapist? Did I need to take him to a doctor? I was at a loss.

And then my mother showed up.

Just as I'd expected, she showed up at the house unannounced. Thankfully, there was no trace of Nina here anymore.

Mom walked straight into James's room and pulled him into her arms. He was glad to see her, glad to see a warm, familiar face. Before I could have a conversation with her, James broke down and cried to her about how much he missed Nina.

Mom looked at me for answers.

"The babysitter," I said softly and she nodded and took in a deep breath.

"Now, James, honey, look at me." She grabbed my son's chin firmly with her hand and tipped his head up so she could look at him. "It's sweet that you miss her. I'm sure she took great care of you, but honey, she's not family. Do you understand what I'm saying?"

James's eyes were filled with tears but he was staring up at her, confused.

"This is your family. Your dad, me...we are what matter. A babysitter, a housekeeper, your friends, they are all on the outside. We are on the inside."

James still couldn't understand her.

"Mom, this is a little too heavy for his age. Stop."

She ignored me. "It's okay to feel sad. She was like a friend to you, I understand, but honey you have so much more. Your dad is working really hard to give you a good life."

James looked at me. I had nothing to say to him. At that moment, I knew he missed Nina and there was nothing I could do to help him.

"Nina is my best friend," James said in a quivering voice.

Mom nodded and stroked his shining blond hair.

"I understand that's how you feel, but you will make many other best friends in your life. She was just the first one."

"Mom!" I was a bit more firm this time. She looked up at me crossly and I indicated that I wanted to talk to her privately.

She kissed James's forehead and then followed me out of his room.

"What is it, son?"

"What are you doing in there?" I snapped.

"Trying to teach him some life lessons. What do you think? The sooner he learns the meaning of change and loss, the better it is for him. And no good can come from getting overly attached to a babysitter or a nanny. Soon you're going to find him a mother, a more permanent figure in his life—"

I cut her off. "We are not discussing this again."

"No, we're not, because you know what to do. Look at what you've done to the poor boy! He's crying over some babysitter leaving. Thinks she was his best friend. He needs a mother in his life, Eric. It is your duty to give him that."

I glared at my mother. My head felt so fucked-up that I couldn't decide if she was right or not. It made sense, of course it did. I wanted James to be happy. I'd made so many bad decisions in my life and now my mother had a solution to all my problems.

I shook my head and rubbed my temples with my fingers.

"Oh, you poor thing. I'm here now, honey. I'll take care of it. You seem so stressed. Just focus on your work, Eric. Focus on your business and what you need to do. I'll deal with James. I'll help you move. Soon enough, you'll be building a family in Washington and you can forget about all the unpleasantness of Chicago."

Mom gave me a hug. Even though I resisted it at the start, I sank into it because it felt like I'd needed it for a while. She smiled up at me reassuringly.

"Everything is going to be okay, son. James is going to be fine. You have nothing to worry about. Just leave it all up to me."

## 35

## NINA

*I* was crashing with Karen. She had a new roommate at the dorm, but the girl usually slept at her boyfriend's apartment so Karen said I could use her bed. Thank God for friends!

I spent the next few days after I left the job just cooped up in the room, reading and trying to keep my mind off Eric and James. Karen could sense I had something on my mind. She could sense I missed working with James and she knew I had a thing for Eric. She tried to quiz me about it a couple of times but when I was unresponsive, she left me alone.

She tried to cheer me up by inviting me to coffee shops and urging me to accompany her to the library, but I didn't care about either of those things. I hadn't touched my course books in weeks. I knew my education had taken a major blow. I was aware that I would end up disappointing Raina if I dropped out, but I just couldn't bring myself to do it. I had no motivation.

Jim called at the end of the week. I wasn't expecting him to. I hoped *that* chapter of my life was over, but I should have known better. Jim wasn't simply going to drop it because I chose to.

"We haven't seen you back at the club," he said. Karen wasn't in the room at the time so I could talk freely.

"I don't think it's for me," I replied. I was lying in bed, staring up at the ceiling.

"Okay, whatever you want, little bird. But how else are you going to pay me back?"

I pressed my eyes closed.

"I will figure it out. Just give me some more time."

"Some more time, eh? How much more time? You're leaving me no choice."

"What are you going to do?" I asked. I sat up, suddenly feeling a chill in the air.

"I could go to your sister or speak to your brother. I'm sure they would love to know the kind of work you did for me. They'll be able to cough up the money."

I clenched my fist. I didn't want Corey or Raina involved. "Leave them out of this!"

"I want to, but it doesn't look like you can help me."

"I just need to find another job," I snapped.

"Or you could come back to work for me. Suzy and the girls had great things to say about you."

I wasn't buying that for a second. I was sure I was terrible at the job. "I didn't exactly make a lot of tips that night," I retorted which made Jim laugh.

"No you didn't, but it was your first night. It takes time to master the art."

"I didn't realize it was an art."

"Well, it fucking is and if you know what is good for you, you'll come back here and work your ass off 'til you're making some money."

His voice was firm and cold. He meant business. I could sense he wasn't going to keep giving me chances. I tried to steady myself as I held the phone to my ear.

"Look," Jim began. "You owe me what your father owed me, but I'm a reasonable guy, I'm willing to make this easy for you."

I remained silent and Jim took it as his cue to continue with the proposition.

"You come work for me, be a good little girl, and you can keep the full paycheck. The tips come to me but I can put you up in an apartment."

I gulped. I needed a place to stay. I'd lost all dorm privileges when I left this one. Karen couldn't put me up here forever and I didn't want to go to Raina or Corey with this problem. They were both too busy with their own lives these days. Besides, I didn't want to owe them any favors.

"What kind of place is it?" I asked.

"Now we're talkin'. It's a small little apartment near the club, but it'll do. You'll be sharing it with Candy and Melissa. You met them at the club."

It didn't sound half bad.

The job was going to be hard but it was the only job I could land on such short notice. And maybe Suzy was right, maybe it was just the first night that was the hardest. I was counting on things getting easier now. Especially if I was actually going to start making money and if I'd have a place to stay.

"When can I move in?" I asked.

Jim laughed a victorious laugh. "Exactly. That's the kind of question you should be asking. Move in whenever the fuck you want. I'll tell the girls to expect you. You have to show up to work every night though, that's the only condition."

"I'll be there," I said.

"Good. Tonight."

"Yes, I'll be there tonight," I replied.

"And Suzy will take care of your outfit and makeup. She told me you have a lot of learning to do."

I tried not to take that feedback personally. I just had to roll with the punches if I was going to learn. What did it matter? My future seemed pretty dim otherwise.

I had nowhere to live. I wasn't interested in school. The man I wanted was gone and didn't want me. At least I could earn some money doing this. Maybe it wasn't that bad and it was all in my head. Maybe it wouldn't be terrible to be under Jim's protection. Suzy and the other girls at the club seemed happy enough.

"I'll find Suzy once I get to the club tonight," I said.

"Good," he replied and ended the call.

I kept the phone pressed to my ear for a few more moments, listening to the beeping sound on the other end. I felt a strange calmness now. At least I was in control of something in my life.

"What club?"

It was Karen's voice. I hadn't seen her come into the room. She stood at the door now, watching me with her brows crossed. I turned to her and knew immediately that she'd overheard too much of the conversation already.

"It's nothing to worry about," I said.

"Maybe I'll be the judge of that," she snapped. "Spill the beans, Nina. Or I'm going to have to go to your brother with this. Are you in trouble?"

I had to tell Karen. She was going to hound me to death about it if I didn't. I had no choice. When she found out what my new job was, I could see how shocked she was. She had a million questions. She was convinced it was too dangerous to be involved in, that I was going to get myself in major trouble. All I could do was reassure her I knew how to take care of myself.

It was late in the evening and I was getting dressed to go to the Club.

Karen stood behind me, watching me apply some light makeup while I held up a mirror in front of my face.

"It's not that I doubt whether you can look after yourself,

Nina. But this place sounds dangerous. This man sounds dangerous. Can't you just ask your sister to pay him? She's rich now, isn't she? At least her husband is, right?"

I snapped the compact mirror shut and turned to face Karen.

"I don't want Raina involved. She is finally happy. She's finally made something of her life. She spent all those years looking after us, forgetting about herself, the least I can do is take care of this alone."

"But it's just money, Nina. Isn't that what you said? If she can just pay off this Jim guy, you wouldn't have to put yourself through this."

"Have you ever considered the possibility that maybe I *want* to do this job?"

"No, that's not possible," Karen said firmly and crossed her arms over her chest.

I rolled my eyes at her. "Well, it's totally possible."

"You said the men there are seedy. That they hit on you and tip you if you reciprocate."

"You're exaggerating my words," I snapped. I stood up from the chair and Karen followed me around the room.

"Nina, I mean, look at you. This isn't my best friend. This isn't the girl I know."

I made sure my dress looked neat and wrinkle-free. It was the same one I'd worn the previous night. I didn't have anything else that was appropriate for a place like that. I could have asked Karen for an outfit-lend, but it didn't seem like she was in a lending mood.

"Maybe you didn't know me at all," I said and Karen's face seemed to sink.

"Take that back, Nina. You're being rude on purpose."

I walked away from her. I had my purse ready with whatever I'd need for the night.

"Thanks for letting me crash here. I think I'll be able to move out of here in a few days. Maybe tomorrow," I said.

Karen looked shocked by that too. She wasn't expecting it. "Nina...seriously, you don't have to do this."

"I think I know a little more about what I do and don't have to do."

"Nina!"

I walked out of the door of the dorm room and I didn't look back at her. I had a strong suspicion that my best friend was on the verge of tears. But she had already promised me she wasn't going to rat me out to Raina or Corey. I knew she wouldn't go back on her word.

I arrived early at the club because I wanted to give Suzy a chance to help me with my outfit and makeup.

She was bossing some of the girls around, directing them to do things around the place. None of the patrons had arrived yet. The front doors of the club were locked and a big burly security man was standing there. He eyed me up and down but let me through when I told him who I was.

"You're back!" Suzy exclaimed when I walked in, my heels clicking on the sticky lino floor.

"I couldn't stay away," I commented and a wide smile spread on her face.

"Good girl."

"I've come as a blank canvas today. You're free to do with me as you please." I wanted to force a good mood on myself. I figured it'd be the only way I could get through this job without breaking down.

Suzy examined me closely and then nodded.

"Sure, yeah, I think I can work with that. Glad you're embracing it," she said.

I followed her to the staff room in the back.

"I might have a few dresses back here that could fit you," she continued. On a rack, I saw the clothes she was talking about. All short, brightly colored and decorated with fringes or sequin. None of it was in my style, nothing I would voluntarily wear.

"Try some on and then we can do something about that hair," Suzy said. She stood with her hip cocked to the side, waiting for me to follow her orders.

I pulled out a yellow number that made me nearly gag. But I didn't care about how I looked. I wasn't dressing up for my sake, I was dressing up for the sake of better tips.

Suzy watched me as I undressed and put on the yellow one. I'd turned away to preserve my modesty and when I looked at her again, she was smiling.

"There is no need to hide yourself, honey. You should flaunt what you have. You're lucky you have those perky tits and a great ass. You won't have to work extra hard," she said.

Was I supposed to take it as a compliment? It didn't feel like it was. It felt more like a professional observation.

"I'll need all the advice I can get," I told Suzy. "I just want to do a good job."

Now that I'd made the decision to spin my life in this direction, there was no point complaining. I just needed to ride the wave and ride it well.

## 36

## ERIC

**Three weeks later**

*W*e were in Washington, in a new house with a new housekeeper and a new nanny my mother had found through her network of other rich ladies she was friends with.

James wasn't happy.

In the last year, the only time I could remember that my son was truly happy was when Nina lived in our house. He hadn't forgotten about her. He asked after her every night when I read to him.

The morning she left, James had woken up and run to her room when he saw she hadn't come to wake him. I thought I was prepared to handle it, but I wasn't. James had spent the rest of the day crying. He'd cried himself to sleep. He was inconsolable. Even when my mother arrived and promised she'd take care of the situation, she couldn't. There was just no convincing James that things were going to get better.

They weren't. Not any time soon, anyway.

Mom moved with us to Washington. She suggested she would stay with us for a few weeks until things settled down and I had the household up and running.

She was the one who interviewed for the housekeeper and the nanny positions. It was some relief because it took the burden off my shoulders. The housekeeper, Cheryl, was a good fit, but the new nanny, an older woman of forty-five who had twenty years of experience with kids James's age, seemed to be an utter failure at the job.

I knew it wasn't her fault. It was James. He just couldn't let go of the memory of Nina. I knew a little bit about what he was going through because I hadn't been able to forget about her either.

I thought putting distance between us, immersing myself in a new city and a new role would help me forget. But I remembered her exactly. Her dark silky hair, how small her waist felt in my hands, the softness of the inside of her thighs, how her perfect breasts fit in my hands. How our bodies rose and fell together.

It was like I'd never met anyone like Nina before. I doubted I would ever meet anyone like her again. Was I in love with her? It certainly felt like more than just lust.

Sometimes, I'd be sitting in my home office, trying to get through the day and make the phone calls I needed to make, and I'd remember something she'd said. A passing remark, or just a 'good morning.' I used to love returning to the house from the gym in the morning and finding her in the kitchen with James.

I used to love listening to their voices filling the house. It was the sound of laughter and happiness. Not only did I want Nina for her body, but I wanted her for how much joy she brought to my son's life. I wanted her for me too.

The new gym in Washington was only two blocks away from our new house. I'd been frequenting it more often than the one in Chicago. Twice a day, sometimes three times if I just wanted to get away from feeling like shit at home.

I ran on the treadmill. Sweat dripped down my back. My t-shirt looked an entirely different color now that it was damp. I was thinking about Nina and what she was doing. Had her nightlife intensified now that she didn't have me as a boss? The last night, after that last kiss we shared, it seemed like she never wanted to look at me again.

Was she relieved to leave the job?

"You look like you're running away from something. Or is it someone?" I heard a voice speak beside me but it took several moments before I realized it wasn't just a voice in my head. I saw a woman standing beside me. She was in damp gym clothes too, a plastic bottle filled with a blue energy drink in hand.

"Excuse me?" I tapped on the buttons of the machine to make it go slower.

"I said you look like you're running away from something," she repeated herself. I had a natural male reaction toward her. I registered how hot she was. Tall, blonde, shapely. The lycra clothing really accentuated her body. She had a big smile on her face and no ring on her finger.

I felt an immediate pang of guilt. Like I was being unfaithful to Nina somehow. Even though she had nothing to do with my life anymore.

"I'm just exercising," I said while the machine came to a stop.

"Are you sure about that?" she urged and I hopped off. "I'm just kidding. I'm Selena. I've seen you here often in the last few weeks. In fact, you're here every time I am. It's almost like you're stalking me."

She was still smiling, but I didn't find her remark very funny.

"Believe me, I'm not," I replied. I reached for my towel hanging off the treadmill and I gave my head a good rub.

"Wow. Tough crowd," she said.

"Sorry, I don't mean to be rude. I just wasn't expecting to make new friends today."

"I wasn't aware you needed to be prepared for that," she said, tilting her head to one side while she examined me.

"I've had a busy day," I said.

"Umm-hmm..." She sighed after that. "Anyway, now you know I want to be friends. So the next time you see me, you'll be prepared. How does that sound?" Selena didn't seem to mind my hostility. I felt bad I was being rude to her. Besides, the more I rejected other women, the stronger Nina would embed herself in me, I figured.

"That sounds good. I promise to be better prepared next time, but right now I have to go," I said.

Selena nodded. "I'll hold you to that," she said and turned

with a smile and started walking away. I couldn't help but stare at her as she did. Her dangerously sexy butt in those leggings swayed as she walked. But I looked away before she turned and saw me staring. I just didn't feel ready yet.

When I returned to the house, I could hear James yelling before I even walked through the door.

"No!" I heard him screaming. There were other voices too, which I presumed were my mother's and the new nanny's, but they were drowned out by the fuss that James was kicking up.

I dejectedly put down my gym bag by the door. The thought of having to deal with another one of his tantrums was upsetting. However, I knew as hard as it was for me as a parent to suffer this, James was simply acting out his emotions. The only thing I could do at this point was try to help him, be as patient as I possibly could.

I found them in James's bedroom. Mom, the nanny, and James.

He sat on the carpeted floor with all his toys spread out around him. Mom sat in a chair with her head in her hand like she was ready to give up. The nanny, Moira, stood over him, trying to pry one of his toys out of his hand.

"No!" James squealed again.

"What is going on?" My voice came like thunder. They all turned to me.

"I hate them! I hate them! I hate everything!" My son turned red in the face from the pitch he was screaming at.

"James, you've lost your manners. This isn't the way you should be speaking to your grandmother." Mom was red-faced too as she spoke. I could see how stressed she was.

"What happened?" I asked the nanny. She was the only one in the room who was managing to keep herself together, to some extent.

"James has refused to eat anything since he woke up, and now he won't take a bath or let us play with him. He wants to be by himself." Moira looked like she was out of ideas. She didn't know how to handle the situation anymore.

I turned to James. He had returned to his toys on the floor, refusing to look at us.

"Buddy, do you want to go out and get something to eat together? Like a burger and fries, maybe?"

"Stop feeding him junk, Eric! He needs a wholesome home-cooked meal."

"I'm just trying to handle the situation the best I can at this moment, Mom. It's better that he eats something rather than nothing at all."

Mom turned her face away from me, her nostrils flaring.

"Why don't you take the rest of the day off, Moira? Thank you."

She nodded and hurried away from the room, clearly relieved to be allowed to leave. I wasn't sure of what to do but I knew that leaving James alone with my mother or the nanny wasn't the solution. I needed to spend some time with him myself. My work would just have to wait. The situation was turning out to be worse than I'd hoped.

"Why don't you play by yourself for some time, then we take a bath and go out and get something to eat?" I bent down to his level and my son finally looked up at me with his wide, blue, curious eyes.

"Okay, Daddy," he said in a soft voice. Behind him on the chair, my mother was shaking her head with disapproval.

"Mom, can I talk to you in private, please?"

I walked out of the room and she followed me. James needed his space and alone time anyway. Mom came at me with her guns blazing.

"You give that child too much free rein, Eric. He needs discipline. He needs rules."

"He isn't a brat. He isn't a bad child, he's not destructive, and he's not always like this. There is a reason why he's acting out and I want to address that reason and make him feel safe and secure. I don't want to punish my child for no reason." I tried to speak calmly to my mother, hoping she would understand.

She just kept muttering under her breath.

"Tell me what you want to say, Mom. I can take it."

She shook her head again. "I just don't want you doing more damage to the poor boy rather than helping him. I know you're trying your best, but it's not like you have any real experience in this, son."

"Well, I've been a dad to him for five years," I replied and Mom humphed.

"Look, Mom, I do appreciate your help around here, and thank you with the moving and setting up of the household. But maybe it's time that you return to Seattle? I don't want you feeling like your help isn't appreciated around here, but I'm going to raise my son the way I want to raise him."

"You mean as a kid who talks back to adults and kicks up a storm every time he has to take a bath?"

"He just needs some time to settle down."

"He keeps talking about that babysitter from Chicago. What was her name? Nina. Nina, Nina, Nina. All day. That's all he wants to talk about. How much he misses her and how great she was and blah, blah, blah."

I looked away from Mom and she must have caught the discomfort on my face because she was staring curiously at me now.

"Yeah, they got close," was all I could say. Mom crossed her arms over her chest.

"And did *you* happen to get close to her too?" she asked. As inappropriate as that question was, there was no way for me to escape it. If I refused to answer that query, it would only make my mother's suspicions stronger.

"She was my friend Miles's sister-in-law, so I guess we were friends and friendlier than just a professional relationship would be."

Mom's brows crossed. She was trying to analyze my answer. I could sense there was something else coming. "Anyway, you're here now and she's all the way over there. It's all probably for the best."

The last thing I needed was a lecture on how I shouldn't start something with a babysitter. I didn't think of Nina that way, as just a babysitter, but Mom wasn't going to understand. So the best thing to do was simply avoid a conversation.

"How was gym, by the way?" she continued. We'd meandered our way to the kitchen. Mom sat down at the table and adjusted the scarf at her neck.

"The gym? It was fine, why?" She never asked about the gym.

"Met anyone there lately? Made any new friends?" There was a gleam in my mother's eyes that made me suspicious.

"What are you talking about, Mom?" I snapped. I clutched the back of a chair tightly. It made my knuckles turn white. Mom's grin grew, like she knew something I didn't.

"Oh c'mon, son, you can be honest with me. What did you think of her?"

"Think of who?"

"Selena, of course. What did you think of Selena? Isn't she gorgeous? My friend Maggie sent me a photograph of her on the email and I was blown away."

I was shocked and enraged at the same time. Couldn't she see the storm brewing inside me now?

"Who is she?" I growled.

Mom looked at her manicured nails admiringly. "Maggie's cousin's youngest daughter. When I heard she was single, I knew I had to set you two up. Then Maggie told me she lived around here, that she even went to the same gym as you. I knew it was fate! I figured it would make sense if the two of you met organically, you know? Rather than a formal setup."

I couldn't believe I was actually hearing this. I'd considered being interested in Selena for a second. Just as a distraction from Nina. I wasn't serious about this consideration either. And now I was finding out that this was a setup all along!

"What has the poor girl been offered to show interest in me? What bribe?" I raged.

Mom rolled her eyes. "Oh, don't be silly, Eric. Don't you know what a catch you are? She was more than glad about the introductions. She said she couldn't wait to start getting to know you. I got a text today the moment she spoke to you."

I could see how happy Mom was with herself. Sure, I loved Mom. I always respected my parents. I believed that they only ever wanted to do what was best for me, but this was too much. She was messing with my life now and I didn't appreciate it.

"And what did you think of her?" Mom continued.

"I think you should leave," I replied.

Clearly, she was stunned by that response. "Eric, honey, you're overreacting now," she said.

"No, Mom, I'm completely serious. I think it's time that you left for Seattle. Thank you for all your help."

"You need more help, son. With everything. With James, and especially with your own life."

"I don't need your help. I don't need anyone's help. I can take care of things myself. I'm a grown fuckin' man!" I was on the verge of yelling. I didn't curse in front of my parents. The tips of Mom's ears had turned red. Her eyes looked like they were ready to pop out of her skull. Obviously, she wasn't happy with my reaction. I didn't care. I wasn't a kid anymore. And just like James wanted her out of his room, I wanted her out of my house.

Mom stood up slowly. "You are forgetting who you are, who I am, where you come from. You would rather encourage a babysitter to become wrapped up in your life than accept help from your own mother."

"I'm trying to do what is best for my kid," I said.

"I'll leave tonight," Mom said.

"Good."

"And what about Selena? What should I tell Maggie?" she asked.

"I don't care what you tell her. It's not my problem. All you need to know is that I'm not going to pursue anything with her. I am not interested. I'll leave the gym if I have to if you want me to keep this civil."

Mom jerked away from me and left the kitchen.

I didn't want to fight with her. I didn't want to argue with family. I knew Dad wouldn't have appreciated my tone with her if he was around to see this. But I also knew that Dad would have told me I needed to do what I thought was right.

I went to James's room and entered once I'd knocked on his door.

He wasn't even really playing with his toys anymore. He was

just sitting there quietly and I could feel my heart physically breaking.

"Hey, bud, what about that bath?"

He looked up at me with his sad blue eyes.

"Daddy, why did Nina have to go? Why couldn't she come here with us?" he asked.

I reached for him and stroked his head.

"She didn't want to be a part of our lives, bud," I lied. Maybe this was the only way I could get him to stop thinking about her.

"But she was my best friend!" he said and now there were big fat tears in his eyes.

"Maybe she wasn't. This was just her job. Maybe it'll be better if you look for a new best friend. What do you think?"

I was smiling at him, trying to make light of the situation, but it seemed like there was nothing I could say or do that could lift his spirits.

## 37

# NINA

*I*t was three weeks since I became a regular fixture at the club. Nearly four weeks since I last saw Eric and James, and equally long since I started sharing a small studio apartment with the other girls at the club.

It would be an understatement to say that my life looked very different now than it did three weeks ago. In fact, I barely even recognized myself in the mirror these days. This was a completely different girl, with a different set of priorities. I didn't have the same hopes and ambitions as the Nina Jones who enrolled in college and took up a job babysitting a five-year-old.

Was it really Eric who'd changed me this much? Was it because I'd allowed myself to fall in love with a man I was just supposed to have sex with?

Now, I had started to get good at this new job. I wasn't quite an expert at it yet, as much as Suzy or Candy or the others, but I was starting to develop a thick skin. Now when a man eyed me up and down and demanded some sweet small talk, I rolled along with it. I was learning what to say, how to say it, how to forget about it a minute later.

All I could do was observe the other girls at work and keep collecting the tips.

It was close to midnight tonight. My shift was supposed to last until one and then I was off for the next sixteen hours. It was laundry day today. The girls and I rotated simple home chores. So in the morning, I'd sleep in until at least noon, then I was going to do all the laundry for the apartment. Funnily enough, I looked forward to the monotony of the chore.

I was dressed in an electric-blue cocktail dress tonight. One that Candy helped me pick out just a few days ago. It was in a thick, shiny material and it clung to my butt and thighs in ways I couldn't have pictured before. The neck was a low dip right over my cleavage. I wore a tight pink bra underneath just to give my breasts that extra spill-effect. Suzy had done my makeup tonight again. I trusted her instinct. She always knew what to do with my appearance. I always got more tips on nights that she fiddled around with my look.

It was a busy night. Saturday. I'd been running to and from the bar all night, collecting and delivering drinks. All I had to do was also keep calm and smile, flirt a little, and bite my lip seductively. The key was to make the men think I enjoyed their attention. Now that I'd been working in this place for three weeks, I had a newfound respect for the girls. It was a tough job.

"Hey, Nina, there's some boy looking for you. Suzy showed him to the back room." Candy shouted at me over the bar so she could make herself heard over the music.

"Boy?" I asked, putting down the empty beer bottles on the counter.

"Yeah, he looks about your age. Said he's your twin," Candy said and rolled her eyes. "As if."

My heart came to a screeching halt. Corey? Was it possible he found me? It had to be Karen.

"Shit. Cover for me?" I begged Candy as I hurried away in the direction of the back room. The only thing I could hope for now was there was nobody else there. That Corey and I could have some privacy.

I barged in through the door and found Corey standing near the mirror that the girls used to dress up. He had his hands stuffed in the pockets of his leather jacket. He was glaring angrily at some posters of models up on the walls.

My shoulders were heaving. I'd forgotten what I looked like at that moment, but I was reminded when Corey's eyes turned to me and he examined my outfit. My makeup. The expression on his face turned sour.

"I had to see it for myself to believe it."

"Who told you?" I asked while he shook his head. "Was it Karen? Did Jim call you?"

I stepped toward him but Corey stepped back.

"What the fuck is going on with you, Nina? Why would you leave a perfectly decent babysitting job to do *this*?"

It wasn't Jim who called, because then he wouldn't be asking me this question.

"I didn't just leave that job because I wanted to. I *had* to leave because they left the city. And seriously, what is wrong with this job? I'm a waitress here like I would be anywhere else."

"A waitress who has to dress in...in that? Who has to look like that?" Corey's eyes had turned red. I couldn't tell if he was embarrassed or angry. Maybe he was a bit of both.

"It's just a part of the role I'm playing. Nothing more is expected of me."

I was afraid of what my brother would do next. Was he going to punch the wall? Was he going to break something? It looked like he was going to erupt.

Instead, he lunged at me and grabbed me by my wrist.

"You're coming with me. You're leaving this place right now!" He started to pull me out of the room, but I managed to yank my hand away. More than anything else, I was afraid of what would happen if Jim saw him trying to take me away. What would he do if he thought one of his 'girls' was being taken away from the job?

"You can't make me do anything!" I screeched. My voice made Corey stop and stare at me.

"What are you trying to tell me? That for some reason you want to do this? Karen told me everything. This guy has been threatening you? With what? What money did Dad owe him? I'll figure out a way to pay him back."

"No!" I screeched again. "I don't need you to pay him back. I don't need anyone to do anything for me. I want to be here. I'm doing this job because I want to do it."

Corey came toward me. Before I could stop him, he'd taken

my face in his hands. "Do you have any idea what you're saying, Nina?"

"I think I do."

"I don't think you do at all. You're saying you want to do this shit job? Dress up like this? Serve sleazy men some drinks? Get groped? Teased?"

"None of that happens here. We are very well looked after," I said, my nostrils flaring. I was as equally angry as he was. "And how dare you walk into my place of work and call the shots? You're not the boss of me!"

He shook his head and I could see he was trying to calm himself. "Okay, Nina, why don't we get out of here and we can talk about it?"

"I can't just leave in the middle of my shift, Corey. I have a job do to. You'd know what I was talking about if you bothered to get yourself a job for a change."

My brother stared at me like I'd pulled a gun on him, when the truth was that there was nothing untrue about what I'd said. Corey wasn't interested in an education, he wasn't interested in a regular real-world job either. In fact, I didn't really know what my brother was interested in. I didn't really know my brother anymore.

"Whatever it is, I wouldn't demean myself to your level and work at a place like this, just for a few bucks," he growled.

"It is honest money for honest work. I don't care what you think of me or this job. I want to do it. I want to be here. You don't have to be the hero and rescue me."

Things between Corey and me had been strained for some

time now, but this argument was taking it to a whole new level. We had never spoken to each other this way before.

"Nina, seriously."

"Yes, Corey, seriously."

"So what do you want me to do?" he asked.

"I want you to leave. Maybe when you've taken some time to think about my perspective, you can give me a call and we can meet up. Maybe you can tell me about this girl you're chasing after."

My brother's cheeks flushed. I knew I'd hit some kind of a soft spot. He wasn't being completely honest with me.

"It's a long story, Nina. I'm sorry we've not been talking much these days," he said.

I rolled my eyes. "I don't know anything about you anymore," I said.

"Ditto."

"I need to go back to work," I said and started pushing the door open with my back.

"Nina..."

"What?"

"You can talk to me whenever you want. I'm here if you need me. You don't have to do this."

I smiled at Corey. "Please, don't feel sorry for me. I am perfectly happy."

"I don't think we should tell Raina though," he added

quickly, before I could go. "She wouldn't want to hear this. Let her be happy thinking you're still in school. Leading the life she wants you to lead."

"I can't keep lying to her," I said and he rubbed a hand over his face.

"For some time. Some more time. Let's just keep this from her for as long as possible."

I shrugged. He was right. I didn't want to hurt Raina if I didn't have to.

I was about to walk away from him without saying goodbye.

"Nina..."

"I have to go," I said.

"I miss you. I'm sorry if I'm being a dick, but I miss my sister," he said.

I half-smiled at him but said nothing. I had nothing to say.

"Yeah, I miss her too," I murmured under my breath.

I walked back into the thick of things. Suzy was talking to Candy at the bar when I walked up to them.

"Who was that? What was that about?" Suzy asked. I knew she was good to me but at the same time was loyal to Jim too. I needed to be careful about what I said around her.

"Some guy I know."

"He said he was your brother?" she said.

"Yeah, he knew I wouldn't want to see him if he told you who he really was."

"Is he like a stalker or something?" Candy asked while she shook a cocktail in a shaker.

"Could turn into one if I'm not careful," I lied.

"Yeah, you should be. I have enough of those in my life, and it's not fun after a while," Candy said.

I smiled at her and took a tray of drinks off the counter. I could sense their eyes on me as I walked away. I appreciated their kindness and help. I didn't mind living with them, but I knew none of us were really friends. Not in the way Karen and I were. I always had to watch my back.

I laid the tray down on a table I was serving.

I'd started to recognize most of the guys now. The big guy with the mustache and in a pinstripe suit smiled at me.

"How's the night going, boys?" I asked, smiling at the man even wider because I'd caught his eye.

"Much better now that you're here, sweetheart," he said. I giggled with forced glee and I walked away. I felt his hand on my hip and I pretended not to notice it. I remembered Suzy's advice to swing my hips because I knew he was watching me.

At least at the end of the night, I knew he'd tip me well. I'd be one step closer to not owing Jim anything. I looked forward to that day.

## 38

## ERIC

*J*ames was now in a new playschool and it seemed like he hated it nearly as much as he used to hate the one in Chicago when we first got there. Before Nina came into our lives.

Only this time, I didn't know how to make it better for him without her help.

This morning, he'd kicked up another tantrum when Moira tried to get him ready for playschool. He wouldn't stop crying and complaining that he was feeling sick. He wasn't sick. There were no signs of it. I even took his temperature.

Instead of punishing him, I decided to take the day off work and spend it with him instead. This had been happening a lot lately, and I was barely able to get any work done. But I was willing to put in as much effort and time as I needed for the sake of my son.

I brought him to the zoo. Watching the animals usually calmed him down and made him feel better.

We'd spent the past hour talking to the monkeys and discussing their lives in great detail. James seemed in a much better mood now. He held my hand, tugging me along and all smiles. I would have given anything to see him like this all the time. I just wanted him to be happy.

We got ice cream and sat down on a bench together. The perfect spot where we could continue watching the monkeys play. James was distracted, but he was in a better mood so I figured it would be the perfect time for me to talk to him about Nina.

"Hey, bud, are you feeling okay?"

James took a big lick of his ice cream and nodded. "Yes, Daddy, I don't feel sick anymore."

"That's good, but I mean in general. You know, like at other times. I know you've been very upset about losing Nina as a best friend."

He looked down at his ice cream and seemed to focus really hard. Even though he was just five years old, I knew my son was very perceptive. He was a thoughtful little boy. "Yes, Daddy, I'm okay."

"Are you sure? Because it seems like you don't want to go to playschool or make new friends because you miss her."

James's nostrils flared. I wanted him to be honest with me.

"I miss her."

I pulled him into my arms and we hugged. "I'm sorry, bud, I miss her too."

James looked up at me and his cheeks were flushed, his lip

was quivering a little. I thought he would cry but he didn't. "But you said I should make a new best friend."

"Yes, you should."

"If I make a new best friend, will I forget about Nina?" he asked.

I stared at my son because he'd asked me the question that was on my mind too. Would I truly be able to forget about Nina? Would being with another woman solve this problem? When would I move on? It was over a month now and I still thought about her every night.

"I don't know, son."

James watched me silently. I couldn't lie to him. The kind of bond he'd formed with Nina, the way I felt about her... wasn't something that was easily replaceable. It would be dishonest of me to tell him that kind of a relationship occurred in life over and over again, because it didn't.

James looked away from me, almost like he understood exactly what was on my mind. "Okay, Daddy," he said.

"I want to help you, James. Tell me how I can help you."

It was a ridiculous question to ask a five-year-old. He had no clue, just like I didn't.

Then he placed a hand on my back and patted me like I was an old pal.

"It will be all right, Daddy," he said. I hugged him again. I loved this little guy. He had no idea how amazing he was. I was glad I'd fought so hard to bring up him, to look after him as a single parent. If I'd let Cynthia do what she wanted to do—give him up for adoption, I would have missed out on all this.

I smiled at my son and nodded. "Yes, it will be. I'm going to take care of it," I said.

James had a trusting look in his eyes like he totally believed me. I didn't know what I was going to do to make things better, but I was sure as hell going to try my hardest. I would do anything to make my son happy.

And a part of me knew that the key to doing that was for me to find happiness too. To find stability. To give James a happy home. Mom was right all along. I was doing the best I could as a father, but he needed a mother too. He needed a team to look after him.

We walked around the zoo for a few more hours...right up until it was closing down for the day. Then we went and got a pizza. After that, we went to the supermarket and bought a big bag of groceries. Mom was right about this too—he couldn't keep eating junk all his life. But he wasn't interested in eating anything the housekeeper was cooking for us.

"Are you ready to help me cook?" I asked him when we returned home.

"I can help?" he asked excitedly. I stacked all of our shopping items on the kitchen island. Fresh fruit and vegetables, meat and spices. Everything we would need to cook up some delicious home-cooked meals for the rest of the week.

"Of course you can, bud. Our new life starts now, and the first step of that is going to be cooking for ourselves."

## 39

# NINA

*I*t had been so long since I'd started working at this club. I'd stopped counting the days, really. A month, maybe?

I knew I'd gotten really good at collecting tips. I was using all the ideas that Suzy and the other girls had given me. I was getting even better at making the men who frequented the place believe that I really wanted to be here.

It wasn't much, but the tips I'd made in my days at the club had already made a dent in the money owed to Jim.

Thankfully, Corey hadn't tried to contact me since the last time we talked. Karen called sometimes, but I let it go to voicemail. I didn't want to hear anything she might have to say. I didn't love this job, but it was something I had to do. I was earning a living and keeping a roof over my head. What more could I ask for?

Tonight, I was working the tables and humming a tune in my head. It was the *Friends* theme song. I usually always picked a happy tune to hum for the night, just to keep me distracted, to keep my spirits up when I started to doubt myself.

Most of the men at the tables knew me by now.

"Nina, sweetheart, come over here and sit on my lap," some would say. There might even be a few who'd grab me by my waist, expect me to giggle and try to pull away—half-teasing, fully flirting. As long as I kept my cool and didn't throw a fuss, these men were happy.

Tonight, while I worked, I caught him walking into the club. The guy with the mustache from my first night working here, Saul. I hadn't seen him since, and even though I'd gotten accustomed to this place, seeing him still gave me a sick feeling in my stomach. I didn't want him to see me. I didn't want to hear his voice.

For some reason, he reminded me of my life before this place. My job before this job. Of how naïve and stupid I was back then.

I tried to keep my head down and keep doing my thing, but not before long, I caught him staring at me from the other end of the room.

He was alone here tonight. Sitting at a lone table in the corner, wearing the same pinstripe suit as before. He was clutching his glass of whiskey and had that same sleazy grin on his face that I hated so much. From the look in his eyes, I could tell he was about to call me over.

I couldn't avoid him for very long. He told one of the other girls to send me to him when I kept looking away. I had to do it. I had to go to him. It was my job. If Suzy or Jim heard about it, they would have forced me to go to him.

So I went. I tried to be as casual about it as possible.

"Hi there," I said.

"Nina, right?"

It made me sick to realize he remembered my name.

"What can I get you?" I asked, trying to engage with him as little as possible.

"I'm happy to see you. Are you happy to see me too?" He was smiling like it was all a joke.

"Of course, I am. I'm happy to see all our loyal patrons."

Saul placed his drink on the table and patted his leg. He wanted me to sit on his lap. I knew the gesture well. My stomach flipped. Although I would have probably done it for some other guy because I knew it was harmless, I knew I wouldn't be able to bring myself to do it for him. My skin crawled with disgust.

"What's the matter, sweetheart? Thought you'd learned the ways of this place by now," he said. I stood my ground, glaring at him instead. I knew it wasn't like any of the other girls would come to my rescue. This was a part of everyone's job around here.

"If you don't have an order for me, I'll come back later," I said. I was about to walk away but Saul reached into his jacket pocket and pulled out a thickish wad of cash. He placed it on the table and looked up at me with that disgusting grin of his.

"Come and sit down on my lap. Let me feel that body of yours. I've missed it."

I looked at the cash and then at his face.

"I'll come back for your order later," I insisted.

When I made to go, he grabbed me again. This time with both hands. They were on my hips. He pulled me back to himself. I saw a flash of memory of the last time. It was a repeat of what happened, only this time, nobody else seemed to notice what was going on.

Saul held me to himself with one hand, and his other hand made its crawling way up my back...toward the back of my head. He was weaving his fingers in my hair. I felt like my voice was stuck in my throat, like I couldn't scream even if I wanted to.

"Don't fight it, sweetheart, you know you want the money, don't you?" His voice was right in my ear while I struggled to get out of his grip. "Come on!" he scolded me a little firmly.

Before I could say anything, I felt like I was being pulled away in a different direction. I squealed with shock before I realized someone else had yanked me away from Saul.

I was wrapped up around someone else's body now. His arm was enclosed around me.

"Are you okay? Nina? Are you okay?" Eric's voice was in my ear. I realized I had my eyes closed and now I opened them to look directly at his face.

"Eric?" I mumbled his name softly like I was in a dream. This had to be a dream, right? How else was this really happening?

"Stand back," he said in a deep, commanding voice. He let go of me and guarded me with his body, putting himself between Saul and me.

"Who the fuck do you think you are?" Saul stood up. He wasn't nearly as tall as Eric, nor as muscular or fit. Eric didn't budge. It didn't seem like he was even a little bit bothered by Saul's threat.

"Don't you know how to treat a lady?" Eric growled.

"She's no lady!" Saul quipped and tried to look at me over Eric's shoulder.

"Focus on me. I'm the only one talking to you," Eric said.

Saul looked like he had smoke coming out of his nostrils. Around us, everyone stood and stared, expecting a fight to break out. I could still feel Saul's grimy hands on my body and it made me feel sick.

I wished to tell Eric I wanted to leave, but no sound came out.

"What is going on here?" It was Jim. Someone had alerted him about this and he came rushing to see. I wanted to hide. A part of me didn't want him to see it was my fault that this was happening in his club. Another part of me was glad that he saw someone came to help me.

I stayed close to Eric.

"Hey, who are you?" Jim spoke directly to Eric now.

"Eric Hall. Do you know that this man here was terrorizing one of your staff members?" Eric spoke calmly, without really raising his voice at Jim.

"Terrorizing? I was having fun and this bitch here was getting paid for it," Saul said.

Eric's punch came out of nowhere. Barely a beat passed between what Saul said and Eric's fist landing squarely on his face. Saul's body seemed to bounce back a little and then it was almost in slow motion that he seemed to sink to the floor.

A big gasp and chatter rang out in the crowd around us.

"Eric!" I screeched his name when I saw the two club bouncers approach him.

He held up both his hands in the air to show he wasn't armed, and that he wasn't going to attack Saul or anyone else again.

"You need to get the fuck out of here, Eric Hall," Jim growled, then his eyes turned to me. "And leave the welfare of my staff members up to me."

"She's coming with me," Eric said. That startled me too, not only Jim.

"I don't think so, buddy," Jim remarked.

I watched as Eric reached in the pocket of his jeans and pulled out a thick wad of cash. The kind of money I'd never seen before.

"This is what you want, right? This is what you think the Jones family owes you?" Eric threw the money at Jim. It landed on his chest and he grabbed it. He was keeping the cash even though this whole scene was likely pissing him off.

"I have more. You can count it," Eric said and pulled out another wad of cash and threw it at Jim again.

I gulped. My knees were shaking. I felt weak.

"There is more money in there than anyone ever owed you. So stop coming after innocent young girls and threatening their families. I don't want you coming anywhere near Nina again. Am I making myself clear?" Eric spoke firmly, looking directly at Jim.

The bouncers were standing by, just waiting to pounce on him under orders of Jim.

I had my breath stuck in my throat as I waited to hear what Jim would have to say. He slowly looked down at all the cash in his hand and then up at Eric again.

"Get the fuck out of here. Take the girl with you. I don't want to see either of you again."

Eric reached for my hand before I had a chance to react. He yanked me to him and started leading me out of the club. I didn't even try to speak to him, I just wanted to get out of here. I didn't realize how much I wanted to get out of this place. Saul was the last straw. I'd just been keeping myself together somehow all these days.

Outside in the cool air of the night, I felt like I could finally breathe again. I realized my hand was in Eric's. He was holding it tightly, leading me along. I would have gone anywhere he wanted me to go.

But just outside the club, Eric stopped in his tracks, forcing me to stop too. He turned to look at me and I couldn't take my eyes off his handsome face.

"Where do you want to go, Nina? Where can I take you?" he asked.

I gulped. He was watching me, scanning my body—my dress, my makeup. I was embarrassed but empowered at the same time. The one thing I knew now was that he couldn't stay away from me, just like I couldn't stay away from him.

"I'll go wherever you're going tonight," I murmured.

He came closer to me. He took my face in his hands and then our lips met. This kiss was deep and slow, unlike any other kiss I'd experienced before. His tongue found mine and then thrust in between my lips. We were fused to each other by our groins. I was sinking into him. That tightness in my belly grew. I wanted to merge with him. I wanted him inside me tonight.

Eric slowly pulled his mouth away from me and looked into my eyes again. "I'm in love with you, Nina," he said.

## 40

## ERIC

*W*e didn't talk much on our way to the hotel room. We'd kissed. I told her I loved her and then we kissed again. She said she wanted to be with me, and the only place I could think of going was back to the hotel I was staying in.

"Where is James? Is he okay?" Nina asked while we were in the cab.

"He's fine. He's in DC at the moment, with his new nanny whom he despises," I told her. It made her smile. I knew she would take it as a compliment.

When we got to the hotel, she followed me to my room in silence. I could feel her warmth and energy close behind me as she waited for me to unlock the door. When we stepped inside and the lights came on, Nina rushed into my arms without saying another word.

"I'm in love with you too, Eric," she said. "But I don't understand how you're here or how you found me."

I made my way to the chairs in the suite. Nina followed me there and we sat down facing each other. Only a small glass coffee table remained between us. I would have pounced on her, I would have pulled her to myself and ripped apart her clothes if we didn't put some distance between us. We had been apart for too long.

"I wanted to come find you, so I came back to Chicago."

"Why?" she asked me and I rubbed the back of my hand on my forehead. I had nothing to hide from her any longer. The only thing I wanted now was complete honesty between us. She deserved that.

"Because James and I have been miserable without you. Ever since the day you left us, all we do is talk about you and think about you. I thought I was doing what was best for my son, but I realize now that keeping you apart from us was the worst thing I could do for him."

Nina's cheeks were flushed, even under all that gaudy heavy makeup I could see her cheeks turning red. That turned me on. Everything she did turned me on.

She looked away from me, as if embarrassed.

"I thought you wanted to start a new life in DC. I felt like you thought I was in the way of that. That you were afraid of this thing between us turning into something you didn't want."

I sighed and nodded. "Yeah, I thought it could never be serious between us. You're much younger than me and you're related to Miles. I figured it would never work, but now I realize it's not worth it. The pain and the sadness of separation. For James and me. I would rather risk every-thing else and have you with us."

She gulped. Was she as nervous as I was? I'd never spoken to a woman like this before. I'd never felt like this before, not even for Cynthia.

"But I don't think I can leave Chicago. I've been an idiot. I wanted to drop out of college. I don't think I want to go through with that."

"Of course not. You need to graduate. We're going to come back to Chicago. DC just isn't for us."

"What about your work?"

"I can do it here. It doesn't really matter, and I can travel to DC for meetings or whatever's needed."

Finally, a smile started to appear on Nina's face. Finally, she was beginning to see this wasn't all a joke. I was completely serious about her.

"I can't wait to see James," she said.

I moved off my chair and toward her. Before she could say anything more, I bent down on my knees and reached for her hand.

"I want to do this right this time, Nina. I've never been able to do it right with anyone else but I want to try with you."

She was still smiling. I could have watched her smiling forever.

"How did you know where I was? I'm so embarrassed."

"It was your brother Corey. He got in touch with me. He said he was worried about you. Your friend Karen told him about us. They both believed I was the only person who could knock some sense into you."

She blushed again.

"Lucky for all of us, I happened to be back in Chicago when he called. I wanted to find you. I was going to text you or get in touch with Miles and ask him what was going on."

Nina leaned forward so that our foreheads were touching now. "What will we do about him? Miles? My sister Raina?"

"I'm going to talk to him tomorrow. I don't want to hide it from him. I want to enjoy our relationship openly."

Nina kissed me now. Her mouth was over mine, her arms were wrapped around my neck. I pulled her to me and she fell on top of me. We rolled around on the carpeted floor. Her hair was over my face, her voice was in my ears. I couldn't believe how happy I was.

I kissed her everywhere. My hand found its way to her butt, I pulled up her dress. She giggled.

"James is going to be so jealous when he finds out we've already spent time together," she said.

I looked into her eyes and kissed her adorable chin. "Yeah, well, he's going to have you all to himself most of the time. When I'm not working, I want to spend every moment with you. Tough luck for him," I replied and Nina laughed.

"We're all just going to have to learn to share," she said. I didn't bother replying. I didn't want to waste another moment. I wanted to devour her, now!

It was going to be a long night and I couldn't wait to get

started. Her hands were on my belt, she was pulling it off and within moments, and my jeans were coming off too.

We twisted and turned, moving together until I was on top of her. She was underneath me, her breasts squished up against my chest.

"I've missed you, Eric," she said and we snuggled into each other. She had no idea.

# EPILOGUE

NINA

**Fourteen months later**

*I* was now a college graduate and nobody was as proud of me as Raina. Eric came to a close second, but then he was proud of everything I did.

In honor of my graduation, Raina and Miles were organizing a party. It had taken them a few months to come to terms with the fact that Eric and I were now a couple, but they eventually came around to it.

It was mostly Miles holding them back because it was difficult for him to accept one of his closest friends being in a relationship with me. He considered me a younger sister. I knew I was lucky to have a brother like him, but I also wanted him to see how perfect Eric and I were for each other.

James was now six years old and the happiest little bug around.

He enjoyed going to school. He had at least three close

friends who he hung out with all the time. His budding social life meant that he was less attached to me these days. I did experience something like separation anxiety from him now that I felt like he didn't really need me anymore, but I knew it was for the best.

James was growing and blooming into a smart and happy young boy. His father and I couldn't be happier.

It was the evening of my graduation party, and for some reason, I was nervous as I got ready in our bedroom.

Eric walked in, looking exceptionally handsome tonight in a navy suit. His hair was a little longer now than when we first met, but his eyes were just as blue, his shoulders just as wide...if anything, he looked taller now, more muscular. How was it possible that I fell in love with him every time I saw him? Even if I saw him just half an hour ago.

I was slipping my feet into a new pair of shoes when he came up to me and kissed my cheek.

"Those are new. I like them!" he commented, looking down at my feet. Among the many glorious things I'd discovered about Eric since we officially began our relationship—one of the most remarkable traits that he had was he was extremely observant. He wanted me to feel noticed, loved, and cherished.

"I bought it for the party. They're brand new and now I'm worried they're going to hurt because I haven't broken them in."

He stepped back and gave me a full examination. I was in a sea-green cocktail dress in a thin chiffon material. I had my hair messily tied up in a bun. I'd put on some makeup, but the bare minimum. Nude lips, a light greenish eyeshadow.

"You would look just as beautiful if you had to keep your shoes off for the night," he said.

We kissed again and I couldn't believe how lucky I truly was.

"James is ready. He's so happy with his new suit," Eric said and we were both smiling. James had wanted to wear a suit to the party when he found out it was what his dad was wearing.

I gave myself the once-over and we finally left to go find James. I still had that nervous feeling in the back of my head. Even though Eric and I had been together for over a year now, this was going to be the first time we would all be together in one place—with my family and my closest friends. I wanted tonight to go smoothly. I wanted everyone to see what I saw in Eric.

James sat between us in the backseat of the limo Eric had ordered to drive us to the party.

Raina had organized it on the garden grounds of Miles's country club. It was an exceptionally fancy affair. I was skeptical about being the center of attention of all this, but I wanted everyone to be happy. Especially Raina, who was so proud of me.

At the venue, everyone was full of praises for me. James had some other kids to play with, friends and their children who'd been invited to the party. Eric didn't take his hand off my waist the whole time and slowly but surely, my nerves started to settle. I was excited about the party.

Raina introduced me to all her friends whom she'd invited

—as 'the new graduate.' There was a cake to be cut and candles to be blown. This party was even more lavish than a birthday party would have been.

Eric had his arm around me while others clapped. I'd blown out the candles, cut a piece of the cake, and Eric smeared some of the icing on my face. While people clapped and cheered, he leaned in close to me and whispered in my ear.

"I am so proud of you, my love. I will always support you in whatever you want to do after this."

I nodded. I knew he did.

"But there is something else," he added and while he hugged me, I felt a sharp object brush against my fingertips. I looked down and saw the big sparkling diamond ring in his hand. "I want to marry you first. I want you to be my wife. I know our lives couldn't get any better, but I want to see us try. Sealed forever..."

He continued to speak, so I put a finger on his lips to shut him up.

"You don't have to convince me, Eric. I would marry you in a heartbeat. Tonight, if you want to," I said and I meant it.

There was nothing more I wanted than to be able to spend the rest of my life with this man. I didn't want to be away from him or James ever again. I was ready to take the leap and so was he. Now all we had to do was tell the family and make it official.

Eric kissed me. Everyone was clapping even though they didn't know what was actually happening...they had no idea this was the happiest day of my life.

*The End*

Want to read another over the top novel? Check out this box set, **Turning Good Series.** With over **10 million pages** already read, I'm sure you'll love it.
**Read the Turning Good Series here!**

## A NOTE FROM THE AUTHOR

Thank you for taking the time to read my book Hot Boss. I hope you enjoyed reading this story as much as I loved writing it.

If you did, I would truly appreciate you taking some time to leave a quick review for this book. Reviews are very important, and they allow me to keep writing.

Thank you again for your support, I am incredibly grateful.

Thank you very much.

Love,
Suzanne

# ABOUT SUZANNE HART

Thank you so much for reading my romances. I'm an avid reader who lives her dream of becoming an indie author. I enjoy writing about gorgeous billionaires that love to protect their sexy women.

I hope you love my books as much as I do!

Get FREEBIE!

https://dl.bookfunnel.com/rfgslpe5al

f facebook.com/SuzanneHartRomance

a amazon.com/author/suzannehart

BB bookbub.com/profile/suzanne-hart

Made in the USA
San Bernardino, CA
11 February 2020

64282394R00191